BAY MATTHEWS
Amarillo
by Morning

Silhouette Special Edition

Published by Silhouette Books New York

America's Publisher of Contemporary Romance

This book is dedicated to Joe Wimberly,
a "Cool" bull rider,
with many thanks.

Thanks also to Paula
for sharing her feelings,
to C. C. Sanders
for his help and interest,
and to Mr. and Mrs. Will Bain
and all the people of Claude, Texas,
for sharing part of their town with me.

SILHOUETTE BOOKS
300 East 42nd St., New York, N.Y. 10017

ISBN: 0-373-09464-7

First Silhouette Books printing July 1988

Printed in the U.S.A.

Books by Bay Matthews

Silhouette Special Edition

BAY MATTHEWS

of Haughton, Louisiana, describes herself as a dreamer and an incurable romantic. Married at an early age to her high-school sweetheart, she claims she grew up with her three children. Now that only the youngest is at home, writing romances adds a new dimension to the already exciting life she leads on her husband's thoroughbred farm.

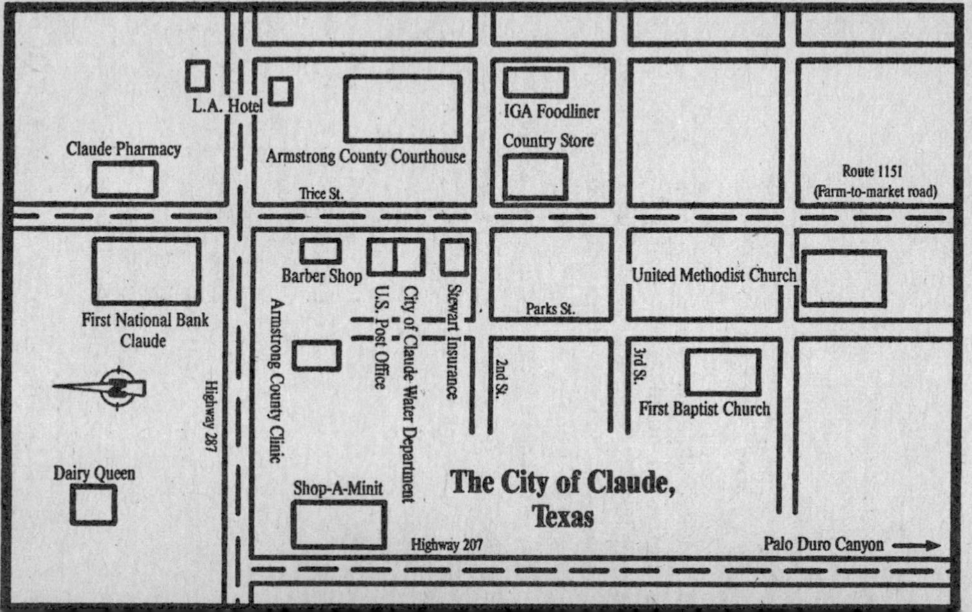
L.A. Hotel
Claude Pharmacy
Armstrong County Courthouse
Trice St.
IGA Foodliner
Country Store
Route 1151
(Farm-to-market road)
First National Bank
Claude
Barber Shop
U.S. Post Office
City of Claude Water Department
Stewart Insurance
Parks St.
United Methodist Church
2nd St.
3rd St.
First Baptist Church
Highway 287
Armstrong County Clinic
Dairy Queen
Shop-A-Minit
The City of Claude,
Texas
Highway 207
Palo Duro Canyon

Chapter One

Arms crossed over his chest, his cream-colored Stetson tilted over his eyes, Russ Wheeler slumped in the seat of the Greyhound bus that rumbled southeast on Texas Highway 287, leaving the night behind and driving straight into the day. The early-morning sun peeking over the horizon shot fingers of gold through an eastern sky marbled with pink, mauve and lavender.

Arching his back and shifting to a more comfortable position, Russ lifted a work-roughened hand and covered a huge yawn. He'd hoped to catch forty winks in as many minutes—about the time it took to get from Amarillo to the place be called home—but sleep, like the welcome bleating of the eight-second buzzer the night before, eluded him....

The bronc he'd drawn in Big Spring was new to Parkerson's string, bought from some outfit back East. Russ figured he was in trouble when the rough-looking gelding had pinned his ears and rolled his eyes until the whites showed before he was ever loaded into the chute. Russ tried to concentrate on getting his rigging just right and his rear end situated firmly in the saddle, tried to block out everything from the dull roar of the crowd to the nervousness he always felt as he eased onto a bronc's back.

The instant they sprang the latch and the horse lurched head down out of the chute, bucking crazily, Russ knew he was in trouble, but after a couple of seconds he'd thought he could feel a rhythm. That was when the ornery son-of-a-gun had gone from a head-down, snorting buck to a straight, up-and-back leap, almost flipping over. It was, as his granddaddy used to say, "all downhill from there," as his bruised and still-throbbing hip proved.

Downhill. Beneath the protective brim of the hat, Russ smiled wryly to himself. Things had been going downhill now for six months and twenty-three days. Ever since Amy decided there was no future in their strange relationship and told him as kindly as possible not to drift into Dallas anymore—at least, not to see her. The perpetual knot of pain in his gut tightened at the memory. It seemed that as long as he could remember, Amarillo Corbett—Amy, as everyone called her—had been a pain of one kind or another to him.

The bus began to slow, and Russ figured correctly that they were nearing the Claude city limits. Straightening his long legs and sitting upright in his seat, he cocked his hat back on his dark-auburn hair and looked out the window at his right side. Sure enough, up ahead was the sign that read Welcome to Claude.

As usual, he was filled with a sense of peace, a sense of coming home. It didn't matter how many miles he trav-

ed, how many pillows across the country he laid his
ead on, or how much fun and excitement he experi-
nced along the way. Claude, Texas, population one
nousand, was home and always would be.

The Dairy Queen was just ahead, and Russ smiled,
ondering if Paula Gentry, a friend from high school
ho managed the restaurant, had had her baby over the
eekend. She'd looked ready to pop when he saw her on
Vednesday. Passing the familiar restaurant on his left,
uss yawned and stretched and hoped that Tandy was
aiting for him at the L.A. Café, which did double duty
s the Greyhound bus stop.

As he stretched, the woman across the aisle, who'd
ept an eye on him ever since they boarded the bus, raked
is lean, hard-muscled frame with an appreciative glance
nat stopped at his ruggedly attractive face. Russ caught
ne tail end of the look and closed one smoky-blue eye in
n audacious wink. The woman's face reddened with
mbarrassment, and she took a sudden interest in the
nagazine in her lap. Russ smiled to himself and turned
o look out the window again.

The big Greyhound passed beneath the caution light
ear the county courthouse and turned into the café
arking lot, the air brakes hissing as it pulled to a stop.
uss, the only passenger getting off, stood and reached
or the small bag stowed on the rack above his head be-
ore edging down the aisle toward the door.

Tandy McGregor, friend, partner and father figure
nce Russ's real father had passed away five years ago,
eaned against the door of a dusty Dodge Ram, cleaning
is fingernails with his pocketknife. Not a hair over five-
eet four-inches, barrel chested, bowlegged, with a luxu-
iant mustache draped over his upper lip, Tandy could
ouble for Yosemite Sam. Over the years, the Texas sun
ad bleached the color from his blue eyes and red hair,
ut the smile he bestowed on Russ was sunshine bright.

As if he were afraid the smile revealed too much Tandy spit a stream of tobacco juice that landed peri ously near his feet and said, "Must've been a bad rode if you hadta ride home on the bus."

"Plane tickets cost money, Tandy," Russ said, sling ing his gear into the truck's bed, "and I have better thing to do with mine."

"You're lettin' it eat you alive, boy," Tandy told hin straightening away from the silver-and-gray truck.

Russ shrugged off the observation, uncertain if Tand meant the ranch as well as the bucking stock Russ wa buying from him bit by bit as his winnings allowed, or th despondence weighing him down since Amy broke thing off. He turned to the older man with a bland look in h eyes that warned him to leave things alone.

"Had breakfast?" he asked, changing the subject.

Tandy shook his head and switched the wad of t bacco from one cheek to the other.

Russ jerked his head toward the café. "Let's eat, the My treat."

Looking askance at Russ, Tandy smirked. "Sure yo can handle it?"

Russ wriggled his hand into the front pocket of h tight-fitting Wranglers and pulled out a ten-dollar bil "If you don't drink but a couple of pots of coffee, we' be okay."

Tandy smiled. "Let's do it."

Amarillo Corbett's West: A One Woman Show

*The Hardeman Gallery
cordially invites you
to view
the most recent collection
of Amarillo Corbett paintings*

The plain white envelope bearing the card engraved
'ith gold had been handed to Amy the day before by
ette Hardeman, part owner of the gallery. Even though
my knew the details by heart, her eyes skimmed the rest
f the information on the invitation sent to the gallery's
1ost faithful patrons and wondered why she didn't feel
1e excitement and nervousness that usually set in before
show.

Thanks to Wayne's belief in her, it was her first major
1ow in Dallas—the other two having been held at a
maller, less prestigious gallery—so where was the ex-
itement she should be feeling? Where were the now fa-
1iliar preshow jitters? After all, it was her work that
'ould be condemned or praised. With a soft sigh, she
icked up the envelope and put the heavy white card back
1side.

The ring on her left hand, a pear-shaped canary dia-
1ond that looked too big for the slender finger bearing
, winked at her in the midmorning light coming through
1e huge expanse of glass that brightened her apart-
1ent. Like the invitation, the sight of the ring didn't stir
1y excitement. Amy ignored the vague unease that re-
lization brought and rose to refill her coffee cup.

Padding barefoot across wood floors polished to a soft
atina, she went into the kitchen, which was nothing
1ore than a section of the gigantic open space—origi-
ally the upper floor of a warehouse—set apart by the
weeping curve of ash cabinets. Her bedroom, like the
itchen, wasn't really a room, either, but a sixteen-foot-
quare raised platform above the rest of the huge area.
)oric columns rose from the floor of the bedroom to the
eiling at each corner of the platform. Her bed looked

like a curtained four-poster, an effect achieved by th
yards and yards of gauzy rose-pink fabric draped fro
hooks attached to the ceiling. The apartment was deco
rated in pastels, with the only vivid color coming from th
miniature gardens of green plants sprouting from ever
conceivable space.

Amy stepped into the kitchen area, the black-and-whit
tiles cool to her bare feet. The kitchen, with its abun
dance of innovative stainless steel kitchen gadgetry, wa
a cook's delight. It was also the apartment's sole conces
sion to modern decor, the rest of the furnishings leanin
toward Art Deco.

Pouring hot coffee into the cool, she leaned against th
tile-topped cabinets and surveyed her domain. It was a
artist's dream, with its huge northern exposure, the bric
walls painted white—a perfect foil for her finished a
work—and a price range that proclaimed her success i
her chosen field. Why was it that lately she hadn't foun
any enjoyment living there?

The doorbell rang, jerking her from her minor bout o
despondence. Putting down her cup, she went to the doo
and opened it to find a tall, handsome man in his mid
thirties standing there...the same tall, handsome ma
who had put the diamond ring on her finger only thre
nights before—Wayne Hardeman, owner of the Harde
man Gallery. At somewhere near six feet tall Wayne ha
an athletic body, kept in shape by several games of rac
quetball each week. Dressed in an expensive summer
weight suit from an exclusive men's clothing store, he wa
the perfect specimen of the successful Dallas busines
executive.

Amy did her best not to let her irritation show on her makeup-free face. This was the second morning in a row he'd stopped by, interrupting her work schedule, and he, of all people, should know she didn't need interruptions now.

"Hello, Wayne."

She watched as Wayne's gaze traveled the length of her slim body—from her bare feet up her bare legs to the long shirt she wore over her shorts and on up to her face. She'd carelessly brushed her short, straight, taffy-blond hair from a side part and let it fall in haphazard bangs over her high forehead. Under his scrutiny, she fingered one of the diamond earrings her Aunt Vicki had given her when she'd graduated high school.

Wayne pulled her into a light embrace and bent to brush her lips with his. "Hello, yourself. Working?"

"Trying to," she said, slipping from his arms and stepping aside to let him in. The brief message was accompanied by a pointed look.

"Sorry." He shrugged and gave a polished smile that looked as if it came with the suit. Besides being wealthy and handsome, Wayne Hardeman was charming, and, according to Aunt Vicki, there was nothing worse than a charming man. Even now the smile was working, urging a matching smile to Amy's lips. He reached for her again, and she allowed him to pull her close.

"Can I help it if I miss you?" he asked in a husky voice, pressing a kiss to her forehead.

"No," Amy said, her voice gusting on a sigh. "But I really do have to work, Wayne, and interruptions tend to knock me off stride."

"I know," he said, releasing her. "I'm sorry, and I'll try to do better," he told her with a little-boy twinkle in his eyes. His gaze drifted to the small table near the sofa and the envelope with the gallery's return address lying there. The look in his eyes was understanding. "You're getting nervous."

Amy looked into his brown eyes, her own troubled. "I guess so. Maybe I'm getting blasé, but I didn't feel the usual thrill this time."

Wayne took the hand bearing his ring, lifted it to his lips and kissed each finger in turn. Unsmiling now, he asked, "How about engagements? Are you getting blasé about those, too?"

She laughed softly. "I've never been engaged before."

I love you, Amarillo. Will you marry me?

Amy pushed away the sudden, unwanted memory of Russ Wheeler's proposal and his offer of a small diamond engagement ring the day after she graduated from high school, ten years ago. She didn't want to think of it. It was in the past, just the way her relationship with Russ was. Over. Done. Finished.

Wayne snapped his fingers in front of her memory-glazed eyes. "Hey! Am I putting you to sleep?"

"No! Of course not," she denied, thrusting the memories aside and running a hand through her hair.

"But you're a working woman whose mind is on her work and who has no time for romance until after six p.m.—right?"

Amy forced a lightness to her voice, which she didn't feel. "Well...with the show coming up and everything..."

"I know. I shouldn't have come by and bothered you, but I couldn't help myself."

She could see the sincerity in his eyes, and that feeling of unease flicked through her again. "I'm...flattered."

Wayne laughed. "Flattered that I love you? Don't be idiculous. Have you told your brothers yet?"

Amy's heart sank. Calling her brothers meant that oon everyone in Claude would find out. Everyone. The nability to keep anything a secret was one of the curses onnected with small-town living. She shook her head.

"Don't you think you should? I mean, it's official 1ow, and the date is just over five weeks away. If they vant to come, they might need to make arrangements for heir farms or... whatever."

"You're right," she agreed, secretly doubting that any of her five brothers would drop everything and drive to Dallas for her wedding. "I'll call Zach this evening."

"Promise?"

"Promise."

"All right, then," Wayne said, a pleased look in his eyes. "I'll head off to work. Are we still having dinner omorrow evening?"

Amy plunged her hands into the pockets of her over-ized shirt and smiled up at him. "Sure."

He cradled her face in his palms. "I wish I didn't have hat damned dinner meeting tonight."

"Me, too," she said.

"I'll call when I get in, okay?"

She nodded. Wayne kissed her, a passion-filled kiss hat Amy realized was executed very well. The kiss was ike Wayne—polished, pleasing and very nice. It was quite good as kisses go, but it just wasn't...

Russ's kiss.

She gave an involuntary moan at the intrusive thought, a moan that Wayne misinterpreted. Tearing his mouth from hers, he pushed her away. "I've got to get out of 1ere."

This time Amy's moan of frustration was real. Wha
was wrong with her today? Maybe if he kissed her agair
maybe if he stayed... "I love you, Wayne," she said, an
wondered if he heard the desperation in her voice.

"Oh, Amy, you don't know how good it feels to hea
you say that."

She didn't answer. Couldn't.

Wayne closed his eyes for a second and resolute!
opened the door. "I'll call."

Amy watched him go and tried to deny the relief tha
suffused her. What was the matter with her? Was sh
sick? Why did she feel as if she were merely biding he
time, waiting for something to happen? She had every
thing she'd ever wanted, snared every brass ring she'
reached for. She was twenty-seven, healthy, had a thriv
ing career and the life-style she'd always coveted, drov
a new sports car and was engaged to Wayne, the kind o
man she'd always dreamed of marrying.

By marrying him she could have the best of bot!
worlds—a kind, witty, cultured and supportive husban
and someone knowledgeable in the world of art wh
could showcase her work and guide her career straight t
the top. So where was the glow of satisfaction she shoul
feel? Why was she having these niggling doubts?

Unable to find an immediate answer, she went into th
kitchen to retrieve her cooling coffee.

It was only later, when she was working painstakingl
on the lined face of an old Indian woman, that the per
sistent voice came back to haunt her.

I've gotta get outta here.

But it wasn't Wayne's transplanted midwestern voic
she heard. It was a husky Texas drawl and, instead o
pushing her away, the hands holding her moved over he

with a fevered intensity. Amy's breath caught in something that sounded suspiciously like a sob.

The piece of hard pastel she was holding slammed onto the table in sudden anger. Russ. Russ who was nothing but a rodeo rider, as different from Wayne as night to day. Russ, a friend almost from the cradle, the one who'd pulled her pigtails, teased her about her braces, gave her her first grown-up kiss. Russ, the sweet-talking, easygoing cowboy who had stolen her heart and her virginity. Russ, part of her past, the man who had dropped unexpectedly into her life every few months for the last six years and somehow, despite all her good intentions to the contrary, wound up in her bed before going on his way.

There had been no strings attached for either of them. No commitments. And that was just the way she wanted it.

No small-town life for her, Amy reminded herself. No husband who followed the rodeo and left her at home with a passel of kids the way her father had her mother. She wanted exactly what she had: her career, her lifestyle, Wayne. Russ was in her past, and he was staying there. She'd ended it once and for all. It was over.

Done.

Finished.

"Zach? It's Amy," she said, fulfilling her promise to Wayne by calling her oldest brother as soon as she thought he would be in from the fields.

"Well, hello stranger," Zach said in the soft, slow speech that led many who didn't know better to think he wasn't too sharp. "What's up?"

Amy couldn't help smiling. Zach, ten years her senior, knew her pretty well. She never called simply to shoot the breeze. When she got in touch, she had a reason.

"I called to tell you that I'm getting married in five weeks."

"Yeee-ha!" Zach yelled in rare show of enthusiasm. "Finally came to your senses and patched things up with Rusty, did you?"

Amy closed her eyes, a misery she didn't fully comprehend squeezing her heart. Zach thought she was going to marry Russ. And why not? They'd been semi-together long enough. "Zach! Zach!" she cried over the sounds of his jubilation. "I'm not marrying Russ, Zach."

Dead silence followed her announcement. Finally he asked, "Who *are* you marrying, then?"

Amy infused her voice with what she hoped was the proper amount of enthusiasm. "His name is Wayne Hardeman. He's sweet, handsome and owns the art gallery sponsoring my new show."

"Rich, you mean?"

"He's very successful, yes," Amy said warily.

"By your standards."

Amy suddenly remembered why she didn't call Zach more often. The anger that usually surfaced when she talked to him began to emerge in slow increments. "By anyone's standards."

"Different folks got different yardsticks, Amarillo," Zach said in the oblique way of his that drove her crazy. "What's Russ gonna say?"

Amy shook her head in disbelief. Instead of being happy for her, he was worried about Russ. Her hurt manifested itself in coolness. "It doesn't matter what Russ says or thinks, or what you think, Zach. It's my life."

She heard him sigh and could almost see his callused fingers rubbing his day's growth of beard. "So it is, little sister," he said by way of apology. "Have you told the others yet?"

"No," she said, her voice returning to normal upon hearing the guilt in his. "I wanted to tell you first."

Seeking Zach out first was a holdover from the days after their parents were killed in a tornado that ravaged the outlying area of Claude during Amy's last year of high school. Zach, the oldest of her five brothers, had been twenty-seven and married. Until she graduated he and his wife, Mona, became the closest thing to parents Amy had.

The sudden gruffness in Zach's voice told her that he remembered, too. "I'll tell them if you want. Save you the long-distance charges."

"Thanks."

"You want Mona to send it in to the newspaper? You're a celebrity here, you know."

"No!"

There was a pause. Then, reading her mind, Zach said, "He'll know by tomorrow, anyway, Amarillo. You know you can't keep a secret in a town this size."

"I know, I know," she muttered. "Everyone's so nosy! It's like living in a fishbowl! How do you stand it?"

"Most aren't nosy. It's just that everyone knows everyone else, and that breeds a special closeness. As for me living here, everything—and almost everyone—I care about is here. Not everyone craves a fancy life-style."

That twinge of something uncomfortable and not understood troubled her again for a second, but Amy couldn't help laughing just the same. "That was quite a speech for a country boy."

"Yeah," he agreed with a smile in his voice, "I guess it was."

She bowed to the inevitable, knowing Zach was right. News of her marriage would be a nine-day wonder. "Go ahead and tell Mona to put it in the paper," she said with a sigh. "Will you be coming for the wedding?"

"Aw, sis, I don't know. I'd sure hate to embarrass you and your fiancé."

"Embarrass me? How?" she asked, though secretly she was hoping that none of her family would come. Not that she *would* be embarrassed, but she knew they wouldn't be comfortable in Dallas or in the company of the people she associated with. She also wasn't sure how her brothers would treat Wayne, knowing how much they thought of Russ.

"The Corbett boys would be out of place in Big D, don't you think?"

"Of course not!"

Zach laughed, a deep, comforting sound. "I can't speak for the others, but I'll tell you what. I'll have Mona get my suit out of mothballs, just in case."

Hearing the teasing note in his voice, Amy laughed again. "You're a mess, Zach Corbett."

"That's what Mona keeps telling me."

What a lie. There wasn't a kinder, more solid, dependable man in the world, and that fact hit her with an unexpected force that took her breath away. "I love you, Zach." There was a husky note in her voice she was hard pressed to explain.

The same huskiness was in Zach's voice as he said, "I love you, too, Sis. See you soon."

Amy hung up the phone and reached for a Kleenex. For the first time since she'd left her hometown to chase her dream, homesickness, like the love she felt for her brother, hit her with unanticipated force. Along with it came a sudden and inexplicable lack of enthusiasm for the life she'd struggled so hard to create.

She ran her hand through her short blond hair, realizing that the nagging headache she'd noticed coming on earlier had arrived in style. She'd been working day and night, trying to get everything finished for this show, and she was tired...burned out. Once she had this behind her, she could devote herself to getting things ready for the wedding, which would be small but would still require a lot of preparation. And she could give more time to Wayne and recapture that first blush of happiness she'd felt when he asked her to marry him.

The next morning, Russ hit the equals sign on his adding machine and watched the paper roll out the figure for the second time. A small smile played at the corners of his lips. Maybe Tandy was right and he was putting too much into the ranch and stock deal, but it looked as if it were paying off. If he kept riding the way he was—not counting the Big Spring rodeo—if he could just keep snaring his share of the prize money, he might be able to pay off the rest of what he owed in the next couple of years.

If. Life was a gamble, he reasoned, no matter what you did.

Rising, he went to the window of the house he was buying from Tandy and, plunging his hands into the back pockets of his jeans, stared out across the expanse of grass separating the house from the nearest barn. *If* it didn't rain too much in the spring, the crops were in on time. If it didn't rain enough, they didn't grow. *If I can keep my butt in the saddle for eight lousy seconds in enough rodeos, I stand to make the National Finals.* He'd done that two years ago and hoped to do it again, *if* he didn't get hurt the way he had last year.

Russ took his hand from his pocket and clasped the back of his neck, kneading the tight muscles that were creating a minor headache, wondering why he was driving himself, why he pushed himself to do better, be more, when deep down he knew that whatever he did would never be enough. Not for Amy. They had different goals, different values.

He was proud of his background, but she was ashamed of her country upbringing, of wearing hand-me-downs. She couldn't understand why her mother had unselfishly worked long hours to help support six kids while Amy's dad plied his trade as a rodeo clown. And, when a particularly mean bull had ended Cal Corbett's career in the arena by puncturing a kidney and crushing a leg so badly it had to be amputated, the man's taking to drink only strengthened Amy's feelings about her situation and rodeos in general. Her near hatred for what Russ did for a living was really too bad, because he'd loved her longer than he'd wanted to ride the rodeo, and rodeoing was all he could remember wanting to do ever since his dad had taken him to see the McAlester Prison Rodeo when he was seven.

Amy had left Claude, Texas for bright lights and the elusive lure of a dream. Russ had a dream, too, but leaving the place that nurtured him wasn't part of it. He had to recapture his dream on a yearly basis, unlike Amy, who had hers in a firm grip.

He supposed that the problem between him and Amy was what Tandy called total incompatibility, except they weren't totally incompatible. They were extremely compatible in a lot of ways—one of them being their rightness in bed. To Russ's way of thinking, there was only one explanation for a physical relationship that was so good, so satisfying, and that, he believed with all his heart, was the fact that, in spite of all their differences, they truly loved each other.

"Russ! You in here?" The sound of Tandy's gravelly voice, riddled with worry, shattered Russ's thoughts. He turned and strode into the hallway, nearly running into the older man, who was hightailing it toward the office.

"Whoa!" Russ said with a smile. "What's the hurry?" Tandy was so worked up and his throat was convulsing so badly that Russ was afraid he'd swallow his plug of tobacco.

"I just got back from the feed store, and you'll never believe what Jess Morrison told me," Tandy said, mopping his perspiring forehead with a faded red bandanna.

"I can't believe or disbelieve until you tell me," Russ replied. "So spit it out—the news, not the tobacco."

Tandy shoved the bandanna into his back pocket. "Hold on to yer saddle horn, son—this one's gonna throw ya." He took a deep breath.

"Tandy..."

Hearing the warning note in Russ's voice, Tandy did spit it out. "Yer gal's gettin' married, Rusty. Amarillo Corbett's marryin' some dude from Dallas."

Chapter Two

Russ lay on his back in the dark, his elbow thrown over his face as if to block out the words Tandy had spoken earlier that afternoon, words that kept flinging themselves against the walls of his mind.

"Married. Your gal's gettin' married. Some dude from Dallas. Hold on to yer saddle horn...Amarillo Corbett's gettin'..."

...married to someone else. It seemed impossible that it would happen after all this time. Improbable, at the very least. She hadn't accepted his proposal ten years ago—thanks, he thought to her Aunt Vicki's influence after her parents were killed—and he supposed that the passage of time had lulled him into believing that the strange and unique relationship they'd shared for six years was a permanent one, even though she'd recently gone to a great deal of trouble convincing him that it was over.

Over. He couldn't—wouldn't—believe it. He loved her too much . . . had loved her too long . . .

Everyone in town conceded that Amarillo Lynn Corbett, with her blond hair and big brown eyes, was the prettiest girl in Claude High School's graduating class of 1977. Russ, sitting in the back row of spectators, agreed. As he watched her accept her diploma, the love he felt for her filled his heart to the bursting point. It seemed he'd waited forever for this night.

He was so busy thinking about the future he wanted to share with Amy that he was hardly aware of sitting through the rest of the ceremony. It was over soon enough; it didn't take long to pass out diplomas to the graduates from a senior class the size of Claude's. Caps were tossed into the air, despite instructions by the principal not to engage in the traditional, frowned-upon activity, and in a matter of minutes Russ was making his way through a throng of parents, grandparents and sundry relatives who had come to see the senior in their lives take his or her first giant step toward adulthood.

The people began to mingle, and hugs, kisses and congratulations were exchanged while Russ's gaze swept the crowd for a glimpse of Amy.

"Russ!" She'd spotted his six-foot-two frame before he did her.

Smiling, Russ zeroed in on her voice and turned, catching sight of her in the sea of bodies. They pushed toward each other through the crowd, and Amy launched herself into his arms. He took her slight weight, swinging her off her feet in a tight circle, while their eyes smiled their pleasure.

He stopped and let her body slide slowly down the length of his, and then, taking her face in his hands, he leaned over to take her mouth in a slow, sweet kiss that set his heart pounding and drowned out the sounds of the people milling around them. They broke apart slowly, and instead of a smile, Russ's face wore a look of seriousness. Amy understood exactly what the look meant.

Without a word, he led her out into the May night toward his beat-up Ford pickup. A sickle moon, waxing fatter every night, hung in the inky, star-dusted sky, and the soft breath of the night carried the faint hooting of an owl.

They reached the truck, and he pushed her against the door, pinning her there with his body, sparking the flame between them that grew brighter every time they were together, a flame Russ found harder and harder to control. Amy turned her face away, her breathing harsh and heavy. Looking up at him in the faint light from the building, she said, "Help me get this thing off."

Russ undid the hooks of the graduation gown, which covered her white scoop-necked blouse and skirt, and tossed it through the truck's open window.

"Let's hurry up and get this party over with," he said, opening the door on the driver's side. "We need to talk."

She nodded and slid onto the seat; Russ got in beside her. He cranked the motor and shifted into reverse, leaving behind the remaining graduation revelers and heading to a deserted road, the place designated for this year's post-graduation party. The exact location was a carefully guarded secret among the seniors so there wouldn't be any unexpected visits from the sheriff's department, even though, as graduation parties went, it was more or less harmless. There was no pot, no blatant sex, but there was a lot of beer and wine, and Claude and the surrounding area was dry; hence, the tradition was established that parties were never to be held in the same spot two years running.

It didn't take long for the party to get into full swing. Russ, four years older than most of the kids there, leaned against the side of his truck and nursed a single bottle of beer, watching Amy laughing and drinking strawberry wine and generally having a good time, something rare in her life. Someone had brought a battery-operated radio, which was currently tuned in to a Dallas station that beamed an amazing number of kilowatts northward into the Texas panhandle.

By eleven o'clock, most of the kids who didn't have a steady had paired off, and the dancing had progressed from rock to slow songs, which necessitated a frequent changing of radio stations. Amy stood nestled in the circle of Russ's arms. Suddenly she broke free and grasped his hands, pulling him away from his new spot against the front of the truck's grills.

She looped her arms around his neck. "Dance with me."

Russ pushed his cowboy hat to the back of his head and grinned. "I've got two left feet."

"Please?" She sweetened her plea with a kiss.

How could he refuse? He pulled her closer and began to move with the music.

He wasn't really a bad dancer. He had a natural rhythm, a necessary skill for riding a bronc or a bull. The truth was, he was uncomfortable in social situations.

Amy, high on the night and the wine, melted against him. The feel of her breasts pressed against him was an exquisite agony, and, as if that weren't enough, she had partially unbuttoned his shirt and was pressing kisses to his bare chest. Unable to take any more, Russ grasped her wrists, holding them together in front of her to put her at arm's length.

"Let's get out of here," he said, his voice sounding as if he were the one who'd had too much to drink.

Amarillo's eyes closed, and she nodded. Russ put his arm around her shoulders and helped her into the truck, backing out of his parking space and heading down the dirt road without a goodbye to anyone. He got back on the asphalt farm-to-market road that eventually forked to a narrow dirt track leading to a deserted barn where he'd taken her parking before. The truck bounced over the potholes, tall grass tickling its underside. The barn, its weathered gray wood silvery on the moonlit night, canted some, as if the wind that blew almost constantly from the south had, over a period of time, pushed it to one side. It stood like a tired, lonely sentinel, guarding field after field of milo.

Pulling into the deep shadow of the barn, Russ turned off the engine and rested his left arm across the top of the steering wheel. Amy smiled in the semidarkness. He smiled back. "You're drunk."

"No, I'm not!" she told him in a huffy tone.

Russ didn't want to argue. He wanted to kiss her. He leaned over to do just that, and Amy's mouth parted instantly, welcoming the probing thrust of his tongue. His hands moved to the buttons of her blouse, and she acquiesced, while her tongue joined his in an erotic dance. He didn't mean to take advantage of her wine-induced weakness. This was a familiar game, one they'd played for several months, but one that had its limit. Russ never pushed beyond the bounds she set for him, even though at the end of each date his body ached with need.

His hands covered her small breasts, protected by a white bra and slip of some silky fabric. She leaned into his warmth while their kiss lengthened then dissolved into a series of small nibbles. Moans of frustration and pleasure rang out from both of them and they resumed a deep kiss with a fevered intensity that rocked Amy's strict moral upbringing to its roots.

She tasted, he thought, of wine and potato chips and hungry woman, and it came to him in a moment's lucidity that they'd played this dangerous game far too long. He couldn't take much more. It was high time they made some changes.

"I love you." His voice was a feverish whisper, his confession breathed between kisses. "God, Amy, I love you so much I hurt."

Without warning she touched him, a touch so light he might have imagined it if his body hadn't responded so quickly. The proposal of marriage hovering on the tip of his tongue was forgotten as more primal sensations flooded him. Her laughter was soft, breathless, and, shrouded as they were in darkness, an unbearably sexy, more-experienced-than-she-was sound.

"That isn't love," she teased, becoming bolder.

Even though a cooling breeze blew in through the open windows, Russ felt sweat break out across his forehead. "If you know what's good for you, you'd better stop— while I can," he said, striving for a tone that matched hers and falling far short.

"What if I don't want to stop?" she asked, sliding her slip straps down her arms.

Suddenly serious, Russ gripped her shoulders. "Stop it, Amarillo. You're wiped out."

She shrugged out of his grasp, threw back her head and looked up at him. Her honey-blond hair streamed over her shoulders and down her back. "Stop saying that. I know what I'm doing."

With that, she reached behind her back to unhook her bra. Something he could only define later as forbidden fascination held him in its grip as she took it off and hung it by one strap over the rearview mirror. Then she gathered her bare feet up beneath her, turning toward him without a hint of embarrassment, her full skirt billowing around her hips.

Her skin glowed with a pale pearlescence in the darkness. Her breasts were small and round, their darker aureoles barely distinguishable. She reached out to unbutton the last remaining buttons of his shirt, but Russ caught her hands in his.

"Stop it!" he said hoarsely.

"I don't want to stop," she said, finishing her task and tugging his shirt from the waistband of his jeans. "And you don't want me to, either."

Then she'd pushed the shirt aside and pulled his head down, her mouth fastening to his with a fierceness that had taken his breath away while she pressed her bare breasts against his chest.

He groaned. "Amy...please..."

"...stop."

The sound of his voice slicing through the darkness jerked Russ back to the present. He licked lips gone desert dry and imagined he could taste strawberry wine on his tongue. Cursing, he sat up and leaned into the corner of the sofa, clasping the back of his neck with an unsteady hand. She couldn't marry anyone else. She loved him, and somehow he was going to make her face it.

"Tired?"

At the sound of Wayne's voice, Amy roused from her thoughts. "A little."

"You haven't been yourself this evening."

No, she hadn't—all through dinner and now walking back to her place, her mind insisted on wandering. In fact, ever since she'd called Zach the night before, she'd been jumpy, edgy and more than a little afraid that every time the phone rang it would be Russ calling to demand why she'd agreed to marry Wayne Hardeman. But Russ hadn't called, and, instead of being relieved, she found herself wondering why he hadn't.

"Earth to Amy. Earth to Amy."

She jumped guiltily and offered her fiancé an apologetic smile. "I'm sorry. I guess I'm just tired. I worked until three this morning and then got up at six."

"Poor baby," Wayne crooned. "When we get to your place, I'll give you a massage."

Her smile faltered. Wayne's offer was made in a tone Amy had no trouble interpreting. She sighed. It didn't take Dr. Ruth to tell her that it didn't bode well for a relationship when the thought of a romantic interlude with the man you were going to marry held about as much appeal as oatmeal for breakfast. She gave him what she hoped was a suitable reply and sank back into her depression.

She was relieved when Wayne decided to forgo any further conversation. It gave her sufficient time for a thorough mental castigation. Wayne was the man she was supposed to marry, and she hated herself for behaving so badly and feeling so...unsettled. He was sweet, wonderful, and they got along perfectly—there were few things they didn't see eye to eye on. She knew that his flair for combining his love of art and business would make him the perfect husband and partner. Besides, his looks also caused a fair amount of feminine heads to turn his direction. The facts were simple: he was her fiancé, and if she didn't want to lose him, she'd better get her act together. Her feelings were natural, she assured herself. The wedding was drawing closer, and she was merely getting cold feet.

With her pep talk still fresh in her mind, Amy let Wayne pull her close once they were in the elevator. She put everything she could muster into returning his kiss and even took things a step further by pulling his tie loose and unbuttoning the top buttons of his shirt. The elevator car rocked to a stop, and the doors slid open. With Wayne's arm around her waist, they walked toward her apartment door while she fumbled in her bag for the key.

Wayne took it, unlocked the door and ushered her inside. Then, without even closing the door, he pulled her to him, kissing her with a hunger she did her best to respond to.

"Wait," she said, pushing him away long enough to reach for the light switch, hitting it with her palm and flooding the room with light.

She started to close the door, but a slight sound from the living area stopped her. She watched, wide-eyed, as a masculine hand appeared on the back of the sofa in the middle of the living room. The hand was followed by the top of a head. A gleaming, auburn-haired head.

"What the hell?" Wayne said.

Which was Amy's thought exactly.

She'd never fainted in her life, but for just an instant she could have sworn that the room pirouetted around her. She clutched Wayne's arm for support as smoky-blue eyes came into view, followed by a bold blade of a nose and a wide, white smile that disclosed deep creases both cheeks and matching crow's feet at the corner each eye.

"Hi," Russ said, as if it were no big deal that he was in her apartment when Amy supposed he was back home in Claude. "You're in early."

Wayne looked from Amy to Russ and back to Amy again. "Who in the hell is this guy?"

Amy was so busy taking in the sight of Russ that she wasn't even aware of the increased cadence of her heartbeats. She should have known he wouldn't call. That wasn't Russ's style. He never dodged trouble if he could run right out and meet it. Even though there was a friendly smile on his rugged face, the coldness in his blue eyes definitely signaled trouble ahead.

She dragged her gaze from Russ and looked up into Wayne's face. His eyebrows were drawn together in a frown, and suspicion was stamped on his handsome features. She forced her frozen lips into a smile. "Wayne—" Did her voice sound as squeaky to him as it did to her? "—this is Russell Wheeler from my hometown."

Wayne wasn't satisfied. She could see the question in his eyes: *How did he get into your apartment?* She flashed Russ another quick look and turned what she hoped was an innocent gaze back to her fiancé.

"Russ is my...cousin. On my father's side," she tacked on for good measure.

"Your cousin?" Wayne echoed.

Russ stood and rounded the corner of the sofa, heading toward them in his sock feet. His rumpled appearance hinted that he'd been sleeping. He held out his hand to Wayne, who took it because manners dictated that he do so.

"You must be the fiancé," Russ said as they shook hands.

"That's right. Wayne Hardeman."

Russ released Wayne's hand and turned to Amy with a bland look. Then, before she realized what he was doing, he pulled her close and pressed a soft kiss to her mouth. The kiss was brief, light, passionless. Even so, it scorched her lips and sizzled its way through her nerve endings. Surprise rendered her speechless. This was what she should feel when Wayne kissed her. Anger, directed at both herself and Russ, sparked in the depths of her brown eyes. She pushed at his chest.

He released her and stepped back a pace, a challenge in his eyes. "How've you been, *cuz*?"

She cast a look at Wayne. He wasn't a happy person, if the glare in his eyes was anything to go by. *How dare Russ kiss her!* Her mind raced as she tried to figure out what outrage he might perpetrate next. She shot him an angry look, their eyes engaging in a brief defiant battle. He was loving this! she realized with something of a shock.

Her eyes blazed. *I'll kill him. I'll carve out his black country heart and feed it to the crows. I'll...*

"I don't believe I've heard Amy mention you before," Wayne said, his voice cutting through tension as thick as black Texas mud. By tacit agreement, they all began the short exodus to the living area.

"Probably not," Russ agreed, sprawling in one of her easy chairs and draping one long leg over the arm.

The denim of his tight jeans splayed across his masculinity in a way that roused dormant memories and made Amy's mouth go dry.

"I'm the black sheep of the family...the rodeo bum." Unrepentant devilment shone in Russ's blue eyes. "My granddaddy used to say I was sorta like the ill wind that blows nobody any good. I blow in; they push me back out the door as fast as they can."

Rodeo bum? He should have been an actor, Amy thought with disgust. It was time to put an end to at least part of this charade. God only knew what Wayne was thinking.

She plastered a smile on her face and tried not to grit her teeth. "Russ likes to tease. Actually, he's a big star in Claude."

There was a bewildered expression on Wayne's face. "Is that so? What kind of star?" he asked with ingrained politeness.

Amy knew the look on Russ's face. Basically shy about his accomplishments, he never tooted his own horn and wasn't crazy about anyone else tooting it, either. She'd pay for this—sometime, someplace.

He shrugged. "I was ProRodeo All-Around Cowboy a couple of years ago."

Businessman that he was, Wayne asked, "Is there any money in that?"

"If you can stay on long enough, often enough," Russ drawled, reaching for his boots and pulling them on.

How could they sit there and talk when she was about to scream? Amy wondered, shifting her attention back to Wayne, who was pulling off his loosened tie. As he crammed it into his pocket, she realized with a panicked horror that his shirt was half-unbuttoned. Her wide-eyed gaze slewed to Russ. She was beginning to feel like a spectator at a tennis match.

Russ pulled on his second boot, looked up and smiled at her, but his eyes were as hard as gemstones. He hadn't missed the fact that Wayne's shirt was unbuttoned, either.

"So," she said, jumping to her feet, "what brings you to Dallas, Russ?" She deliberately injected a bit of anger into her voice to counteract her nervousness.

"I heard you were getting married, darlin'," he said with another of those engaging smiles, "and since we've been so...close for so many years, I wanted to come and congratulate you myself."

It took everything in her not to look at Wayne. Had Russ stressed the word *close* the way it sounded to her? "You shouldn't have bothered," she told him with saccharine sweetness.

"No problem," he assured her. "I have another appointment on Thursday. I figured I could combine the two." He pushed himself to his feet. "Now that I've wished you my best, I guess I'd better be going. I've disturbed you long enough."

Thank goodness!

He scooped his hat up from a nearby table and set it on his head. Then he extended his hand to Wayne. "Nice meeting you, Wayne. You take good care of her, you hear?"

"My pleasure," Wayne said, suckered in by Russ's considerable charm. "Make sure you tell everyone that I'll do my best to make her happy."

"I will," Russ promised. He turned to Amy and, without touching her anywhere else, dropped a light kiss to her cheek. "Be happy, darlin'."

Amy watched him go to the door, open it and disappear out of the room and her life. She swallowed. Was it for good?

"Nice guy," Wayne said, taking her hand and pulling her down beside him.

"Yes," she said, "he is."

"Nice, but I'm glad he's gone." He pulled her into his arms and began planting kisses on her neck. Amy closed her eyes, but Russ's image was stamped indelibly in her mind. *"Be happy, darlin'."*

Did he mean it? Had he come just to wish her happiness and report back to Zach and the others?

A deep sigh in her ear alerted her to the fact that something was wrong. She pulled away from Wayne to see what it was.

His lips quirked in a humorless smile. He kissed her cheek, urged her to her feet and stood beside her. "Get some rest. I'm going home. It's obvious you're exhausted."

Amy felt tears stinging behind her eyelids. She nodded. He really was a wonderful man. She fought back the emotion flooding her and touched his cheek with her fingertips. "Did anyone ever tell you that you're a really good guy, Wayne Hardeman?"

"Sure," Wayne said, taking her hand and lightly kissing her palm. "But everyone knows that good guys finish last."

Amy laughed, albeit weakly. "I'm sorry I'm so... moody. I guess there's just too much going on in my life right now."

"I understand. You get some rest. I'll call you in the morning."

She nodded and watched as he followed the path Russ had taken only moments before. When he reached the door, she called his name.

He turned, his eyebrows raised in question.

"Call me. Don't come by. Please?"

He laughed. "Sure. Good night."

"Good night."

The door closed, locking automatically behind him. With a sigh, Amy turned toward her bed, unbuttoning the cuffs of her silk shirt as she went. She stripped down to her underwear and took a pair of white satin pajamas from the bureau drawer. After a quick change, a haphazard face cleansing and a cursory tooth brushing, she was climbing the steps to her bed. She set the alarm and flipped back the comforter, sliding between the cool, crisp sheets before reaching for the switch near her bed and plunging the entire apartment into total darkness.

"Be happy, darlin'."

Why did the well-meaning words leave her with such an empty feeling? Isn't this what she wanted—Russ out of her life and marriage to someone like Wayne? Hadn't she turned down Russ's proposal because his life-style wasn't what she wanted? And wasn't that why she'd never been able to give him more of herself than a few hours of unplanned but glorious lovemaking each year instead of committing herself to a more permanent relationship?

It was. Of course it was, but even after all this time, she could still remember his changing expressions on that morning after her graduation, the morning she'd told him she wouldn't marry him. She hadn't been drunk on wine and starshine then. She'd been cold sober, and, as far as she was concerned, the night before might never have been....

It was midmorning and Amy had just finished cleaning up the breakfast dishes. She'd put on a fresh pot of coffee for her brother's return when she heard a knock at the kitchen door.

Drying her hands on a dish towel, she opened it and saw Russ standing there, one hand behind his back. The other arm pulled her close, and his mouth came down on hers, soft and gentle. After a few moments, he pulled away.

"Good morning."

"Good morning," she said.

"I have something for you."

"You do? What?"

He brought his hand from behind his back and offered her a red rose. A small box dangled from a ribbon tied to the stem.

She looked up at him, her eyes wide. "A ring?" she asked. "Is it a ring?"

He nodded, so excited himself that he was unaware there was no reciprocal joy in her eyes. "I've been paying it out. Let's see if it fits."

Instead of helping him, instead of eagerly clawing the ribbon aside, Amy thrust the flower at him and stepped back, her hands clenched tightly at her sides.

"Russ, I can't."

Surprise. Disbelief. Hurt. The emotions followed each other across his tanned face as his mind searched for, and failed to find, a logical reason for her denial of what they shared.

"Why?"

The look in her eyes begged him to understand. "Because I don't want to be stuck here for the rest of my life, Russ. I don't want to cook for a herd of people every meal and scrub floors with no varnish on them the way I have all my life."

Russ didn't answer. She continued to look into his eyes, her own eyes anguished but steady.

"But most of all, I don't want to be married to someone who works the rodeo circuit. I don't want to have to worry about whether my husband is going to get his face stepped on or his brains kicked out. I want something better."

At that, Russ looked as if she'd slapped him. "Something better than love?"

He gaze faltered. The coffeepot made a final sputtering sound, and she noticed that the smell of fresh-dripped coffee permeated the room. She didn't answer. She couldn't. Instead, she turned and went to the coffeepot, flipping the switch from brew to warm.

She heard him moving across the room, felt his hands on her shoulders. He turned her and tilted her head back until their eyes met. "You're making a big mistake, Amy. What we feel for each other is rare, special. Don't throw it away. Marry me."

There was a searing pain in the region of her heart, but the prospect of following in her mother's footsteps was more than she thought she could bear, and the carrot of success her aunt was dangling before her looked very appealing. She looked up at him through a glaze of tears. "I can't."

Russ's hand dropped. "What are you going to do?"

"Aunt Vicki has offered to pay for me to attend art school in New York. They think I have a talent worth developing."

She watched him turn away and clasp the back of his neck with a strong, callused hand, a gesture she knew signified deep thought or worry. At that moment he looked far older than his twenty-one years. When he turned back, there was a new emotion in his eyes—determination.

"I've loved you for as long as I can remember, Amy. It seems as if I've waited forever for you to grow up so we could get married and have a family. I never counted on anything like this. Are you sure this is what you want?"

She nodded, but a part of her wasn't sure. As much as she wanted to pursue her art, the thought of pulling up her roots, even roots she claimed to hate, was painful.

"Be sure, Amy, because I'm through waiting. I won't
be here next year or two years from now if things don't
go as you planned. I'll find someone else to take your
place—I promise you that."

Amy bit her bottom lip and blinked back the threat-
ening tears. He meant it. She knew him well enough to
know that much. He'd get over her or die trying, probably leaving in his wake a string of hearts that would
stretch the boundaries of the country's rodeo circuits.

She stood silently while he leaned over and kissed her
on the cheek. "If this is what you want, I wish you all the
success in the world, because as much as I love you, I just
want you to be happy...."

"Be happy, darlin'."

Vagrant thoughts and too real dreams merged with the
very real present. Amy lifted leaden eyes, surprised to
find the night was gone and the day had progressed to a
time somewhere between the gray of dawn and the first
rays of sunshine. She had drifted into sleep with Russ on
her mind and had awakened to find him still in her
thoughts.

"Be happy, darlin'. Be happy...."

"Leave me alone, Russ!" she cried to the gauzy dra-
peries over her head.

"Believe me," his wry-sounding voice said from
somewhere in the room, "I wish I could."

Amy bolted to a sitting position. Bare-chested, bare-
footed, he was coming up the steps to her sleeping area,
carrying two cups of coffee. The smell, she thought ran-
domly. The smell in her dream had been real.

"What are you doing here?" she demanded, trying to
ignore the way the copper-colored curls on his chest narrowed and disappeared into his low-riding Wranglers.

Russ offered her a cup, which she took automatically. Then he took a sip of his coffee, swore when he burned his mouth and looked down at her with a time-for reckoning look in his eyes.

"I don't know about you, Amy, but I think it's high time we had a talk."

Chapter Three

I don't think we have anything to talk about, Russ.'' Amy set her coffee on the nightstand. Her actions were as deliberate as her words. "I'm getting married, and that's that."

"How can you possibly consider marrying someone you don't love?"

"I do love him!"

Russ put his cup down beside hers and planted his hands on his slim hips. "Liar."

"Liar, liar, pants on fire."

She could hear the taunting sound of his voice from their childhood. But this wasn't a child whose blue eyes swept her with icy intent. This was a man—one of the few of the dying, chauvinistic breed still in existence...

The kind of man she didn't want.

"Liar, liar, pants on fire."

"I'm not lying!" Her denial to both Russ and her taunting mind was admirably vehement.

"Then prove it."

"I don't have to prove anything to you."

He sat down on the bed. The look in his eyes couldn't be misunderstood. He was going to kiss her. Amy inched away.

Reaching out, Russ put a hand on either side of her, imprisoning her with his arms. She sank back against the nest of frilly floral pillows, moving as far away as she could from him, and watched with a strange combination of despair and fascination as he leaned nearer.

She couldn't let him. If he kissed her, it would be history repeating itself, and she couldn't let that happen now. Just before his lips reached their target, she turned her head, and his hard lips grazed her cheek.

It didn't seem to bother him. Amy tensed as he inched a string of kisses over her cheek to the spot just below her ear, his lips meandering over her neck. She swallowed and held herself stiffly, determined to prove him wrong as he nudged aside her collar, pressing kisses down to the hollow where her neck and shoulder met. Never once did she give in to the longing swamping her in the face of his tender assault. Finally, as if he were giving up, he lifted his head, straightening and razing her with an insolent look.

"Satisfied?" she asked in a frigid tone.

Russ reached out, touching one pebble-hard nipple.

Amy gasped, knowing she'd just offered proof positive that, while she had full control of her mind, her body had turned traitor on her.

"Yeah," he told her with a smile. "I'm satisfied."

The smug smile was her undoing. With the heat of anger boiling through her, she sat straight up in bed, push ing against his chest with the full force of her hundred and fifteen pounds. The surprise attack took him off guard, and Russ found himself flat on his back while Amy scrambled for the opposite side of the bed.

"I don't recall you being so testy in the mornings," he said, rolling to his side and pushing himself to his feet.

"Maybe I'm only testy when I wake up to find you here!" She rounded the corner of the bed and stormed down the steps. "Did you ever think of that?"

Russ picked up the coffee cups and followed her. Before he could answer, she whirled around to face him, demanding, "How did you get in here, anyway?"

"My key. Remember, Amy? The key I used to use when I was the welcome friend from back home?"

"I'm trying to forget," she said angrily, turning back toward the kitchen, the white satin shirt of her pajamas just brushing the bottoms of the matching French-legged panties.

Russ tagged along behind her. "Six years of memories is a lot of forgetting," he told her, liking the sway of her hips even after all this time.

"Don't remind me. And leave your key on the living-room table. I've had all the surprises I can take for a few days."

Her sarcastic tone broke the slim control he had on his own temper. The two cups of coffee thudded to the countertop. Reaching out, he grabbed her shoulders and hauled her around to face him.

"I've had enough of this. I want to know what's going on, Amarillo, and I want to know now—and don't give me that crap about our relationship not going anywhere, because I don't buy it."

"It *wasn't* going anywhere, Russ. After six years, everything was exactly the same. You sashay into town whenever it's convenient or the mood strikes you to look up an old friend from home. We chitchat, have dinner, talk over old times, old friends, have a few drinks and the next thing I know, I'm waking up with you in my bed."

Russ's lazy grin returned in all its glory. "You never could hold your wine," he said.

Amy's heartbeats faltered when she realized he was alluding to the fact that she'd had too much wine the night he'd first made love to her. She hardened her heart and turned away again. "I'm sorry, Russ. I want more than that."

"You could *have* more than that, dammit!" he said, spinning her back around. "I offered you marriage ten years ago, and, darlin', you turned me down flat. I haven't offered it again because you made it very clear that marriage wasn't in your get-ahead-in-my-career game plan."

"Why are you harping about marriage?"

"Isn't that what this is all about? Isn't that why you broke off with me—so you could marry that...that clotheshorse?"

"Russ," she said with a patient shake of her head, "I hardly knew Wayne when you and I broke up six months ago."

"Seven."

"What?"

"Almost seven months ago. Six months and twenty-six days, to be exact."

Amy couldn't believe he knew exactly how many days had passed since she'd told him it was over between them, and Russ could have shot himself for letting her know he was keeping count.

He cleared his throat. "Let's get back to the issue here."

"What *is* the issue here?"

"Your marriage. What else?"

"Fine." Amy shifted her weight to one leg and folded her arms across her breasts. "Let's settle it. I'm marrying Wayne Hardeman in about five weeks. Do you have a problem with that?"

"As a matter of fact, I do." He measured about an inch of air between his thumb and forefinger. "Just a minor one: the fact that I love you and you love me—not him."

"I don't love you," she said, but she couldn't look him in the eye.

"That isn't what your body said a few minutes ago."

Amy turned a bland gaze to him. "That was lust, Russ, not love. I've never denied that you're an incredibly sexy man or that you can turn me on. But it takes more than lust to make a marriage, as you once found out, if you'll recall."

Russ blushed to the roots of his auburn hair at the mention of his brief, disastrous marriage. "Let's leave Tammy out of this."

"Maybe you've forgotten your former wife, but I haven't."

Russ shook his head slowly. As usual, when he thought of Tammy, he got fighting mad. "I haven't forgotten her. As a matter of fact, I learned some pretty valuable lessons at her hand. And one of them is that women are scheming, two-timing—"

"I learned something from her, too," Amy interrupted angrily.

"Yeah?"

She took a step closer. "Yeah. I learned that this undying love you supposedly felt for me lasted until you got to the city limits." She poked with a slender finger the center of his chest. "As a matter of fact, if ProRodeo had a standing for Best Cowboy Stud, you'd have won hands down!"

"It bothered you, did it?" he said, circling her wrist in a gentle hold.

"Only because I was fool enough to believe it when you said you loved me," she told him, jerking her hand free.

"I did love you!" he yelled, thoroughly out of patience with her. "But when you turned me down, I swore I'd forget you. You remember that, don't you?"

"Yeah, I remember. And *that's* why you went through women like a box of Kleenex?"

"Well, why the hell else, darlin'?" he drawled sarcastically. "Being a wallflower was never my style."

Amy was silent. In the face of his honesty her anger was fading, and in its place was shame for stooping so low as to throw what must surely be the hurtful memory of his failed marriage into his face. He'd never mentioned it while they were together, but of course she'd learned about it from Zach. Strangely enough, she mused, she and Russ never talked about their personal pasts or the future when they were together, confining their reminiscences to friends and family. She'd supposed it was because their past was over and done with and their futures were headed down diverse paths. For six years they had confined their relationship to the parameters of their few brief, love-spangled hours together.

"It didn't work."

His statement intruded on the thoughtful silence and brought her eyes to his. "What?"

"All the women I saw to try to forget you. It didn't work."

Amy wanted to tell him that she was sorry he was still longing for something that couldn't be, but before she could speak, he continued.

"You're jealous of Tammy. No," he said, holding up a hand in protest when she started to speak, "don't try to deny it. I married someone else a year after you left town and that eats at you the same way that your planning to marry this Wayne guy eats at me."

It isn't true. I'm not jealous. . . .

"Do you want to know why I married her when I was supposed to be in love with you? You never asked."

Her heart spasmed in sudden pain. She shook her head. She didn't want to hear this. She didn't want to hear it because it was hurting Russ too much to tell.

He breathed deeply, an act that stretched the taut muscles of his broad chest. He dropped his head and spoke to the floor. "She was pregnant."

Her surprised gasp brought his head up.

"Tammy said the baby was mine, and even though I found out later that my future wife wasn't, as grand-daddy Wheeler used to say, 'pure as the driven snow,' I had sufficient reason to believe her." A wry smile twisted his lips. "Hell, I guess my upbringing was stronger than my new morality. I thought I ought to do what was right, so I asked her to marry me. God knows why she accepted."

His voice was even, emotionless, and, knowing him as she did, Amy realized that his total lack of visible emotion was in itself a measure of how much the memory still hurt.

"Russ," Amy said, "you don't have to tell me this."

He didn't listen. He continued as if she hadn't spoken, as if he needed to tell her. "Tammy had a troubled pregnancy from the start, but she was damned well going to try to be the top barrel racer in the circuit. She started spotting one day when she was about three months along, but she rode anyway. She told me that nothing was going to stop her from getting what she wanted. She lost the baby that night.''

Amy wanted to go to him and put her arms around him and hold him until his hurt went away, the way she had a hundred times in the past, but all she could think to say was, ''I'm sorry.''

He nodded, and the smile on his face was bittersweet. ''Yeah. So am I.'' He reached for his coffee cup, deliberately ending the tale, deliberately altering his tone to one of matter-of-factness. ''I divorced her as soon as it was legally possible... best thing I ever did. We never would have made it.''

''Neither would we,'' Amy said lowly, the comment a natural segue to get them back to their original difference of opinion.

''How can you know that, Amy? I would have gone to hell and back for you.''

''You would have gone to hell and back,'' she said softly, ''but you wouldn't give up the rodeo.''

''What?''

''You knew I hated it, but when I turned you down, you kept right on riding. You didn't try to change for me.''

''Why should I change for anyone, especially you, after you'd let me know you had no intention of marrying me or anyone else who stood in the way of your dream?''

''If you'd wanted me badly enough, you'd have gone into some other work, moved somewhere else. There's nothing back there in Claude for me.''

Russ shook his head. ''Your Aunt Vicki's been telling you that for so long, you've come to believe it. And as for me changing to please you—" he laughed bitterly "—I didn't know your turning me down was a test."

"It wasn't a test!" she cried. Then her voice softened, and she shrugged. "I just thought that maybe you'd want to change for me if you loved me, but you haven't...not in all these years."

Instead of the remorse Amy thought Russ would feel, he came back at her with, if not anger, full-fledged irritation. "Have you changed for me?" he shot back. "Are you willing to give up your dream for mine? Of course not, but that doesn't make me love you less. You're a grown woman, not a kid, and you should know by now that you love someone for what they are, not for what you'd like them to be."

"What are you trying to say?"

"I'm saying that if there wasn't one other thing in Claude for you, I was there. I know you loved me back then, and I think you still do, but you were—still are—so wrapped up in what you and your Aunt Vicki think you need, you can't see what will really make you happy."

"You?"

"I think so. I just have to convince you."

"You've had a lifetime to convince me."

"I never knew we were playing for keeps until yesterday."

Amy saw the seriousness in his smoky-blue eyes. She was suddenly tired of their verbal sparring and afraid to look too closely at what he'd accused her of. "Go home, Russ. Leave me alone," she begged.

Russ reached out and cupped her cheek in a callused palm, his thumb grazing the zenith of her cheekbone in a gentle caress. "Like I said earlier, I've tried."

She watched as he turned and picked up his hat from the bar, set it on his head and went to the door.

Then, framed by the aperture, he turned and said, "I'll see you tomorrow night, and remember, Amarillo, that the buzzer hasn't gone off yet."

She watched as he closed the door, leaving her with her jumbled feelings. It wasn't until he was gone that she realized there was no way she would see him the following night. That was the night of the showing.

The Hardeman Gallery was a large, sprawling building situated in a suburb of Dallas. Built of rough Louisiana cypress and Arkansas rock, it somehow managed to evoke a sense of the past while looking completely modern. It consisted of a massive reception room for newer works and a long hallway with smaller galleries branching off to each side. The culmination of an artist's success at the Hardeman was to monopolize a room of his or her own, which, after the showing, was the next step in Amy's plan.

The excitement Amy usually felt was still missing, she thought, but the nervousness was back—with a vengeance. This was her night—her success or failure. The fight with Russ the day before had been banished to the back of her mind, the way the Gorman's, the Nordahl's and the Seabourn's had been banished temporarily to the back rooms.

Amarillo Corbett pastels and oils dominated the silver-gray fern-bedecked reception area. The only work not Amy's were three pieces of sculpture by Ken Ottinger in one corner of the room.

The affair was black-tie, and tuxedo-clad men were the perfect foil for their companions, whose gowns represented every hue of the rainbow. Conversation was a pleasant hum punctuated with an occasional tinkling laugh, the air was redolent with costly perfumes, and

jewels glittered with equal brightness on wrinkled necks
and young, expressive hands.

Wayne, resplendent in his own tuxedo, and Amy, her
nearly platinum hair rivaling the jewels, wandered
through the room. She held a glass of champagne in one
hand and rested the other in the crook of Wayne's arm as
they made their way through the throng of well-wishers.

Her silk chiffon dress was long and champagne-hued
with a front and back that plunged almost to the waist
from softly shirred shoulders. The wide sleeve openings
left her golden-tanned arms bare, and the gathered waist
was banded by a gold belt. Diamond-and-emerald earrings, a gift from Wayne, dangled at her ears, and a
matching drop on a delicate gold chain nestled in the
slight cleft of her breasts.

Whispers followed their every step. Wasn't she beautiful? Wasn't Wayne Hardeman a dream? Was it true
they were engaged? Hadn't he been married before, and
didn't he have a son somewhere? Amy's success seemed
to have bred an avid curiosity about the details of her life.

As was customary at the Hardeman Gallery, the first
showing was a private, by-invitation-only affair, limited
to those people considered true patrons of the art. Wayne
and his sister, Bette, bestowed that status only on those
who had spent several thousand dollars on art spon-
sored by the gallery. The following afternoon, on Friday, the gallery would open its doors to the public, and
Amy would once again be in attendance, a thought that
made her sigh.

"Bored?" Wayne's voice was light and teasing.

She flashed him a quicksilver smile. "Scared."

The arm around her waist tightened, pulling her closer.
He laughed, a low, intimate sound that drew the atten-

tion of nearby women like children to candy. "Why are you afraid?"

"They might hate me."

"Not if the comments we've been hearing can be believed. I think the Collinses are taking *Quiet Village*, and the Greeleys are trying to choose between *Medicine Man* and *Signing the Treaty*."

Amy arched her eyebrows in surprise and pleasure. As the invitation had stated, the works on display represented Amarillo Corbett's perception of the people and customs left behind by the westward march of civilization. Her work sought out the most profound statements of many types of Indian and Western culture. They were her contribution to posterity, her way of preserving a way of life otherwise lost forever.

Quiet Village, one of the many different renditions she'd done of a village of teepees, remained one of her favorites, no matter how many different mountains, plains or villages she did, no matter how many different color palettes or mediums she used.

Her gaze found *Medicine Man* hanging on the opposite wall. The work showed an old Navaho man, crouched, shrunken and wrinkled, painstakingly creating a sand painting, an art form created by trickling pollen, crushed sandstone or charcoal from burned trees to create a picture whose only pattern is in the mind of its creator, a painting whose purpose was to call forth divine healing.

She was mentally comparing it to *Signing the Treaty*, when Bette, thin, dark and vivacious, approached them with an avaricious twinkle in her brown eyes and a smug smile on her carmine-painted lips. "My God, Wayne, I just sold *Rescue the Morning Star*."

Amy's eyes widened. *Rescue the Morning Star* was her most ambitious project, an oil painting that had required an ambitious amount of research and wore an ambitious price tag. She turned to Wayne with a wide smile. He matched it with one of his own, gripping her hands tightly. "Congratulations, darling. You're on your way."

"Who bought it?" Amy asked, turning to Bette.

She shrugged and tucked a lock of chin-length, sable-brown hair behind her ear. "Some gorgeous hunk I've never seen before, although he must have bought something from us, or he wouldn't be here."

She spied a couple across the room and waved. "Gotta go," she said. "I'm going to try to steer the Greeleys toward *Signing the Treaty*, because Charla Jefferson is dying for *Medicine Man*." She swept away, leaving a cloud of expensive perfume in her wake.

With a smile, Amy watched Bette zero in on her next victim. If there were doubts in anyone's mind about the reason for the Hardeman Gallery's success, one had only to consider the dynamite combination of Wayne's ability to spot potential success at a glance and Bette's spectacular salesmanship. Separately, they were impressive; together, they were awesome.

Amy sipped her champagne, her mellow gaze sweeping the room's occupants. She saw several easily recognizable faces—a prominent Dallas-based dress designer, a slightly shady politician, a popular Hollywood star whose family still lived in Dallas and a handsome man who looked familiar. A man her first gaze passed over, then returned to with a snap.

Russ. Russ looking exceedingly handsome and undeniably sexy as he stood leaning with careless negligence against a pillar, one hand thrust into the pocket of his slacks, staring at her with palpable intensity.

Amy stared back, wondering what to say, what to do. As she stared at him, he straightened and started toward her. Her stomach lurched, and her panicked gaze flew from him to Wayne, who was indulging in some light-hearted flirting with Charla Jefferson, a wealthy Dallas divorcée whose reputation for having a good time was the only thing exceeding her bank balance. Only fleetingly did it occur to Amy that she wasn't the least bit jealous of the attention Wayne was paying Charla.

As Russ approached, she grabbed Wayne's arm, as if by holding on to him she might keep herself from being affected by the feelings racing through her. Disbelief came first. What was he doing here? Panic followed on its heels. How was she going to explain his gate-crashing to Wayne? Wonder was not far behind. Why had she always supposed Russ would look out of place in a tuxedo?

Her feelings must have transmitted themselves to Wayne, who turned just as Russ stopped in front of them, sweeping her from toe to crown with a look that, in her mind, fell just short of indecent.

"Hello, cuz," he drawled, taking a sip of his champagne, his eyes, bright with mischief, meeting hers over the top of his glass.

"Hello, Russ," she replied with as much equanimity as she could muster. *What* was he doing here? "Wayne, you remember Russ."

Wayne acknowledged Russ's presence with a puzzled frown that repeated Amy's mental question. Then without faltering, he introduced Russ to Charla, whose eyes lit up with pleasure when Russ bestowed his slow sexy smile on her.

"Nice dress," Russ told Charla, his eyes moving over her with the same slow deliberation they had Amy—from the strapless, black sequined bodice that pushed her ample breasts upward, to the slit exposing a generous portion of creamy thigh encased in the sheerest of silk stockings.

Charla moistened her scarlet lips with a flick of her tongue. "Thanks."

"Are you enjoying the show, Russ?" Amy asked in an attempt to divert his attention.

"Very much," he said, his smile and tone of voice sincere. "You're a talented lady."

Charla scooped a martini from the tray of a passing waiter. "Are you here to buy, Russ, or just looking?" she asked before her tongue curled around the olive.

Amy glowered. Charla made the simple act look X-rated.

Wayne cleared his throat.

Russ's firm, chiseled lips curved slightly. "That depends."

"On what?"

"Whether or not I see anything I want to take home."

Charla laughed and, moving nearer to Russ, linked her arm through his. "Come with me. I want to show you the painting I'm taking home."

Russ looked from Amy to Wayne. "Excuse us, please. Amy, it looks as if the show's a great success." He indicated the admiring crowd. "You finally have everything you've wanted. All this and Wayne, too. Congratulations, cuz."

What he said was true, so why did she feel like crying? "Are you going?" she couldn't help asking.

"Maybe," he replied enigmatically, casting Charla a sidelong glance. He shook hands with Wayne and dropped another of those chaste kisses on Amy's cheek. "I'll be seeing you," he said, turning and crossing the room with Charla on his arm.

Amy blinked. This was it? He'd finagled his way into a party where he didn't belong just to congratulate her on getting what she wanted from life? Why?

Because he found a more willing woman, that's why.

Charla Jefferson wasn't a woman; she was...an overpainted sexpot who...

"Why the frown, darling?" Wayne asked, smiling down at her. Then he followed the direction of her gaze, and they both watched as Charla fed Russ a bite of caviar, watched Charla's tongue skim her upper lip in the same way Russ's did to catch an errant morsel.

Amy knew that Charla was all but licking that tiny bit from his mouth herself. Her eyes narrowed. "Charla Jefferson is a man-eating witch."

Wayne chuckled. "They're both free and over twenty-one, but your country friend may be taking on more than he can handle."

Amy doubted it, but the thought failed to reassure her. For the next thirty minutes, as she talked, laughed and listened to her fans sing her praises, her mind and her surreptitious looks were on Russ and Charla as they wandered from painting to painting, group to group. From the way things looked, Russ fit in very well. Even from across the room there was no mistaking the admiring glances he garnered from the women—or the men, for that matter. Funny, she'd never thought of him as a ladies' man; he'd always been a man's man, unlike...

Wayne.

She squelched the disloyal thought. Comparing Wayne Hardeman to Russ Wheeler was like trying to compare imported bonbons to peanut brittle. Wayne and Russ were both men; bonbons and peanut brittle were both candy. The similarities ended there. Wayne was cultured; Russ was a diamond in the rough—although, she admitted, as she watched him mingling with the elite of Dallas society, he wasn't as rough as she'd imagined.

"You're never going to believe this night!" Bette chortled from behind them. "I mean, the critics *love* you! Even Sondra DeVrees was talking about buying *Rescue the Morning Star*, but I had to tell her to find something else."

"It did sell, then?" Wayne asked.

"It did," Bette said with a wide, red smile. "I can't remember the buyer's name, but it was someone from something called Shoestring Enterprises. Have you ever heard of them?" At the negative response from Amy and Wayne, she said, "Me either, but the company name was so unusual, it stuck in my mind."

Bette saw another gallery employee standing nearby and motioned her over. "Joan, do you remember the name of the man who bought *Rescue the Morning Star*?

Joan looked at Wayne, mock consternation on her face. "Check Bette's pulse—she may be dead." Then, looking back at Bette, Joan asked, "Surely you remember the good-looking guy with the auburn hair—Russell Wheeler?"

Amy's world tilted and whirled. Russ had bought *Rescue the Morning Star*? For ten thousand dollars?

"Amy, are you all right?" Wayne's voice came out of a loud, roaring vacuum.

With a supreme effort, she forced her mind to stop its mad spinning and focus its attention on the trio looking at her with concern. "I . . . I'm fine," she stammered. "I think it's just the excitement."

Russ didn't have ten thousand dollars.

Her voice cracked on a giddy laugh. "Who would ever have thought that Amarillo Corbett from Claude, Texas, would sell a painting for ten thousand dollars!"

Wayne, Bette and Joan laughed, thinking they understood her mood. But they didn't. They couldn't, because she didn't understand it herself. Her eyes, wide and searching, skimmed the crowd, hoping she could find Russ, hoping he could explain how and why...

She spotted him at the door, Charla still clinging to his arm. While Amy watched, he leaned down to hear something Charla was saying. He smiled, draped his arm over her shoulders, and together they disappeared into the night. Without realizing she was doing it, Amy clamped her teeth down tightly on her lower lip.

It seemed Russ had found something he wanted to take home after all.

Chapter Four

The rest of the evening was a blur of faces and warm wishes, but Amarillo hardly heard any of them. All she could think of was Russ leaving with Charla Jefferson, Russ kissing those beautiful red lips and caressing that to-die-for body. Amy's apprehension over the success of the showing, combined with her worry over Russ, left her completely exhausted by the time Wayne deposited her at the apartment door with a kiss, a few words of congratulations and a softly uttered, "I'll call."

She watched him walk down the hall to the elevator, a feeling of relief eddying through her. Then she went inside and closed the door behind her, sagging against it with a deep sigh. The indrawn breath communicated one thing to her olfactory senses: Someone had dripped a pot of coffee—recently.

Russ. It couldn't be anyone else.

She wanted to laugh in relief, wanted to yell at him for being so crazy as to leave with Charla Jefferson in the first place, but mostly she wanted to know how and why he'd bought her most expensive painting. She reached up to unhook the diamond and emerald earrings, asking the question aloud to the darkened room.

"Why?"

"Because the woman in the picture is you," he said, the sound of his voice coming from the vicinity of the easy chair.

She might have been asking why he hadn't gone home with Charla for the night or why he was at the apartment uninvited again, but he knew intuitively that she was asking about the painting.

Moving through the dark apartment, Amy dropped the earrings onto a small table and perched on the arm of the sofa. She should have turned on the light, but there was something comforting about the cloak of darkness. Bending to unbuckle her high-heeled gold sandals, she said, "That painting is of an Indian woman, Russ—not me."

"It's your body," he told her.

She was surprised to find that he was sitting in one corner of the sofa, not in the easy chair. The darkness, she realized, while comforting, was also deceiving.

"I've made love to you enough to know that your breasts tilt just that way and that your waist curves into your hips exactly the same way the Indian woman's does."

Heat rose in Amy's cheeks at the husky observation and, in an almost desperate attempt to prove him wrong, she conjured the painting's image in her mind. The woman on the platform was naked and daubed with ceremonial symbols. A slight wind blew her dark hai over the most feminine portion of her body. Warriors circled her; one had his bow and arrow ready, while another had his tomahawk poised. Both awaited the ascent of the morning star just rising over the field of corn sprouting in the background—waiting for just the right moment to deal the sacrificial blow. A solitary warrior on a prancing paint horse was riding in, leaning low to one side, his knife blade slashing at the leather thongs binding the maiden.

Before she could decide whether or not he was right and the body she had painted was indeed hers, he said, "Tell me about it."

She felt a sense of relief that he wasn't going to pursue his comment and launched into the story that had seemed to cry out to be painted. "It's based on a true story about a young Pawnee warrior."

"The guy on the horse?"

"Yes. The Pawnee had many important ceremonies, but their most dramatic was the sacrifice to the morning star."

"The woman, obviously."

Amy nodded, forgetting that he couldn't see in the darkness. "At the summer solstice, a captive maiden was stripped and painted with symbols. For three days she was shown the greatest honor and respect, but on the fourth day they tied her and put her on the platform, where the priests pretended to torture her. Then, just as the morning star rose, one warrior shot an arrow through her breast while another clubbed her. Her heart was removed as a sacrifice to the morning star, and her body was filled with arrows by the men and boys."

"Charming practice."

"It was an act of atonement."

Russ grunted, unimpressed. "So what did this guy on the horse have to do with it?"

"In the early part of the mid-nineteenth century, a respected young warrior who was shocked at the cruelty rode in and set the woman free—the deed I tried to capture in my painting."

"So what did they do to him? Go for a double sacrifice that year?"

"Surprisingly," she said with a slight smile, "they honored him for his bravery. They discontinued the ceremony from then on, and everyone seemed relieved."

"Interesting. Do you think the brave ended up with the woman?"

"Who knows?"

"He did." Russ's voice held conviction. "If he saved her, she was grateful and gave him her undying love."

Amy felt her mouth curving into a whimsical smile. "Did anyone ever tell you that you're a romantic, Russ Wheeler?" she said, her animosity vanished and nothing between them but that easy, comfortable camaraderie that comes with a long-standing friendship.

"Not lately."

She laughed, the sound low and intimate in the darkness.

"It's a great painting," he said. "I'm glad I got it."

They had finally come full circle. "Why did you buy it, Russ? And how? I know rodeo has been pretty good to you, but ten thousand dollars is a lot of money."

"I told you *why*, Amy. I'm not about to let some other man look at the body I know is yours every day for the rest of his life. And the *how* needn't concern you."

"In other words, it's none of my business."

"Right."

"I just hate for you to be in a financial bind because of a painting, when you know I'd paint you one for nothing."

"I'm not in a bind," he assured her. "And as much as I'd like to throttle your Aunt Vicki for pushing her grandiose ideas of success and feminine freedom off on you, I have to admit that you're an excellent artist. The world would have been poorer without Amarillo Corbett's paintings in it."

"Why do you keep bringing up Aunt Vicki as the reason for my leaving home and going into art?"

"Because you were only mildly dissatisfied with your circumstances at home until your parents were killed and Aunt Vicki showed up to help out. She'd broken away from the small-town mold and made a certain success of herself, but nothing on the scale you have."

"You're wrong, Russ. She just wanted to help me make the most of my talent."

"Then why does she keep pushing you?"

"She doesn't."

"Yeah? Why does she keep arranging for you to meet bigger and better people in the art world? Any fool can see that she's a bitter old woman who couldn't quite make the grade, and she saw a way to have a bit of glory secondhand. And if she can arrange for you to marry a well-known gallery owner, so much the better."

"Aunt Vicki had nothing to do with my marrying Wayne."

"No? How did you meet him?"

The good will she'd been starting to feel toward Russ vanished like a puff of smoke. Reaching out, she touched the base of a lamp, and the room was flooded with soft incandescence. Russ was sprawled on the opposite end of the sofa, one arm on the padded armrest, one along the back, his cummerbund and tie discarded, his pleated white shirt unbuttoned halfway to his waist, and a challenge in his smoky eyes.

Amy looked at him in silence. She couldn't tell him that Aunt Vicki had met Bette through catering a big party for the gallery and from there it had only been a matter of time before she'd managed to meet Wayne and introduce him to Amy. The facts did seem incriminating now that Russ had managed to throw them into a different light, but she would never believe that Wayne took her on because of anything anyone would say. He was too protective of his own reputation as an art connoisseur to chance tarnishing that reputation by accepting any work he didn't truly believe was salable.

"Wayne only represents talent. Even if Aunt Vicki did wangle an introduction, he wouldn't be showing my work if I didn't have potential."

"I know that. I'm just saying that your aunt was instrumental in setting all this up."

"She introduced us, Russ. That's all. The way someone introduced you to that bull rider when you wanted to get your ProRodeo card. That's how people get ahead in this world," Amy said, her voice dripping sarcasm. "What do you think she did to get him to propose to me? Held a gun to his head?"

"No. I figure he did that on his own, once the seed was planted."

"What seed?"

"That you were going to be big-time, that you would make a lot of money—"

Amy stood and struck a dramatic pose, her forearm against her forehead. "Oh, please . . ." she groaned. She abandoned her act and faced him with her hands on her hips. "He has money, Russ, in case that fact didn't make an impression on you."

"But he likes it, Amy, and that kind of person is never opposed to making more."

Amy looked at him as if she couldn't believe what he was saying. She neared the place where he sat and glared at him through narrowed eyes. "He loves me, Russ. That's why he's going to marry me. He loves me, and I love—"

His strong hand snaked out and grasped her wrist, jerking her down on top of him with one sharp movement, imprisoning the word she was about to speak beneath his hard, hurting lips.

His mouth, the mouth that had kissed her scrapes and bruises with brotherly concern when they were children, the mouth that had shyly given her her first grown-up kiss, the mouth that had moved over her lips and body with exquisite tenderness, introducing her to the more sensual versions of kissing, now possessed hers with a passion conceived in anger, a punishment bred of hurt, and a thoroughness born of desperation.

The touch of his lips banished the tender feeling of content she'd experienced in the darkness and swept away her own anger. Gradually she realized that her bottom rested against the quickening hardness of his masculinity, and that when he'd pulled her down on top of him, the daring V-bodice of her dress had shifted, partially baring one breast to the heat of his exposed chest.

Her mind, or the portion of it that could still function, recognized her capitulation with a sense of acceptance. This was always the way it happened with them. They both knew the rules—her rules—and they were both well versed in the limits she'd set on their relationship ten years ago. On the surface, they both were willing to abide by those boundaries.

When he came to see her, they went out to dinner, talked about mutual friends and family, and she silently vowed that there wouldn't be a repeat performance of their fierce and glorious lovemaking. But the instant he touched her, her need overcame her common sense and her vows vanished beneath the pure pleasure he made her feel. He was so unrepentantly male that only the coldest woman could fail to feel an exultant joy in the knowledge of his touch.

The same joy she was feeling now.

She felt his hand move between their bodies, his fingertips brushing the tip of her breast. She moaned, a sound trapped in her throat, a sound that manifested her despair and lamented her need. It wasn't fair, she thought; it wasn't even decent for any woman to feel what he made her feel. It wasn't right that he could make her feel things that Wayne...

Wayne!

Amy brought her palms up and pushed with all her might against Russ's shoulders, turning her head and tearing her mouth from his. Shame rushed in on a wave of remorse. Dear God, what was she doing, letting Russ kiss her this way when she was engaged to Wayne? She scrambled off his lap, scrubbing at her lips like an angry child and racing across the room to the window that overlooked the glittering, bejeweled city. She stood with her arms locked across her waist, her forehead resting against the glass, fighting her disappointment in herself and damning Russ for coming to see her when she'd told him not to.

Without warning, without so much as a sound, she felt his arms go around her from behind, crossing over hers and pulling her back against him. She heard him sigh and felt him rest his chin on the top of her head. Her first inclination was to pull away, but she realized she couldn't.

Their eyes met in their reflections in the plate glass—a tall auburn-haired man with steady blue eyes and a woman in a fashionable gown, her own devil-ridden eyes searching his... as if she might find the answers to the questions churning through her.

Why had he come back? Why does his slightest touch arouse such uncontrollable feelings? And why don't I have enough willpower to fight those feelings? It came to her slowly, that her response to him seemed in some way to be a culmination of the uncertainty she'd been experiencing the past week or so. She didn't know what it meant, but she knew that tonight was a turning point. It was time to make some decisions and stick by them. It was time she cut her ties with the past, time she gave up on the dreams of yesterday and stopped longing for what might have been, if only... If only Russ were a different kind of man, a man like Wayne. If only she were a different kind of woman, one content to be what Russ wanted. If...

"If you marry him, you'll be making a big mistake, Amarillo." Russ's voice was a low rumble above her head while his lips nuzzled the softness of her hair.

"No!" Her voice throbbed with conviction, a conviction she was far from feeling.

"Every time he touches you, you'll wish it were me." The statement was followed by a tender kiss to her temple.

"I won't." This time her denial was pathetically weak.

Russ turned her to face him and cupped the side of her face with one hand. "You love me. Why is that so hard for you to admit?"

She didn't answer, and he smiled at the stubborn look on her face that he knew so well from the past. His thumb brushed the short hair near her ears, and he trailed his rough fingertips over her cheekbone, around her jaw, and brought them to rest on her lips. Amy willed herself to ignore the treacherous feelings his touch brought to vibrant life.

Looking into her eyes with disarming directness, he said, "You've been fighting this—fighting me—for ten years. You owe it to yourself to give this a chance to work, Amy. You owe it to both of us."

As much as she wanted to, she couldn't look away. She could think of no flip reply, no words of anger to make him or the feelings his nearness evoked go away. "Even if I *did* love you, Russ, it would never work," she said, sounding like a broken record even to herself.

"You've never given it a chance. I think you're afraid it will work."

"That's crazy! It's—"

"Then prove it," he said, interrupting.

"What?"

"Let me prove that I can fit into your world. And I'll prove to you that even though you don't want to live in a small town, that's exactly where you belong."

"Clients are in the city."

"You've made your contacts. Let the gallery do the selling, and you concentrate on giving them something great to sell."

"I'd curl up and die in a small town!" she cried. "What is there to paint in the country?"

Russ smiled. "I thought artists relied on their imagination. Besides, I read somewhere that artists should never deny their environment or be limited by it. You're doing both—by choice. I'll show you that a small-town climate is perfect for your work."

Amy couldn't help smiling back. She knew a ruse when she saw it. "This is a challenge, right?"

"Double dog dare you," he said with a nod, flinging a familiar taunt from their childhood straight at her, knowing she'd never been able to refuse a dare.

Amy's teeth worried her bottom lip. Maybe he was right. She knew it would never work, even though a part of her might wish it would, but Russ still harbored the belief that they belonged together. Maybe what she needed to do for both their sakes was to go along with whatever he suggested, to prove once and for all that anything lasting between them was impossible.

"What do you suggest?" she asked.

"That I stay here with you for one week, to show you that, country bumpkin or not, I can fit into your world."

Her eyes widened in surprise. "You make it sound as if I'm ashamed of you and the fact that you're from the country."

"Aren't you?"

She looked appalled at the suggestion. "No. I don't think you'll fit, but not because of your background. I think it's more a question of you feeling as stifled here as I would back home. It has nothing to do with being ashamed of you."

"Well," he said with a slow grin, "that's something. So what do you say?"

She shrugged. "It might be a good idea. But we have to get one thing straight."

"Yeah?" he asked, unable to believe she was agreeing so easily.

"No more incidents like—" Her eyes met his, then danced away from the humor gleaming there. "—like what just happened between us."

"You're saying you'll go for the deal if I don't make any passes."

She nodded.

"I don't believe you're really going to give this a try."

"Only if you—"

"Keep my hands to myself." He thrust them into his pockets and turned the full impact of his lazy smile in her direction. "Piece of cake."

"So when do we start this ... arrangement?"

"As soon as you can figure out how to break it to your fiancé."

"I'll think of something. What about your riding?"

"There's not a lot of money involved, but I've already paid my entry fee to ride at Mesquite tomorrow night."

"You're awfully sure of yourself," Amy told him.

"I just kept my fingers crossed."

"So we start right now? Tonight?"

"Suits me," he drawled laconically.

Amy looked at his familiar rugged face and the twinkle of mischief in his eyes. Was she getting in over her head with this, or was she finally showing some sense in ending their strange relationship in a roundabout way? She took a deep, fortifying breath.

"Okay, then, I'll get the sheets." Halfway to the linen closet she turned back, a Cheshire cat-like smile on her face. "I hope your feet don't hang over the edge of the sofa."

They did. As a matter of fact, Russ thought, turning on his side and punching his pillow with his fist, his elbows, his arms—*everything*—hung over the edge. He let one arm hang over the side, and his fingers brushed the floor. Damn! His only consolation was that Amy was willing to give his idea a try—that, and the fact that she wasn't sleeping any better than he was. He could hear her thrashing around in her big bed. He could even hear an occasional sigh, and he wondered if her inability to sleep came from the fact that he was so near.

Russ didn't deceive himself. He'd slept in horse trailers, slept sitting up crammed in the back seat with three other guys, slept on sofas smaller than Amy's. He knew that a big part of his sleeplessness was due to the fact that she was alone in her bed, a bed he'd shared with her on more than one occasion. He wished he were sharing it with her now.

Shifting to his back, he folded his arms behind his head and wished for the thousandth time that he hadn't stopped smoking. Sometimes smoking helped a man get things in perspective, helped him to think.

"This is crazy," she said, her voice coming unexpectedly out of the darkness.

"You backing out, Amarillo?"

"No."

"Good."

"It's still crazy."

Silently, Russ agreed, but he was a desperate man, and desperate men used any means at their disposal. Even though she wouldn't admit it, he was as sure she loved him as he was that the sun would come up in the east the next morning. He was positive they could make their different life-styles mesh, but all he had going for him in the way of convincing her of that was the fact that they were dynamite in bed. If he had to hang around Dallas for a week, pretending to be her cousin and following her around from luncheon to luncheon, waiting for her to weaken, he would. And when she did weaken and he got her in bed, he might not let her out until she agreed to break her engagement to Hardeman and promised to marry him, instead.

It was an underhanded trick, he admitted, but hadn't Granddaddy Wheeler always said that all was fair in love and war? And this was both. An all-out war on Amy's senses, to make her realize she loved him. It was underhanded and unbelievably conceited of him. Crazy...

The sounds of Amy trying to be quiet in the kitchen woke Russ from a deep sleep. Flat on his back, he opened his eyes to a brilliant morning and promptly closed them again. With a groan, he turned to his side and drew his knees up in a fetal position, deciding that he'd have to get better to die. He felt as if he'd been thrown and stomped by the meanest bull in the country. There was a crick in his neck from the unnatural angle forced on him by the sofa's padded arm, his backbone felt permanently damaged and his muscles protested every move he made. His feet, hanging over the end of the sofa, had blessedly gone to sleep at some time, but now they were waking up, and the needles and pins shooting through them were nothing short of torture. He swore roundly and leaped to his feet, hoping to get his circulation stirring.

"And a good morning to you!" Amy, who was getting something from the refrigerator, called the mock cheerful greeting over her shoulder.

Russ limped back and forth in front of the sofa, glaring at her back. She could afford to be cheerful. She hadn't slept on the rack the night before.

"Did you sleep..." Her voice dwindled to nothing as she turned and saw Russ pacing the living area dressed in nothing but a snarl and a pair of revealing, bright red jockey shorts.

Turning, he caught a look that was closely related to longing on her face. The look temporarily diverted his attention from his throbbing feet, but even as he was mentally chalking up a point for his side, he saw her rein in her wayward emotions and watched the curtain come down over her face.

Narrowing her eyes at him in a gesture that was rapidly becoming familiar, she said frigidly, "Do you mind?"

"Mind what?" he asked, stopping and putting his hands on his hips, knowing full well what she meant.

"Putting on some clothes."

He shrugged. "I don't mind. Do you care if I shower first?"

"Be my guest," she said with false largess.

Russ headed for the bathroom, leaving her with a frown on her pretty face. He returned in a matter of seconds, and Amy watched in disbelief as he retrieved a small suitcase from the end of the sofa. When he started back toward the bathroom, suitcase in hand, and saw her watching him, he asked innocently, "Have you had your shower yet?"

"No."

"I don't suppose you'd like to join me?"

She shook her head in despair. "Don't you ever give up, Wheeler?"

"Maybe. Someday."

By Thursday of the following week, after one week of self-imposed exile with Russ, Amy was ready to give up, give in, or get out, she wasn't certain which. True to his word, he had carved a small niche for himself in her life, which, along with the flack she was getting from Wayne, made her feel like a Thanksgiving wishbone.

She'd imagined that Wayne would take Russ's temporary stay with his usual equanimity. She was only partly right. He didn't buy her story that Russ had business in Dallas and couldn't afford a hotel room, and, she reasoned, why should he after Russ had bought *Rescue the Morning Star*? Wayne figured that anyone who could fork over for a painting of that price could afford a few nights at the Holiday Inn. Even her reminder that Russ was her cousin didn't help the situation. She didn't think Wayne was jealous; it was just that Russ was always *there*.

It had come as a surprise at how easily they'd fallen into a routine. After breakfast, a meal she'd never eaten until he moved in, Russ loaded the dishwasher and finished cleaning up the kitchen. Then he sat quietly in the living area, just a few feet away from where she worked, reading magazines and the *ProRodeo News* or watching television game shows with the headphones on so the sound wouldn't disturb her. At nine-forty-five he slipped into the kitchen and brewed a pot of fresh coffee, silently bringing her a cup and then going back to his reading. At noon, when she broke for a stay-at-home lunch, usually a sandwich or a salad, he ate without so much as a grumble. Afternoons were spent in much the same way.

His determination to be a part of her life, to fit in, was driving her crazy. He went to lunch with her and Bette charming that jaded jet-setter with his droll sense of humor and his charming, if outdated, manners. He attended a dinner party at Wayne's town house with her on Wednesday night, the same dinner party at which Wayne had planned to announce their engagement—but hadn' when Russ talked everyone into going to Billy Bob's to watch him ride the mechanical bull, a feat he managed with style and grace, even in a tuxedo.

How lucky could one woman get? she wondered. All that and Wayne, too.

By Tuesday she'd been ready to tear up her contract with the Hardeman Gallery and set Russ's suitcase in the hallway, just to be rid of them both for a few days. Wayne, much to her dismay, had renewed his habit of stopping by on his way to the gallery. She supposed his reasoning was that she didn't need to work so hard now that the showing was over. He'd also taken to calling her several times a day, "just to see what she was doing and to tell her he loved her," and to ask when the devil Russ was leaving. It was hard to talk, and impossible to tell him she loved him, too, with Russ sitting nearby, reading or watching television—and listening to her every word.

True to his promise and much to her reluctant concern, Russ hadn't made so much as a halfhearted pass. If they brushed against each other in the kitchen, each drew away as if afraid the contact might ignite some uncontrollable fire. Sometimes she would look toward the bathroom and see Russ—who claimed he got claustrophobic if the door was closed for very long—clad only in a towel, shaving. Once she'd even found herself thinking of his shower invitation that first morning—"I don't suppose you'd like to join me?"—and remembering the way she had joined him on occasion after they'd made love far into the morning.

It was almost as if he were biding his time, waiting for something, and she was waiting for it, too... whatever it was.

* * *

What Russ was waiting for was the opportune time to make a move on her, which was damned hard when he was trying his utmost to be noble at the same time. If he wasn't trying to prove that he wasn't jealous of the time she spent working, he was busy trying to win her friends and influence the people she dealt with on a daily basis. With that and traipsing around after her to lunch and parties, trying to keep from yanking the phone out of the wall every time Wayne called or smashing the man's elegant face when he showed up unexpectedly at the door, it was hard to find just the right moment to instigate a little "accidental" pass.

He knew this uncharacteristic good behavior was bothering Amy. He could see it in her eyes when they touched and he drew away, and when he didn't deliberately go to her the few times he'd caught those looks of longing on her face. At those times, he could have made his move, but backing off seemed a better ploy—it left her wondering.

Now, on Friday, the last day of his week, a week during which he'd nearly gone insane with boredom half the time, he wondered if maybe he had made the wrong decision. Nothing had changed. She hadn't changed. But he had proved that he could go the distance on her turf.

He was tossing a handful of frilly underthings into an open suitcase on her bed when she came through the door with the mail in her hands. When she saw what he was doing, she stopped in her tracks and closed the door behind her.

"What are you doing?"

"Packing for you."

"Packing for me?" she repeated.

"Yeah. My week is up. It's your turn."

"My turn?"

He grinned and turned his head, as if listening carefully. "Is there an echo in here?" He looked her directly in the eye. "I've proved that I can fit into not only your life-style, but your life. It's your turn to go back home with me so that I can make you see that you belong there."

Without answering, Amy carried the mail to the countertop and set it down. She turned and leaned against the cabinets. Since Russ was on the bedroom level, she had to tilt her chin to look up at him. The gesture gave her a haughtiness that set his teeth on edge.

"I'm not going back with you. Not for a week or a day. I'm going to Nashville tomorrow to see a country singer about doing her portrait."

Russ reached out and slammed the top of the expensive tweed suitcase down. From the corner of his eye he had the satisfaction of seeing Amy jump in surprise. He turned and rounded the foot of the bed, heading toward the living area, his booted feet thudding at every downward step he took. He didn't stop until he was standing mere inches from her.

By this time Amy had worked herself into a healthy case of fear. She'd seen Russ hurt, depressed, angry—even angry at her. But she'd never seen this cold fury before.

"I knew you were headstrong, Amarillo," he bit out. "I knew you were mixed up and hungry for glory. I knew you were searching to find out just who you were and what Amarillo Corbett was all about. I'll bet you were as surprised as I am to find out that you're a liar and a cheat."

Her eyes closed. She couldn't believe Russ would say such things to her, but a tiny voice from deep inside whispered that he was right. She had led him to believe she would hold up her end of the bargain, and she hadn't. Did that make her a liar and a cheat? "I'm not a cheat. I just..."

"Just what, Amy? Make up some lie that will salve your conscience if you want, but that won't make it okay with me. You agreed of your own free will to give us a chance. I didn't have to twist your arm or beg. What's the matter? Didn't the week turn out the way you expected? Were you hoping I'd forget my promise to leave you alone and get you in the sack so you'd have one more thing to hold over my head as a reason it won't work between us?"

The accusation hurt. Maybe because it was so close to the truth. Amy didn't think; she reacted. Her hand shot out and struck him across the cheek with a stinging blow. Wide-eyed, she watched the white marks left by her fingers turn a bright red.

Punishing her in the only acceptable way he knew how, Russ grasped her shoulders and jerked her up against him, crushing her mouth with a bruising kiss that made his kisses a week ago seem tame in comparison. His lips ground against hers in anger and punishment, but after a while, when he found no resistance in her, his kiss gentled and he felt a tentative response that grew along with the passion they'd denied themselves for so long. He kissed her sweetly, lingeringly, kissed her until Amy's head began to swim. When he released her, they were both out of breath.

"Is that what you wanted, Amy?" he asked.

Ashamed of her lack of control where he was concerned, she looked up at him. "Bastard," she said on a ragged breath.

His reply was to kiss her once more, but this time he pulled upward on the oversized peach-tinted shirt she wore, seeking and finding her bare breasts. He cupped them in his hands and felt her nipples hardening against his palms. He squeezed them gently, caressed them thoroughly, while his mouth plied hers with tender kisses. When she arched against him, he slid one hand to the juncture of her denim-covered thighs and began a slow rotation with the heel of his hand. She gasped against his lips and, tightening her thighs around his hand, sought a rhythm that matched his.

His mouth left hers, and his lips blazed a heated trail along her jaw to her neck. She reached down a hand to cover his, pressing harder. Her head dropped back, exposing the delicate column of her throat to his kisses while the exquisite pressure in her lower body built with each rotation of her hips against his marauding hand.

She moaned and sought his lips blindly.

Bzzz... The sound of the doorbell shattered the sexually charged moment. Dazedly, Russ released her and, placing both hands on the countertop, lowered his head, dragging in deep draughts of air in an effort to regain control of his runaway emotions.

Bzzz.

He looked at Amy when the buzzer sounded the second time. Her mouth was red and swollen, almost bruised-looking from his kisses. Her caramel-brown eyes, dark with passion, moved from his to the door and back.

"Amy! Are you in there?" Wayne called.

A bitter smile curved Russ's lips. He straightened and, reaching over, pulled down her wrinkled shirt, which was bunched around her waist. "Better answer that."

Obeying his command without really thinking, Amy turned toward the door. She was halfway there when his voice stopped her. "You can run from it, Amy—as long and as far as you want—but it won't go away."

She didn't answer.

Bzzz.

"You said you'd do this for me, and you will. Some way, someday, somehow, you're going to give me that week you promised."

She did turn then, remorse and pain on her pale features. "It's over, Russ. Why can't you accept that?"

"It's never over until it's over, and what we shared a few minutes ago proves that we've got a helluva long way to go before we're finished."

"Amy!" Wayne called again.

With a sigh, she turned and went to the door, opening it to admit a furious Wayne. "What the hell's going on here?" he demanded, looking from Russ to Amy.

She stood near the door with her hands in her back pockets, a tall, disheveled woman with swollen lips, a glazed look in her eyes, and a heart full of tears. What had just transpired in the room was about as obvious as it could be without a proper announcement. Wayne's gaze moved back to Russ, his angry brown eyes clashing with eyes a cool, daring blue.

"I demand to know what's been going on in here."

If she hadn't been hurting so badly, Amy would have laughed at Wayne's Victorian manner.

"That's pretty obvious, isn't it, bub?" Russ said, throwing caution to the wind. He started toward the doorway, where his suitcase sat waiting.

Wayne couldn't have looked more shocked if Russ had punched him in the stomach. "B...But you said he was your cousin," he sputtered.

Amy didn't answer; she just looked at Russ with tear-glazed eyes, watching as he picked up the suitcase.

"Oh, we are, Hardeman," he said, turning and meeting Wayne's questioning look with a cocky smile. "The kissing kind."

Chapter Five

The Tennessee mountains were as beautiful as Amy had always heard they were, and the two-story log house that country singer Darcy Lightfoot called home was a perfect complement to the woodland around it. The green valley with the black board fence and the rough wood barn and outbuildings exuded a calm serenity, a much welcomed serenity after the week she'd just spent with Russ and the fights she'd had with him and Wayne the day before.

She hadn't had the courage to face her reaction to Russ's lovemaking or to wonder what he would do next. She hadn't had the time. She was too busy trying to explain her way out of the situation he'd pushed her into with his uncaring comment to Wayne about the two of them being kissing cousins. Wayne wasn't stupid, and after Russ had gone, he'd asked her very coldly, very dispassionately, what the hell she'd been up to.

What could she do but tell him the truth—up to a point. She came clean about her past association with Russ. It was true they'd known each other all their lives, but no, they weren't really cousins. Yes, she had once had a relationship with him, but it was over. Had been over for several months. When Wayne demanded to know why, if it was over, Russ had been in her apartment that first night, Amy told him that he'd never given back his key. And when he'd asked who had instigated the scene he'd interrupted, Amy was able to tell him truthfully that Russ had. Then she had crossed her fingers and prayed that he wouldn't ask if she'd responded. He hadn't.

She'd watched his cold fury gradually wane, replaced with a curious hurt. When he'd asked her if she still wanted to marry him, Amy had pushed aside her curious vacillation and nodded. Things had gone from there to a trucelike stage—he might have forgiven her, but he hadn't forgotten. He'd dropped her off at the airport a few hours ago, and she got on the jet feeling battered and bruised, all the way from her lips to her soul.

To top off her week, her flight had been late because of a storm, and she'd had no time to do more than hail a cab to get to her scheduled meeting with the country singer on time. Amy felt rumpled and tired and was definitely out of sorts, not in the best frame of mind to be charming and friendly to someone who'd commissioned an expensive portrait.

Her cab pulled to a stop in front of the house just as a dust-kicking horse carrying a slight form rounded a barrel in a far paddock and then raced on to the next one. Amy got out of the cab and, shielding her eyes from the late afternoon sun, watched as the horse made a tight circle around the final barrel and streaked to the far end of the paddock before coming to a skidding halt.

Barrel racing. Amy sighed. It seemed she couldn't get away from memories of Russ and rodeo no matter how hard she tried. The woman patted the horse's gleaming brown neck, and began to jog the horse toward the house.

Amy fumbled in her purse for money to pay the cabbie, who had already taken her suitcase from the trunk and set it on the shady porch that ran the entire length of the front of the house. Feeling a sudden urge to cry, she thanked him and watched as he got back into the cab, turned around and headed back out the long gravel driveway.

She was exhausted. She'd hardly slept the night before, and the nerve-wracking flight around and partially through the storm had depleted what was left of her composure. Now here she was, hundreds of miles from anyone she knew, standing in the driveway of a famous singer, tired, worried and more than a little in awe of the woman—very definitely Darcy Lightfoot, if that long braid hanging over her shoulder was any indication— approaching on a sweaty brown horse.

Dear God, she's gorgeous, was Amy's first thought as horse and rider drew closer. Even though she wore no makeup and was dressed in a cotton shirt and well-worn jeans, the pictures on her album covers hadn't begun to do justice to the coppery tint of her skin, blushed now with a touch of rose from her exertions, or the ebony darkness of her waist-length hair that hung in a long braid over one breast. Amy, dressed in pure silk slacks and a matching jacket of pale aqua, suddenly felt over- dressed and wondered if her short hair made her look as masculine as Darcy's long hair made her look feminine.

Darcy pulled the horse to a stop, a soft smile on her beautifully shaped lips. She slid from the animal's broad back, her moccasin-encased feet hitting the ground with unbelievable lightness before she turned and held out a well-manicured hand. "Hi. You must be Amarillo Corbett. I'm Darcy Lightfoot."

Amy took her extended hand, and they exchanged a firm handshake. "Yes. It's so good to meet you," Amy said. "I've been a fan ever since I heard *Sweet Lies, Satin Sigh*."

"Thanks," Darcy replied with a smile, brushing a wisp of hair away from her face. "Let's go in and get something to drink. You're probably tired from the flight, and I'm thirsty."

"That sounds great." Amy could feel her uneasiness disappearing with every word that fell from Darcy Lightfoot's perfectly shaped mouth.

Darcy tied her mount to an old-fashioned hitching post at the edge of the lawn and started up the brick sidewalk leading to the house.

"You have a beautiful home," Amy offered, looking around with undisguised interest and just a hint of envy. As much as she loved the city, there were times—usually when she was upset—that she really missed the openness and freedom of the country.

Darcy glanced over her shoulder at Amy and smiled. "Thanks. I'm afraid most people who don't know me aren't too impressed, but I'm just not the penthouse type. I was brought up in Arizona on a cattle ranch, and I guess I'm still a country girl at heart."

They reached the porch, and Darcy turned around and walked backward toward the door, her arms outstretched, another of those breathtaking smiles on her face. "This is the real me, Amarillo—blue jeans and moccasins. Think you can get a suitable portrait for posterity out of it?"

Amy blinked. As far as making a suitable portrait, anything Darcy Lightfoot chose to wear would take on whichever facet of her persona she desired, any of which would make a fantastic portrait. Amy told her as much.

"Thanks again. You're good for my ego," Darcy said, opening the door to a spacious living area with a brick fireplace and a hearth that ran the width of the room. The decor was antique and country, with plaid lamp shades over crockery lamps, woven rugs on polished wooden floors, and bits and pieces of memorabilia sitting or hanging on every available surface and tucked into every corner of floor space. The effect was one of cluttered comfort and reflected a love and regard for the past.

Amy glanced around the room, her eyes lighting on a three-gallon crockery butter churn laden with pampas grass and cattails that sat near the fireplace. She remembered that her mother had owned one just like it that had been handed down by her grandmother. Amy's mother had also filled the churn with natural grasses, but at the time, Amy had thought it tacky. Zach had asked Amy if she wanted to take it when she got her apartment, but she had wanted no reminder of her mother's kitchen with its worn linoleum and chipped sink. She wondered suddenly and with a spurt of anxiety where the churn was. She turned to her hostess with sincerity shining in her eyes. "It's lovely."

"I'm glad you like it. Make yourself at home. My maid is off today, so I'll get us something to drink. Is iced tea okay?"

"Fine, thanks," Amy said over her shoulder, already wandering around the room. Darcy disappeared into the next room, and Amy completed her tour.

There was a brass pot filled with magazines sitting next to an easy chair. An old piece of embroidery bearing the message Home Sweet Home was carefully stretched and framed and hung over the mantel, which bore a massive collection of wooden, pewter and brass candlesticks and holders. The room's decor shouted warmth and home and told her volumes about Darcy Lightfoot. And all of it was good.

She fingered a lacy doily and remembered the doilies her mother had starched and stretched over flat cardboard with straight pins holding their pointed edges "just so" until they dried. Where were they? Gone the same way as the churn? And how was it, Amy wondered, that Darcy used many of the same items and decorating techniques that Amy's own mother had, creating a picture-perfect country look, when in the Corbett home it had just looked old and worn?

She heard the soft whisper of Darcy's moccasins and turned to see her bearing a tray with a squat yellow pitcher and two frosted glasses. "Here we are," she said, setting them on a trunk covered with a thick piece of glass that served as a coffee table.

"It looks wonderful," Amy told her, sinking into the reupholstered sofa. "Is that mint?"

Darcy nodded. "I have an herb garden out back." She crushed the sprigs of mint between her fingers, dropped them into the glasses and poured the tea on top. "I forgot to warn you, it's already sweetened."

"No problem. I like it sweet." Amy took the proffered glass and took a healthy swallow. "Fantastic."

"It is good for a change, isn't it?" Darcy said. She picked up her own glass and leaned back in the chair. "How long have you been painting, Amarillo?"

"Please call me Amy. The only time anyone calls me Amarillo is when they're mad at me."

Darcy laughed. "Okay. How long have you been painting, Amy?"

"For as long as I can remember," she said truthfully. "Or I've been drawing that long, anyway. I had a very good art teacher in school, and, after I graduated from high school, I studied for a while in New York. I went to Dallas because there was some interest from a small gallery there. They gave me my start, but it hasn't been until the last couple of years that my work has begun to attract attention nationwide. As a matter of fact, I had my first really big one-woman show last week." She took another sip of her tea and asked, "How did you find out about my work?"

"Through a mutual friend," Darcy said. "Russ Wheeler."

Amy was certain her mouth fell open in surprise. How on earth had Russ come to be friends with someone like Darcy Lightfoot?

"I met him at the Texas State Fair two years ago," Darcy explained. "I was there as part of the grandstand entertainment, and Russ was making appearances, promoting ProRodeo as Best All-Around Cowboy. He conned one of my people into meeting me." She laughed. "You know, I think Russ could charm the rattles off a diamondback."

How well Amy knew that charm. She wondered what Russ had charmed off Darcy but squashed the upsurge of jealousy at the singer's next statement.

"We hit it off really well. We call each other often, and a couple of times a year we get together to drown our sorrows." She smiled reminiscently. "One time when we were both pretty well three sheets to the wind, we even discussed the unlikely possibility of having an affair, but we decided we liked each other too much to risk losing our friendship for a roll in the hay. Unfortunately, Russ and I are both the kind who fall hard and forever, and we'd both already taken the tumble.''

Since Russ swore he loved her, Amy decided that Darcy was saying in a roundabout way that Russ, true to his avowals, had never stopped loving her. It was a subject she didn't want to think about now—if ever. "How did my name come up?"

"I told him my mother had been harping on for months for me to have my portrait painted, and he told me you might be interested, so I called."

"I see."

"Well, relax. The commission is yours," Darcy told her with a smile.

"B...But you haven't seen my work!" Amy sputtered.

"Yes, I have. In *Southwest Art*. I'm impressed."

Amy struggled to find the words to express her thanks but found herself smiling instead and saying, "Does that mean that the slides and projector I brought are just excess baggage?"

"I guess so," Darcy said. "When do we start? And how do we do this? Do you come here or what?"

Amy set her glass on a woven coaster and leaned forward in eagerness. "I'd like to follow you around for a few days to get a feel of what you do, to watch your gestures and see your different facial expressions, if that's possible. That way, I can decide just what we want to capture on canvas."

"That sounds logical to me. When do we start?"

"Some time during the next few weeks is good for me, but let's make it fit your schedule."

"I just finished a short tour and don't plan on doing another for a while. I'd like to have a couple of weeks of quiet to concentrate on writing some new songs, and after that I'll be taping a couple of new ones for an upcoming album, but there wouldn't be any problem with you coming along to watch."

"Good. We should be able to start in a couple of weeks then," Amy said. She sighed. "This was certainly easy. I thought we'd talk about it for a while, haggle over a price, and you'd call me with a yes or no after you consulted with two or three other artists."

"I don't care about the cost nearly as much as I do the finished product," Darcy told her. "I could have called any number of reputable portrait artists, but I know that you try to keep the past alive through your work, especially the traditions of the Indian. It means a lot to me. Besides, you're extremely talented," she tacked on with a laugh.

Amy felt curiously humbled by the praise. She was beginning to find that Darcy Lightfoot was a special person in more ways than her extraordinary singing talent. "Thank you," she said.

They looked into each other's eyes for a moment in one of those rare occasions when two people see and recognize something in the other worth exploring, the first tender shoots of friendship.

Finally they both smiled, and Darcy laughed. "More tea?"

Amy glanced at her watch. "No thanks. I'd better call and see if they held my room at the hotel. With the plane getting in so late, I didn't have time to check in before coming out here."

"Go ahead and call, and if they're still holding it cancel. You're more than welcome to stay here for the night."

"I couldn't do that," Amy said.

"Why not? Success has its price, and it's usually costly o relationships." Her dark eyes held a curious vulnerability. "It gets pretty lonely sometimes, and I miss feminine companionship. My road crew and band are all guys, and sometimes I just want to talk girl talk—you now, what's on sale at Neiman's, what's a good movie o see . . . that kind of thing."

Amy did know. She wasn't surrounded by men the way Darcy was, but her work was solitary. "Are you sure you on't mind?"

"Positive," Darcy said with a smile. "If you'll stay, I'll uy you dinner and then we can come back here and rash."

"Sounds good to me," Amy told her. "Where's the hone?"

In the end, they didn't go out. Darcy called for pizza, hich they ate in their pajamas, sitting cross-legged on e floor in front of the sofa, like two teenagers at a umber party. They sipped colas and groaned about the lories hiding in each morsel of the everything-but-the-tchen-sink pizza, devouring slice after slice and giging as the cheese stretched out farther and farther, 'entually breaking and trailing down their chins.

"How on earth did you get the name Amarillo?" arcy asked at one point.

Amy, who was looping a string of mozzarella back on p of her slice of pizza, explained that her mother had ffered a bad bout of pneumonia, and when she got well al had taken her to Amarillo for a second honeymoon ekend. Amy's conception had resulted, and as a sennental reminder, Sally Corbett had named her only ughter Amarillo.

Darcy laughed and in turn told Amy stories about her uth.

Amy didn't remember when she'd had such fun, and, looking back, couldn't recall a single time when she was growing up that she'd spent the night with a friend. There had always been so many chores, so much to do to help her mother. She'd never wanted to spend the night with her friends, because then she would have to return the invitation.

"Are you all right?"

The sound of Darcy's voice startled Amy from her reverie. "I'm fine." She put down the last bite of her pizza and wiped her fingers on a napkin. "I was just thinking that I never spent the night with anyone when I was growing up. We were so poor I didn't want anyone to see our house or my dad, who was usually drunk."

Darcy looked thoughtful a moment. "You know, I don't think I did, either. We had a little house on the reservation—not much of one, but it was home. I guess we were pretty poor, too, but I never really thought much about not having things, because no one else did, either. Actually, I guess we were better off than most, because Mama worked as a housekeeper for as long as I can remember. Still does."

"We just scraped by," Amy said. "Mom and I kept the house as clean as two people can with five boys and a man tracking in from daylight to dark. And then, when my dad got hurt, and Mom had to get a real job, I inherited it all—the housework, the laundry and the cooking."

"Do they still live in the same place?"

Amy shook her head. "No. My parents were killed in a tornado when I was a senior in high school. My older brother built a house on the land, but our old house has been standing vacant for about eight years now."

"Do you go back often?" Darcy asked, an undisguised wistfulness in her voice.

The fight with Russ over going back to Claude came to mind, and Amy pushed it ruthlessly away. "Not if I can help it. It's taken me ten years to forget that lifetime. I have no desire to go back. What about you? Do you spend much time in Arizona?"

Darcy shook her head. "I don't go back much, either. But unlike you, I'd like to go and stay," Darcy said, her eyes soft with longing.

"Then why don't you?"

It was Darcy's turn to wear a wry smile. "You sound like Mama. Do you remember me telling you that like Russ I was the kind that fell hard and forever?"

"You're still in love with someone back there," Amy guessed.

Darcy took a deep breath and let it out in a sigh. "Yeah. The rancher's son."

"What happened?" Amy asked.

"I guess it all comes down to the fact that I loved him, but he was just looking for a summer fling," she said with a shrug. "What about you? Tell me about the man in your life," Darcy urged, turning the topic of conversation away from herself.

"Russ?" Amy blurted before she realized what she'd done.

"Did Russ give you that ring?" Darcy asked, her surprise evident.

Amy felt a quick rush of heat warm her cheeks. "No, Russ didn't give it to me. I guess I said his name because he's been the man in my life for so long. I'm engaged to Wayne Hardeman, the owner of the Hardeman Gallery in Dallas."

"But..."

"But, what?" Amy asked.

"I don't know. I sense a hesitation in you. Are you having second thoughts?" Darcy asked.

"No!" Amy said quickly. Too quickly.

"Good! When's the wedding?"

"In about four weeks now," Amy told her, realizing that the time was passing swiftly. The thought was sobering.

"So soon?"

"Yes. Soon."

Somehow Amy skirted the questions in Darcy's eyes and steered the conversation back to neutral territory. "Speaking of Wayne, do you mind if I use the phone to call and tell him I'll be flying back tomorrow afternoon?"

"Of course not," Darcy said. "You call, and I'll clean up this mess."

"If you'll wait, I'll help."

"Don't be silly," Darcy said, reaching for Amy's glass. "You're company."

Wayne, who seemed to have put the incident with Russ from his mind, seemed genuinely glad she'd called and ecstatic over news of the commissioned portrait. He was thrilled that she was coming home the next day, telling her he had a big surprise for her. She couldn't help smiling at his enthusiasm. Hearing the warmth of his voice as he told her how much he loved and missed her, Amy, from the distance of several states, experienced again the feelings she'd convinced herself were love. She hung up more settled in her heart than she had been since before Russ had sauntered back into her life. And she went to bed with Wayne, not Russ, on her mind.

And then she dreamed....

She was in her mother's bedroom with the balding chenille spread and the dresser with the cracked mirror, sitting cross-legged on the bed watching her mother wrap the meager stash of Christmas presents for her brothers.

"Why did you get them Levi's and shirts again?" she asked. "You get them the same thing every year."

Sally Corbett smiled at her sixteen-year-old daughter, a pretty, serene smile that made her careworn face look the forty-two years it should look instead of the fifty it did. "Because they need them. And just to keep the record straight, I got them sweaters, not shirts."

"You should get things for Christmas that you'd never get any other time of the year," Amy said. "Something special."

"Really?" her mother asked with bland innocence.

"Yeah. Stuff like jewelry, stereo systems, a television for my bedroom."

"A maid?" Sally asked hopefully.

"Mom!"

Sally finished crafting the bow, something she was very good at, and held up the finished package wrapped with green foil paper and ribbon saved from a present Amy's Aunt Vicki had given her the year before. The package was decorated with clusters of chinaberries picked from the tree in the backyard, sprayed with gold-and-silver paint. To Amarillo, the very fact that they saved their Christmas wrapping was a mark of their poverty, no matter how pretty the package actually was.

"How does it look?"

"Okay," Amy admitted grudgingly.

"What's the matter?" Sally Corbett asked, reaching for a sweater in a Sears box.

"I'm tired of being poor."

"Poor? Who says we are?"

"Aunt Vicki."

Sally's face wore a worried look. "Well, honey, your Aunt Vicki has a lot of grand ideas. She might be my baby sister, but living in the city has changed her in a lot of ways, not all of them good."

"She's beautiful, successful..."

"And unhappy."

"Unhappy? How can you say that?" Amy demanded.

"Because it's the truth. She's gone out and filled her life with things because she doesn't have anyone to care for," her mother said. "Why do you think she's been married twice and each time taken the poor guy to the cleaners for support? You don't need things when you have people to love who love you back, Amy. And in that, I'm rich. Much richer than Vicki."

Amy tossed in the unfamiliar bed, fighting the sadness brought on by the unexpected vision of her mother, even though some part of her mind told her it was only a dream. And dreamlike, she remembered that her mother had somehow bought her an expensive set of oil paints that year and two real, stretched canvasses. Something she would never have done at any other time of the year. Something special.

The next morning Amy slept in, since her plane wasn't leaving until late afternoon. At midmorning she and Darcy shared a pot of coffee, and, after dressing for the day, they loaded Amy's luggage into Darcy's minivan and Darcy treated her to a whirlwind tour of Nashville. They stopped by a boutique, where Amy paid an exorbitant price for a long, straight skirt in rust-colored suede, drove by several well-known recording artists' homes, saw legendary Sixteenth Avenue, the Grand Ole

Opry's new location as well as the old building, and Darcy's recording studio. Darcy ended Amy's orientation with a late lunch at a refurbished fifties diner where she was relatively certain she wouldn't be recognized while they stuffed themselves with old-fashioned hamburgers, fries and real, honest-to-goodness milk shakes instead of a premixed concoction from a machine.

After that they drove to the airport where they checked her luggage, and then had coffee until it was time for the flight, which was scheduled to leave at two-forty. They were just gathering their purses and arguing over who was going to pay for the coffee when Amy was paged on the intercom.

She looked at Darcy, a question in her eyes, unrelated thoughts of terrible things happening running rampant through her mind.

"Amarillo Corbett, please report to the airport information booth," came the summons once more.

"You go on. I'll pay for the coffee and meet you at the waiting area," Darcy suggested, seeing the stricken look on Amy's face.

Amy nodded and almost ran to the designated area. A petite Oriental woman with a glossy pageboy hairdo and dressed in an official airline uniform stood talking to a man dressed in jeans, boots and a T-shirt with a design of a small airplane and the words Flying High Charters ironed onto the back.

Ignoring him, Amy approached the desk and said, "I'm Amarillo Corbett. I believe you have a message for me."

The woman smiled and pointed to the man who was chewing gum ninety-to-nothing. "There it is."

Amy turned to him, a question in her eyes. He was on the lower rung of his forties, whipcord lean with sunburned brown hair, weathered skin and eyes a Montana-sky blue. He was a complete stranger. He held out his hand and, ceasing for the moment his frantic masticating of his gum, smiled a friendly smile that crinkled the skin around his eyes.

"Hi. Cody Jarrell."

Amy took his hand out of politeness. "Mr. Jarrell."

"Call me Cody."

"Cody, then," Amy acquiesced. "Look, Cody, why—"

"I guess you're wondering why I'm here, huh?" he asked, interrupting just that question.

"Yes," Amy said with a nod.

"I'm here to pick you up."

Amy frowned. "Wayne sent you? Why?"

"I don't ask questions, ma'am, I just contract the jobs. But I believe he mentioned something about a surprise."

"I'm glad you're coming back tomorrow, darling. I have a surprise for you."

How like Wayne to do it up really big. No telling what he had in mind, or where Cody Jarrell was flying her.

Darcy walked up, her hair crammed beneath a wide-brimmed straw hat, her face partially concealed by funky sunglasses. "Hi. What's going on?" she asked.

"Wayne sent Cody to pick me up."

"Isn't that sweet?" Darcy said. "It sounds like something interesting is about to happen."

Cody was looking at her with undivided interest. "Don't I know you?"

Darcy smiled sweetly up at him. "I don't think so." She turned her attention back to Amy. "So what's the problem?"

"No problem," Amy said. "I was just trying to get things straight when you got here." She looked at Cody Jarrell. "What about my luggage?"

"It's all taken care of. I got it stowed away a little while ago."

"Well, then, I guess I'm ready." She smiled at Darcy, and they hugged briefly. "Call when you're ready to start on the painting," Amy said.

"Thanks for a great time. I will."

"Sure."

They smiled at each other, and Amy shifted her purse to the other shoulder before looking up at Cody. "I guess I'm all set."

"Good."

They started down the corridor, and Cody suddenly turned back to look at Darcy. "Are you sure I don't know you?"

Darcy smiled. "Positive."

Amy had never flown in a small plane before and spent the first hour clinging to her seat while Cody handled the controls with easy nonchalance and sang slightly off-key beneath his breath. Gradually, she began to relax and sift through her memories of the last few days. For the first time she felt that enough time had passed so that she could examine what had happened between her and Russ, and that self-examination brought home one crystal-clear fact: she might claim to love Wayne Hardeman, but there was no way he could compare to making her feel what Russ did.

The realization puzzled her, and she supposed it could be chalked up to that old science-defying cliché called sexual chemistry. Why did she feel it in quantum amounts for Russ, when she didn't want to, and to a much lesser degree for Wayne, whom she should be feeling it for? There was no rhyme or reason for it that she could see, but she did know that she couldn't blithely ignore it anymore. She was still pondering how to overcome it so that there wouldn't be a repeat performance of what had happened a few days ago when the low thrumming of the plane's dual engines hummed her to sleep.

It was the slow loss of altitude and a sharp banking to the right that finally roused Amy from her rest. Opening sleepy eyes and looking out the window, she saw that dusk was falling, and only a few lingering fingers of sunlight held on to the end of the day.

"Are we here?"

"Sure 'nough," Cody drawled. "We'll be on the ground in no time."

Amy opened her purse and took out a mirror. She combed through her short blond hair and touched up her blush and lipstick. She was spraying a cloud of musky smelling cologne on her wrists when the plane's wheels touched the tarmac, bounced a couple of times and began to grind to a stop.

She glanced out the window again, wondering where Wayne would meet her. Her eyes widened when she realized that they hadn't landed at the Dallas/Ft. Worth airport.

"Cody?" she asked, her gaze taking in other familiar landmarks.

Cody broke off his rendition of the song "La Bamba" to murmur, "Hmm?"

"Where are we, anyway?"

"Amarillo."

"Why are we in Amarillo?" she asked with a frown.

"That's where the guy who hired me said to bring you."

Guy? All sorts of wild thoughts began to parade through her mind. Why would Wayne meet her in Amarillo? Was he—she paled at the thought—going to confront her and Russ together? Had he seen Russ?

The plane came to a full stop, and Cody took off his headphones and undid his seat belt. Amy followed suit. She slung her purse over her shoulder just as the door opened from the outside and a familiar auburn head came into view.

"Russ!" she cried, her worry over this whole unorthodox situation melting with surprise. He filled the small doorway in a way that was somehow intimidating.

"Hello, Amarillo," he said, a gleam in his blue eyes she couldn't quite define.

"Where's Wayne?"

"Dallas, I imagine," Russ said with a shrug. He held out his hand to help her down the short flight of steps, and Amy accepted it in an automatic gesture.

"Dallas?" she echoed. "Then what am I doing here? Wayne hired Cody to take me someplace to meet him."

"Uh-uh. *I* hired Cody."

Amy's mind raced, skirting a possibility she didn't want to face. "You? Why?"

Russ's rugged face wore a pleased smile that Amy didn't trust one bit.

"Russ Wheeler, what's going on?" she demanded.

"Well, darlin'," he said with disgusting cheerfulness, "it's like this. You've been kidnapped."

Chapter Six

You can't do this!'' Amy stormed.

It was the same song, somewhere around the seventeenth verse. Russ had listened to it and what she was
going to do to him when she got the chance, all the while
he took her luggage from the plane. Her tirade continued sotto voce during the time he "escorted" her out of
the terminal and increased in volume on the way to the
parking lot where his dusty truck sat waiting. He slung
her suitcase into the back, unlocked the door and waited
while she climbed inside. Then, pulling out of the parking lot and into Amarillo's evening traffic, he shifted his
attention from the road to her indignant face. "I just did
darlin'," he reminded her gently.

"Kidnapping is against the law!"

"So turn me in," he quipped.

"You can't make me stay in Claude. I'll leave the first
chance I get."

The gleam of satisfied mirth in his eyes died. "You won't get a chance, Amy. I intend to see to that."

"People will miss me. Wayne will call the police and report that I'm missing." A rising note of hysteria urged aside the conviction in her voice.

"Your precious Wayne has already received a call telling him where you are."

"What?" she cried. "Who called?"

"Jason."

"Jason," she repeated with a sinking heart. Jason, her youngest brother. She could believe it. Russ and all her brothers were as tight as husk on corn, and Jason had an ornery, fun-loving streak a mile wide in him.

"How did you find out when I was leaving Nashville?"

"Darcy," Russ supplied, guiding the truck around a corner with a deft motion.

"What!" Amy shrieked.

"Simmer down, simmer down. She's only an accomplice by trickery. I called her last night to see how things were going between the two of you. She said great; she liked you a lot. I asked—very innocently—how long you were staying, and she, in true innocence, told me what time she was taking you to meet the plane. She also told me that Wayne had a surprise for you, a piece of information I understand was the stroke of genius when Cody said he'd come to take you back."

Amy was dumbfounded. Speechless. She stared at Russ's masculine profile and tried to make sense of the whole thing. Darcy had unwittingly helped Russ perpetrate this...this charade! Well, he could watch her twenty-four hours a day if he had to, because there was no way she was staying, just as there was no way Wayne would believe that she... Believe what? What had they told him?

"What reason did Jason give Wayne for my not showing up in Dallas?" she asked, breaking the silence.

"That one was easy. He told him they were planning a surprise party for Zach's seventeenth wedding anniversary and that you'd forgotten it in all the hubbub with the art show." He grinned. "Pretty slick, huh?"

Amy lowered her lashes to block out the sight of his victorious face. "Pretty stupid," she murmured.

"Wayne bought it," he said with a shrug.

Yes, he probably would. Wayne wasn't conniving like some people she knew. Sharp, yes. Manipulative, even. But he wasn't a sneaking, low-down, good-for-nothing conniver. She sighed and opened her eyes to look at Russ once more. "Why are you doing this?" she asked.

He turned briefly to look at her. "Because you owe it to me. You agreed to give me a week, and you reneged. I told you I'd get it somehow."

She sank back into the corner of the truck's cab and closed her eyes again. "I think I hate you," she said in a weary, conversational tone.

Russ honked at someone who pulled in front of him. "I know you think you do, but you don't. Not really."

"Why don't you just leave me alone and let me live my life?" she asked without opening her eyes.

"That's what I've done for the last ten years, Amy. I knew when you turned me down ten years ago that you had to have some time to figure things out for yourself, to come to terms with who you were. Even when I was out raising hell, I knew I owed you that much." He sighed. "After the deal with Tammy, I realized that granddaddy was right about that old saying, 'Marry in haste; repent in leisure,' and I decided to straighten up and give you all the time and space you needed."

He glanced over at her and saw that even though she still reclined against the seat, she had turned her head toward him and opened her eyes, listening, really listening, for perhaps the first time.

"When we first...got back together that night six years ago, I thought everything would be okay, that it was only a matter of time before you realized we were right for each other and we could get on with our lives—together. But the more I listened to you and your goals for your life, I began to see that it was a life that left no room for me except the little bit you gave me whenever I came to town and looked you up."

He laughed, laughter tinged with bitterness. "Hell, even that was given to me more or less against your will. There wasn't a single time that I came to see you really expecting to wind up in your bed. You made it clear every time I left that it wasn't going to happen again, but I kept coming back, hoping I could change your mind by playing the one ace I had up my sleeve."

"What was that?" she asked.

"The knowledge that you wanted me as much as I wanted you. That if I could ever get you in my arms, you opened up and let me have more of yourself than you planned or wanted to."

Amy didn't reply to that. Instead, she straightened and turned to look out the window, surprised that they were already on the highway that led to Claude. He was right about her determination not to give in to him, and he was right about her capitulation. She turned to him once more. "So you came to town deliberately planning on seducing me?"

He had the grace to look chagrined. "It was the only thing in my favor, the only way I had to try to make you see how it could be between us."

"I've told you before, Russ, that good sex doesn't make a good marriage."

"I know. And I know you don't think you can be happy in Claude. Isn't that what this is all about?"

"It isn't Claude. It's small-town living—anywhere. I don't want to live the way my mother did. I won't."

"I think you're talking about two entirely different things, here. One doesn't really have anything to do with the other, and in spite of what you think, her life wasn't a bad one, Amy. A hard life, yes, but not bad. And your mother was a very special person. She didn't let life get her down; she grabbed hold of it and shaped it into something worth living."

"What do you mean?"

"Good Lord, woman, if I have to tell you, you really don't know who you are."

"Tell me!"

"I'll tell you this. I want this week to prove to you that we can merge our life-styles into a workable, happy whole. I want to show you that we're compatible, and that you haven't grown as far away as you think from that innocent seventeen-year-old who went to New York ten years ago, in spite of the fancy apartment and expensive clothes. And I want you to realize that you have t care for people as they are."

"I do care for you, Russ. I just don't think we're righ for each other."

"You're wrong," he said with a conviction she er vied. "You said it before. Deep down in your heart, yo think that if I loved you enough, I'd have stopped ridir the rodeo or moved to Dallas and become the man you'

ike me to be. Well, I can't give it up just for you, Amy—
not and be true to myself—just the way you couldn't give
up your own dream of success for me."

He was right. She couldn't have. The need to prove her
worth had driven her for far too long.

"I know everyone has to do what they have to do, and
that's why I never pushed you into making a decision
before. The secret to any good relationship is to not
expect the other person to change to suit your whims."

He looked directly into her eyes for the span of a
heartbeat. "I love you, and I'm willing to take you the
way you are. If you love me the way I think you do,
you're going to have to accept it. You're going to have to
stop expecting me to change, and you're going to have to
stop looking for a replacement. Second best just isn't
good enough if you can have the real thing."

"You think Wayne is second best?"

"I think Wayne will make someone a helluva good
husband."

"But not me?"

"Let me put it this way. If at the end of the week you
don't agree that we can be happy together, I'll let you go,
and I won't bother you again. Ever. Time's hurrying by,
Amarillo, and I've hung on about as long as I can. The
old 'marry in haste; repent in leisure' platitude is valid,
but ten years is long enough for anyone to make a decision."

Amy turned to look out the truck's window at the
countryside that grew more familiar the nearer they drew
Claude. He was right. It was time to settle things between them, which was what she'd intended when she
first agreed to his ridiculous scheme, so why had she
backed out? Was she afraid she might learn some things
about herself she'd rather not know? Another uncom-

fortable thought nagged her, a thought whose truth she needed to face. *Had* she hoped he would change for her? A tiny voice deep inside whispered that he might be telling the truth, even though she didn't want to think she was that self-centered. And, like Russ, hadn't she nurtured a belief that they might have a second chance on that first night he'd come back into her life after four long years?

When he had first called, she hadn't been back in Texas long. She'd left New York and John—fellow art student and lover for a brief two months—behind without a second thought.

Extremely talented, John suffered from an ego that rivaled her home state in size. He'd proposed marriage within two months, proposing also that Amy find work as a commercial artist to help support them while he pursued his studies of real art. His casual disregard of her own talent and goals, plus visions of herself in the same role she'd played as a teenager, had prompted her to tell him very calmly to get his clothes and take them with him—straight to hell.

At twenty-one, she'd finished her year at the art school, then packed up and flown to Dallas to look for an apartment and a job, both of which she'd found sooner than she expected.

She was working on a layout at home when the phone rang, and with one huskily drawled, "Hello, Amarillo," Russ Wheeler had once more insinuated himself into her orderly, goal-oriented life....

Four years. Long years. Forgotten memories, half remembered longings and a sudden, irrational joy swamped her. "Russ?"

"How've you been, Amy?" he asked in a quiet voice

"Fine. I've been fine." She ran a hand through her shoulder-length, layered haircut and wondered if he would like it. "You?"

"Good. Never better."

Silence.

"How are—"

"What have—"

They both began to speak simultaneously. Both gave an uncomfortable laugh.

"Ladies first," Russ offered.

Amy felt her mouth curving into a smile. "I was going to ask what you'd been up to. What are you doing?"

"Still working for MacGregor. Still trying to get into the National Finals."

"You're still rodeoing, then?"

"Yeah."

For some reason the knowledge produced a vague letdown. "Oh."

"How was New York?"

"Big," she said with a smile in her voice. "Big and crazy. Terrible. Wonderful."

"You had a lot of fun, huh?"

"I guess I did. And I learned a lot."

"Leave any broken hearts behind?" he asked, probing into her romantic status as unobtrusively as possible.

"No," she told him truthfully. Then she probed a bit herself. "I heard your marriage broke up."

"Yeah. But there wasn't much to break up."

Another lengthy silence ensued while they both struggled with their memories—Russ with the bitter disappointment when she'd turned down his marriage proposal and Amy with the remembrance of her hurt and irrational jealousy when she'd learned of his marriage to Tammy Carter.

"What are you doing in Dallas?" she asked at last.

"Zach told me you were living here now, and I was in Mesquite for a rodeo, so I thought I'd give you a call and see how you were doing."

"I'm glad you did. I . . . I'd like to see you—"

"Yeah, me too."

"...I mean we could catch up on what's been going..." Her voice trailed away as she realized he'd agreed. "You would?" She took a deep breath and plunged. "I could fix something here if you'd like to come over for dinner."

"Why don't I take you out?" he offered with a laugh. "I've made a little money the last few weeks."

Amy had agreed, and he'd arrived to pick her up at eight. She didn't know what she expected, but, at her first sight of him, her heartbeats had kicked into high gear. The four years had changed him, and yet they hadn't. He looked taller and was definitely broader through the shoulders, even though he was still slim. She supposed that what he'd done was mature, because as she took in his appearance from the top of his too long auburn hair to the tips of his ostrich boots, she was fully aware that Russ Wheeler was no longer on the verge of manhood; he'd toppled over the edge.

Without warning, her mind catapulted back to her graduation night and the way he had gently taken her virginity. She dragged her wayward thoughts back and looked at Russ. If the hungry look in his eyes was anything to go on, he was fighting the memory, too. It should have warned her of the inevitability of the evening's end, but if it did, it was a warning she ignored.

They went to dinner and later to a club where country-western dancing was the craze. She hadn't forgotten how to do the two-step, but she had forgotten what it felt like to be held in Russ's arms while their bodies brushed and the scent of his masculine cologne reminded her of the way his skin tasted of soap and clean, warm man. The evening was wonderful; it was terrible. And when it was over and they stood outside her door saying goodbye, she felt like crying.

Russ grasped her shoulders and leaned forward, and she knew he was going to kiss her. She also knew she shouldn't let him. It would simply bring her more grief. She didn't need a man in her life, especially not Russ Wheeler. With those thoughts filling her mind, her eyes drifted shut.

His kiss was gentle, sweet, undemanding and totally unsatisfactory. Amy wanted him to kiss her the way he had in his truck, surrounded by an ocean of milo that rippled in soft, undulating eddies in the breath of the Texas wind. Her mouth parted beneath his, and she melted against him.

He didn't disappoint her. His mouth slanted over hers in a series of hard, drugging kisses that made her stomach quiver and her breasts ache. After several long moments, he touched her, his hands moving beneath her sweater to her breasts. They met no resistance, because Amy's hands were too busy with the buttons of his shirt.

From that point, it was only a matter of moments until they were inside her apartment, their clothes scattered from the door to the bed, where Russ's body invaded her with breathtaking thoroughness. They loved each other far into the night. It was wonderful, and Amy couldn't remember feeling so . . . whole.

But when they had awakened the next morning, Amy felt a tremendous anger. Nothing had really changed. She still wanted to have the art world kneeling at her feet, and Russ was still the guy from back home, the man without a real future. The rodeo rider. She never should have let him make love to her.

And she told him so.

To her surprise, he seemed to accept her feelings. He told her he understood and left after a quick shower. She hadn't seen him for seven or eight months, and she'd just begun to think he wasn't coming back, when he breezed into Dallas again, and, just as they had the first time, they had given all they could give to each other until the pink of dawn came stealing through the curtains.

For the next six years, two or three times a year, it had been the same—until she met Wayne Hardeman seven months ago and had told Russ unequivocally that it was over between them. . . .

"Almost there."

Russ's quiet commentary roused her from her troubling thoughts, and she noticed they were driving past the Claude city limits sign. Like it or not, she was here. In a matter of minutes Russ had turned right onto Trice Street, headed, she supposed, to the ranch where he still worked.

As she gazed at the streets, deserted at this time of day, she realized that nothing had changed much since she'd been here three years ago for Jason's wedding. The hardware store was having a sale, a couple of storefronts had been painted and the barber shop sported a new pole. She felt like an outsider, a stranger, and yet everything was familiar to her.

They passed the Methodist church and soon left the town proper. A man mowing his yard in the comparative coolness of the summer evening recognized Russ's truck and waved. Russ smiled and waved back. A child played on a swing set in a spacious backyard, where love and care had encouraged several trees to grow.

The secondary highway, or farm-to-market road, as Texans called it, sliced through the heart of the panhandle, dividing it into tracts that reached out and caught the hem of the horizon. Listlessly grazing cattle dotted fields turning brown from the heat, and acres of milo and maize stretched as far as the eye could see. The houses, infrequent reminders of habitation, relieved the flat landscape with unexpected splashes of color. The trees, what few of them there were, boasted branches reaching horizontally toward the ground, like a woman doing stretching exercises, their strange pattern evolved by the never-ending Texas wind whose only restraint was a barbed-wire fence every few miles.

They passed a rutted road, which, she realized with a start, led to the place she'd first given herself to Russ. The barn, listing more than even, was a gray silhouette in the gathering dusk. She looked at Russ, but he was concentrating on the highway. Had he forgotten what happened there?

She was still pondering that question and wondering why it even mattered, when he turned down the lane that led to the MacGregor Ranch. Dust billowed up from the gravel driveway, and a dog, dozing beneath a shade tree, awoke and ran barking out to the truck.

Russ pulled to a stop and turned off the ignition. Then he turned to her, a strange look in his eyes and a smile on his lips. Amy's heart stopped, then began to beat in a heavy sluggish cadence. They were on his turf now. And it was common knowledge that the home field had the advantage in any type of confrontation. The fear she'd been unable to face at the thought of spending another week in close proximity with him now hit her with staggering force. She'd barely been able to hold him at arm's length in Dallas, so how could she expect to here? And more important, if she did give in to him, what would it mean?

Russ saw the turmoil in her eyes. The look in his own eyes softened. "Welcome home, Amarillo."

Home. Was she home? she asked herself.

The sound of someone hitting the hood of the truck broke the spell of the moment, and Amy turned to see Tandy MacGregor standing at the window, a wide smile on his gnomelike features.

"Tandy!" she cried, wrenching open the door. She stepped out of the truck's cab into smothering heat and hugged the old man with genuine happiness. Though small and wiry, there was still a hard strength to him that Amy found comforting. Tandy had been around for as long as she could remember, and even though she knew it was an impossibility, she'd like to think he always would be.

Tandy stepped back and held her at arm's length. "Let me git a look at you, girl," he said, regarding her with twinkling pale blue eyes. "Lord above us, if you ain't as perty as them pictures you paint."

Amy laughed.

Taking off his hat, he slapped it against his thigh and shook his head. "I couldn't believe it when Rusty said you were comin' fer a visit."

Amy looked at Russ, who was just getting out of the truck, murder in her narrowed gaze. Her lips curved in a false smile, and she infused her voice with matching humor. "You know Russ. He just won't take no for an answer."

From the corner of her eye, she caught the grin that flirted with the corners of Russ's mouth as he moved to get her suitcase from the truck bed. Then he started up the sidewalk to the house and spoke for the first time since Tandy had joined them.

"Come on, you two. You can talk inside, where it's cool."

"He's right, Amy. Let's go inside."

As they made the short trek from the truck to the house, Amy's gaze took in more details of the ranch. The barn looked newly painted, and part of the fence had been replaced at some not too far past. Horses grazed in nearby pastures, and the sun, sinking in a blaze of glory, stained the western sky with pink and purple. She'd forgotten how gorgeous sunsets were in the open spaces and tried to recall the last time she'd seen one.

The sound of the screen door squeaking on its hinges drew her attention back to the house, a big two-story structure of white-painted wood, bordered on the front and west sides by covered porches, nestled in its own small grove of protecting trees.

Russ held open the door, and she stepped into the long hallway with a steep staircase that bisected the house—living area and kitchen to the right, bedrooms and bath to the left. The house was old; like Tandy, it had been here for as long as she could remember, but someone had obviously spent a considerable amount of money refurbishing it.

The hardwood floors gleamed with new varnish, and the hallway had been newly papered with a gray-and-maroon stripe that managed to look both masculine and up-to-date, while still retaining the old house's integrity.

"You've been remodeling, Tandy," she said with a smile. "It looks great."

"It was Russ's idea," Tandy said, opening the door of a bedroom done in yellow and pale green. Amy glanced at Russ who carried in the suitcase and swung it up onto the bed. As he turned, his eyes met hers.

"Was this your idea, too?" she asked, remembering the cabbage roses and dark wood the room had boasted in the past.

He shrugged. "I told Tandy the house hadn't had a makeover in thirty years, and it was high time we did something about it."

Her eyes glowed with approval. "I think you were right." She turned her attention to Tandy. "Does the rest look this good?"

"Better," he assured her. "We got a new fridge with an ice maker right in the front door and one of them microwave ovens that does everything but serve up the food—the whole nine yards."

Amy laughed, her gaze climbing from Tandy's face to Russ's eyes, which gleamed with humor. "You mean you guys are really getting civilized?" she asked.

"Russ said we had to if we expected you to—"

"You got any tea made, Tandy?" Russ interrupted.

Frowning at the timing of the inquiry, Tandy said testily, "Does a bear sleep in the woods? Hell, yes, I got tea made. Don't I always?"

"I'd like a glass, and so would Amy, I imagine." He raised his eyebrows and looked at her for confirmation. "Iced tea?"

"That sounds wonderful," she told him truthfully.

"I'll go get it," Tandy offered, turning and crossing the room. Stopping at the door, he looked back. "Y'all et?"

"I had a hamburger in town," Russ said.

Amy realized with a start that she hadn't eaten since her late lunch with Darcy, but she shook her head. "I'm not hungry, Tandy, thanks."

"Good enough," he growled, and stomped off down the corridor.

"I'm going to go on into the kitchen," Russ told her once Tandy was out of earshot. "You can freshen up, but don't try to leave." He held up the keys to the truck.

Amy's brown eyes flashed. "Don't worry. I'm not crazy about walking back to town or the nearest house in the dark."

He smiled, and the attractive crinkles appeared at the corners of his eyes. "Didn't think you would be."

He half turned to leave, but her voice stopped him. "Russ."

"Yeah?"

"What reason did you give Tandy for my staying here?"

"The truth," he said without a pause, his blue gaze holding hers.

"What truth? That you had me abducted from the Nashville airport?"

"No. That we were trying to get things worked out." He left her standing there, a look closely akin to defeat in her face.

At eleven o'clock that night Amy gave up trying to wade the turmoil in her mind and her churning stomach, which by now was protesting her skipped supper. Donning a robe in the glow of her bedside lamp, she slipped from the room and into the hallway. A sliver of light escaped from beneath the door of a room down the way, the room she assumed was Russ's.

Careful not to make any noise, she edged to the kitchen door, tiptoed through the spacious room, which was bathed in the glow of the security light outside, and opened the refrigerator door with a stealth that would have done any burglar proud. She surveyed the contents with interest: a platter of leftover fried chicken; a drawer with various kinds of lunch meats and cheese; Tupperware containers holding odds and ends, a gallon of milk from a nearby dairy.

Deciding that a piece of chicken would be the least trouble, she picked up two golden-brown legs and closed the refrigerator door behind her. Edging around the butcher block, she reached under the upper cabinets and tore off a paper towel, wrapped the chicken in it and headed for the back door that opened onto a screened porch.

As she stepped outside, the sweet scent of tobacco wafted instantly to her nostrils. Startled, she turned toward the glider at one end of the porch and saw Tandy sitting there, smoking his pipe in the shadow of a leafy oak. A sudden gust of wind sent the leaves and shadows dancing.

"What's the matter, girl? Strange bed keep you from sleepin'?"

"That and hunger," she said, holding up a chicken leg and following his lead by speaking just a decibel above a whisper. "What about you?"

"Arthritis kickin' up. I took a pill, but it hasn't got to work yet. The wind must be blowin' in a rain," he said, taking a deep pull on his pipe stem that made the tobacco in the bowl glow. He coughed, and she could hear sadness in his voice when he spoke. "It's hell to get old, Amarillo. Especially when there's so many things you want to do."

"I know."

"How 'bout you? Have you got to where you was headed when you left?"

She chewed thoughtfully a moment. What had she wanted when she left here? To make a name for herself with her art. To sell it. And to escape the life she'd been living. Well, she'd succeeded on all counts. There were write-ups about her in the papers, articles about her work in art magazines, and living in a plush Dallas apartment was a far cry from a country farmhouse. "Yes," she said, with a bit of surprise, "I guess I've accomplished what I set out to do."

"And now yer thinkin' of settlin' down with Rusty?"

While she was considering the right way to answer him without telling him an out-and-out lie, Tandy went on. "He's a good man."

Amy wondered at the sudden tightening in her throat. "I know."

They sat in silence, Tandy smoking, Amy eating her chicken, listening to the june bugs batting themselves against the screen and the coyotes yipping in the fields. Peace, a commodity she hadn't felt in a long time, wrapped itself around her soul.

"It's nice out here," she said with a sigh.

The glider squeaked back and forth. Back and forth. Back...

"How come you left?" Tandy asked.

"Because I watched worry eat my mother up every time my dad left for a rodeo," she said, her answer sounding as if it belonged to an entirely different question. "She asked him to stop. *Begged* him to. But he wouldn't." She turned to Tandy in the darkness, finally reaching the crux of the matter. "Russ rides the rodeo for a living—if you can even make a living riding rodeo."

"So what's that got to do with anything?" Tandy growled. "Are you sayin' you ran away from here—from him—because he rides the rodeo?"

"I'd never marry a man like my father."

"And what was wrong with yer father, missy?"

"He was a drunk." The statement was flat, emotionless.

Tandy's voice sounded practical as he said, "Cal had a hard time acceptin' them takin' his leg off."

"Don't make excuses for him!" she said angrily.

"I ain't makin' excuses for him or anyone else. I'm just askin' you to open your eyes to the facts and maybe to have a little bit of give for human frailties in that heart of yours. Yes, yer daddy drank. And maybe he should have given up bein' a rodeo clown. I know it was hard on yer mama and all you kids, but that shouldn't have anything to do with you and Rusty. You got to realize that even though he's connected with the rodeo, he's a damn sight different from Cal Corbett. And if you can't see that, then you may's well go back to Dallas to the man who give you that big diamond." He stopped and drew in a big gulp of air.

Amy couldn't remember hearing Tandy say so much or seeing him so angry in all the years she'd known him. Of course, as close as he and Russ were, she might have known he'd take Russ's side.

"There's something else," Tandy said, almost as an afterthought. "Yer mama loved yer daddy, and she darn sure didn't run away because she thought things might be bad."

The way you did, Amy.

Tandy cleared his throat and tapped his ash out into an empty coffee can sitting beside the glider. "The pill's a workin' now, so I'll be tellin' you good-night."

His voice was heavy with weariness and pain, and Amy wondered how much of it was physical. "Good night, Tandy," she said.

He limped to the door, where he turned suddenly. "What I wanted to tell you is that dreams, even if you catch 'em, are cold company when yer bones start achin'."

Amy watched him step through the door, leaving her to the night and her thoughts. He had accused her of not having the ability to see the difference between her dad and Russ, and maybe he had a point. The experience of ten additional years of living had given her a different perspective.

Cal had been a drifting kind of man, a dreamer. His dreams were lavish, and she knew from the scope of her own dream that lavish dreams didn't cost any more than plain ones. But the difference was that Cal hadn't wanted to pay the price. He'd wanted to have, but he hadn't wanted to do what was necessary to have. As Russ's granddaddy probably would have said, Cal thought the world owed him a living. According to Tandy, Russ was different.

"Dreams, even when you catch 'em, are cold company when yer bones start achin'."

The lesson he was trying to make her see came to her as quietly as the way the clouds sped through the night sky. She'd reached her goals, caught her dream. Tandy was telling her in his own peculiar way that success was nothing if you didn't have someone to share it with, someone to grow old with.

Wasn't that why she was marrying Wayne?

She tried to conjure up a picture of herself and Wayne in years to come and succeeded only in arousing that nagging feeling of frustration that had been such a part of her lately. She wondered how long it took to gather as much wisdom as Tandy possessed.

A gust of wind whipped the tail of her thin robe, and a sheet of lightning briefly illuminated the countryside. Amy shivered in spite of the lingering heat.

Tandy was right. They were in for a rain.

Chapter Seven

Amy awoke to a measured *creak...creak...creak*. Opening her eyes, she stared up at the noiseless ceiling fan whirling slowly above her. Turning her head, she focused her sleepy gaze on the unfamiliar, flower-sprigged wallpaper and struggled with the question of her whereabouts. A sleepy smile curved her lips. She was at the MacGregor Ranch, and the creaking noise was the windmill in the backyard that, like most of the windmills dotting the panhandle landscape, seemed forever in need of oiling.

Covering a yawn and stretching, Amy wondered what time it was. If the sunshine streaming through the window was any indication, it was high time she was out of bed. She was on her feet and reaching for her robe before it occurred to her that she had no real reason to get up. She had become so locked into her daily routine in Dallas that the prospect of a week devoid of anything

familiar loomed before her with all the excitement of a
case of mumps.

Sighing, she donned her robe and, poking her head out
the door, looked up and down the hallway to see if Russ
or Tandy were in the house before heading toward the
bathroom.

She showered quickly and dressed in the same clothes
she'd worn the day before, fuming as she rolled up the
sleeves of her silk blouse. If Russ expected her to stay
here, he could darn well get her some clothes! Holding
her irritation close, she marched into the kitchen. The
clock there read eight-forty, and she was surprised to find
a pot of coffee already made and a note in Russ's hand-
writing.

I wanted to start the day with you, but when I
peeked in you were sleeping like a baby. I set the
coffeepot to start dripping at eight-thirty, so it
should be fresh when you wake up. I know you don't
have anything to wear, so Tandy left some of his
things on his chest of drawers for you to "re-
model." See you at lunch.

Russ

P.S. If you get lonely, we'll be out in the north field
baling hay.

Her anger evaporated in an instant. Feeling much better for some strange reason, she turned on the portable
radio sitting on the countertop and poured herself a cup
of coffee. She carried it to the screened-in porch and
sipped the scalding brew, while her eyes reacquainted her
with the surrounding countryside. With the buildings of
Dallas obscuring the horizon, she'd forgotten how fla

the panhandle was and how dry it could be in the summer.

A film of dust covered the tables on the porch, choked the grass and dulled the leaves and blossoms of the vibrant red cannas growing along the corral fence. From inside, the radio weatherman lamented the heat wave and predicted the possibility of scattered thundershowers in the area for the next few days.

Amy couldn't help smiling at his phrasing. Possibility. The threat of rain the night before had been just that—a threat. No more than a few sprinkles had fallen before the wind blew the thunderheads farther east. The weatherman made a bet with the sportscaster on how long the rains would hold off.

It occurred to Amy that the unpredictable weather was a lot like the tension growing between her and Russ, a tension so tangible, it couldn't be denied. Would the emotions she tried to deny erupt into blazing feeling, or would the doubts and fears brew into a storm that would destroy forever the strange relationship they shared? She didn't know, but she did accept the fact that Russ was right. It had gone on long enough. It was time for it to end, one way or the other.

Two cups of coffee later, she felt sufficiently up to facing the day and decided to see what Tandy had left for her to wear. She started to set her cup in the sink filled with the dirty dishes left from his and Russ's breakfast but, on second thought, rinsed them and put them in the dishwasher. By the time she finished, the kitchen was spotless and she'd killed another twenty minutes.

By poking her head into the bedrooms, she located Tandy's. The clothes he had donated to her meager wardrobe consisted of two pairs of faded blue jeans and two long-sleeved western-style cotton shirts—one a lav-

ender, blue and gray plaid, the other brown and tan—
both complete with piped yokes and snaps. Amy held the
pants up and looked in the full-length mirror on the
closet door. Tandy was so slight that they just might
work. She smiled at her reflection. If she could just lo-
cate a pair of scissors, she'd show him some "remodeling."

Russ walked to the back door, hot, tired and worried
about the reception he'd get from Amy. He stripped off
his sweat-stained shirt, turned on the water and sprayed
a fine mist over his face and chest, using his hands to
slough off the film of water. He knew he was delaying the
inevitable, but he couldn't help it. He'd rather ride the
meanest bull on the circuit than go in there and face her
resentment and anger. Still, he thought, turning the hose
off again, he had to face it sooner or later.

The sound of the kitchen door opening brought Amy's
head around. Russ stood in the open door, his wet hair
scraped away from his face, water droplets glistening on
his shoulders and matting the pelt of hair on his chest.
Her heart faltered, then began to beat in double time.

She watched his blue-gray eyes take on an even smo-
kier hue as his gaze traveled from her bare feet up and
over her body. Suppressing the urge to tug at the bottoms of her shorts and wishing fervently that she hadn't
cut them off quite so short, she tried to regain control of
her runaway heartbeats. "Lunch will be ready in a minute," she told him as calmly as she could.

He looked surprised. "You didn't have to fix lunch."

"I didn't have anything else to do," she told him with
a shrug.

"Thanks. I appreciate it."

Yes, become a Silhouette subscriber and the celebration goes on forever.

To begin with we'll send you:

4 new Silhouette Special Edition novels—FREE

an elegant matching pen and watch set—FREE

an exciting mystery bonus—FREE

And that's not all! Special extras— Three more reasons to celebrate.

4. Free Home Delivery. That's right! When you subscribe to Silhouette Special Edition, the excitement, romance and faraway adventures of these novels can be yours for previewing in the convenience of your own home. Here's how it works. Every month, we'll deliver six new books right to your door. If you decide to keep them, they'll be yours for only $2.49 each! That's 26¢ less per book than what you pay in stores. And there's **no charge for shipping and handling.**

5. Free Monthly Newsletter. It's the indispensable insiders' look at our most popular writers and their upcoming novels. Now you can have a behind-the-scenes look at the fascinating world of Silhouette! It's an added bonus you'll look forward to every month!

6. More Surprise Gifts. Because our home subscribers are our most valued readers, we'll be sending you additional free gifts from time to time—as a token of our appreciation.

You'll love your new LCD quartz digital watch with its genuine leather strap. And the slim matching pen is perfect for writing to that special person. They're yours free in this amazing Silhouette celebration!

SILHOUETTE SPECIAL EDITION®

FREE OFFER CARD

4 FREE BOOKS

ELEGANT PEN AND WATCH SET—FREE

FREE MYSTERY BONUS

FREE HOME DELIVERY

FREE FACT-FILLED NEWSLETTER

MORE SURPRISE GIFTS THROUGHOUT THE YEAR—FREE

Yes! Please send me four Silhouette Special Edition novels **FREE**, along with my pen and watch set and my free mystery gift as explained on the opposite page.   235 CIS R1XC

NAME
(PLEASE PRINT)

ADDRESS   APT

CITY   STATE

ZIP

Postage will be paid by addressee

BUSINESS REPLY CARD
FIRST CLASS   PERMIT NO. 717   BUFFALO, N.Y.

SILHOUETTE BOOKS®

901 Fuhrmann Blvd.,
P.O. Box 1867
Buffalo, N.Y. 14240-9952

NO POSTAGE
NECESSARY
IF MAILED
IN THE
UNITED STATES

She nodded and went back to peeling and slicing the homegrown tomatoes she'd found in the crisper drawer. "I don't mind helping out while I'm here, but if I had some watercolors or pastels it would help pass the time. Is it okay if I drive in to Amarillo this afternoon to get some?"

Russ, who was getting a glass from the cabinet, gave her a disbelieving glance. "No, it isn't okay."

"Why?" she asked, turning and meeting his eyes.

His mouth twisted into a wry smile. "I believe you told me there was no way you were going to come here, let alone stay," he reminded. "And now you're wanting me to let you go get some paints?" He shook his head. "No way, darlin'. By the time I found you, you'd be back in Dallas and have a warrant out for me on kidnapping charges."

Amy stared at him for a moment before shrugging again and going back to her slicing.

Russ took his glass to the refrigerator for some ice. He hated to deny her anything, but there was no way he could just turn her loose. Not with her threats to leave hanging over his head. Besides, he liked coming home and finding her here—and it had nothing to do with her fixing lunch. It had more to do with long, slender legs that seemed to go on forever, below the jeans that had been cut into very short shorts. She'd cut the entire sleeves from the plaid shirt and tied it below her breasts, leaving her midriff bare. Even with her extremely short haircut, she looked every inch a woman and so sexy he could hardly stand it.

"That stuff looks a helluva lot better on you than it did on Tandy," he told her, unable to hold back the compliment.

"Thanks," she replied without looking up.

"Did you sleep well?" he asked, pouring himself a glass of tea from the pitcher.

"Yes, once I finally got to sleep."

He walked up behind her and looked over her shoulder. "What's for lunch?"

Even though she'd heard him cross the room, the sound of his voice at her ear sent her spinning around, which was definitely a mistake. He was too close. She could feel the heat of his body, could smell a lingering trace of deodorant. An errant drop of water trickled a crooked path through the hair on his chest, and, without thinking, she reached out and caught it on her fingertip.

"Amy..."

His voice was something between a sigh and a moan, and the sound of her name falling from his lips drew her eyes back to his. There was torment there, and indecision, and a hunger she could feel eating away at her own fragile defenses.

"Damnation, it's hot out there!"

Tandy's voice preceded him as he burst into the kitchen, and before Russ could mutter more than a single soft curse, the wall telephone began to ring. He swung around and grabbed the offending instrument, giving Tandy a heated look at the same time.

"What'd I do?" the old man grumbled, lifting one shoulder and blotting his perspiring face on his shirt-sleeve.

Thankful that they'd been interrupted before Russ wove that web of irresistible charm around her again, Amy shook her head and turned back to her vegetables.

"Mike who?" Russ was saying into the phone. "Oh. Right. You want me to what? I think you've got the wrong guy." He turned and saw that Tandy was listening with unconcealed interest. "Mike," he said into the receiver, "can you hold on? I need to change phones."

Russ thrust the plastic receiver at Amy. "Hang this up when I get to the office."

She took the phone and looked at Tandy, who only shrugged. Obviously, he was used to Russ's shortness.

When Russ returned to the kitchen five minutes later, Amy had everything on the table and he had conformed to politeness by putting on a faded blue T-shirt. He eyed the ham sandwiches, potato salad and sliced tomatoes with appreciation. "This looks great. I'm starving."

They waited for Amy to sit down, and then both Russ and Tandy ate as if there were no opportunity beyond the moment.

"Who was that on the phone?" Tandy asked later, helping himself to more potato salad.

"You're pretty nosy, aren't you?" Russ responded, but there was a smile in his eyes.

"Well, I could tell you was upset."

"Not really upset. Just surprised. It was Mike Fenton, the agent who tried to sign me up the year I won Best All-Around Cowboy." He looked at Amy and said, "They did some posters of me that year."

When she looked surprised, he asked, "Didn't I give you one?" He laughed, a low rumble that sounded unbearably sexy. "I guess you could say I was the pinup of the rodeo set. This Mike guy was looking for someone to do what he called a 'different' sort of Western movie and wanted me to give acting a try—can you believe it?"

Actually, Amy thought, she could. Deep down, she thought Russ had whatever was needed to pull off just about anything.

"I'm no actor, so I turned him down. Now he has a friend who wants to do some kind of rodeo documentary for one of the cable networks, and he wants to use me as a commentator or narrator or something."

"So what did you tell him?" she asked.

"I told him no, but he and the other guy—Stan something or other—want to come and talk to me more about it. They'll be here day after tomorrow."

Day after tomorrow. Tuesday. "What do you plan to do with me while he's here?" she asked with a hint of asperity, disregarding Tandy's presence.

"I thought I'd introduce you," Russ said evenly.

"You aren't afraid I'll beg him to take me away with him?"

He lifted his glass of tea and took a drink, his eyes probing hers over the top of the glass. Then he set it on the table and said, "Should I be?"

She shook her head. The time for games was over. "No. You were right. I owe you this week, and I'll give it to you. Just don't count on it changing anything."

"I never count on anything where you're concerned, Amarillo," he told her.

"I'll be damn glad when you two quit all this fussin'," Tandy growled, rising and carrying his plate to the sink. He gave them both a disgusted look and headed for the back door, sweeping his cowboy hat from the coat tree as he went. "Ten years is long enough!"

Russ left soon after Tandy's dramatic exit, reminding her that Thursday night was the big barbecue Jason was throwing for Zach and Mona.

"Do you mean there really is going to be a seventeenth wedding anniversary celebration?" she'd asked.

He had looked comically affronted. "You don't think Jason would lie to Wayne about something like that, do you?"

Thinking about it as she cleaned up the lunch dishes, Amy couldn't help but smile. Leave it to Russ and Jason. She threw in a load of laundry and listened with crossed fingers as thunder began to rumble outside. Maybe a rain would cool things off. Then, remembering that Russ was baling hay, she changed her mind about wanting it to rain, at least for now. If it rained on the cut hay, they would have to turn it before they could bale it, and it wouldn't be as good as if it hadn't gotten wet. It was surprising, she thought, just how much about country living was coming back to her.

Unfortunately, uncrossed fingers and moans of dismay didn't stop the long-awaited shower. It blew in on a cloud of wind and dust and, for its short duration, was impressively violent. When it stopped, Amy went outside barefoot to pick some cannas for the dinner table. She was marveling at their color and the texture of the petals when she found herself wishing again for some means to capture the beauty of the big red blossoms and the huge spear-shaped leaves.

Flight to Dallas or anywhere else was the furthest thing from her mind, but there was no way she could convince Russ of that. Her main concern beyond dinner and her desire to capture the beauty of the flowers was what to take to the cookout Thursday night.

A quick phone call to Jason, who told her he would try to get by to see her later that evening, certified the fact that there would probably be at least fifty people in attendance. He was furnishing the meat, and everyone else was supposed to bring a dish. He begged Amy to find their mother's recipe and bring a batch of homemade vanilla ice cream and a butter cake. Sally Corbett had so many cookbooks, and none of the boys knew which one she'd used for her ice cream.

Amy knew she'd recognize the book if she saw it and decided to drive out to the hay field and ask Russ if she could get out of solitary confinement long enough to make a visit to the old house. She dreaded the memories—she hadn't been inside the house in years—but she dreaded letting Jason down even more.

After brushing her short blond hair, she applied some pink lip gloss and headed toward the pickup. Wincing at the heat of the vinyl seat against her bare legs, she leaned under the dash and began to fiddle with some wires. The engine caught, and with a smile on her face at the thought of Russ's shock when she drove up, she backed up and headed down the driveway.

She turned off the driveway onto the farm-to-market road, which gave her smooth sailing for perhaps a mile, before guiding the truck onto a rutted road that cut between the fields. Surprisingly, the farther she drove, the drier it got. Apparently, the rain had been an isolated shower and probably hadn't interfered with the hay baling in the least.

She could see Russ in the distance, driving the tractor while the baler gobbled up the mown hay and spit out nice, rectangular bales. An old truck pulling a flatbed trailer followed, and two high school-age boys were hoisting the bales onto the trailer while two others stacked it.

Amy pulled to the edge of the field and waited for Russ to see her—which he did in record time. Pulling over, he stopped and jumped down from the tractor. His shirt, which had the sleeves cut out as hers did, was soaked through. His jeans, too, were wet in places, and he wore a blue bandanna tied around his forehead to catch the blinding sweat. His surprise and anger were clear to Amy as he strode toward her with menacing grace. She spoke first, hoping her teasing would erase the thunderous look on his face.

"You need one of those air-conditioned tractors."

Russ ignored her comment and snapped, "How the hell did you get the truck started?"

"I grew up with five brothers, Russ. They taught me to hot-wire as soon as I was big enough to tag after them."

He looked surprised, then shook his head in a relenting movement, obviously fighting a smile. "I should have remembered. So what are you doing here? Why aren't you halfway back to Dallas by now?"

"I told you I owe you this week," she said, looking him straight in the eyes. "I'll give it to you."

He took her measure for long seconds, as if trying to decide whether or not she was telling the truth. Then, apparently satisfied, he nodded. "I assume you want something, since you drove out here. What is it?"

"I want to know if I can drive over to the old home place and look for one of my mother's cookbooks."

"Why?"

"Jason has his heart set on some of her homemade ice cream for the cookout, and they don't know which one the recipe is in."

"Sure. Go on."

The fact that he didn't hesitate told her without a doubt that he believed her promise not to leave. "Thanks," she said, impetuously stepping closer and rising up on tiptoe to kiss his cheek.

For one brief second she felt his hand at her bare waist, steadying her, and in that moment, despite her goals, her dreams, and the fact that she wore another man's ring on her finger, Amy found herself fighting the urge to lean against his broad chest. Instead, she stepped back and turned toward the truck. She was halfway there when his voice stopped her, and she turned.

"Catch," he said, tossing her the truck keys. "You may as well have these. And don't worry about dinner tonight if you were planning on cooking. Tandy is taking us out to the L.A. Café."

"Do they still have the best chicken-fried steak in town?" she asked with a hint of wistfulness.

Russ smiled. "If you disregard Dairy Queen's steak fingers, they have the *only* chicken-fried steak in town."

Amy laughed. "It's a date, then."

She went to the truck, her smile still in place. The lightness in her heart lasted until fifteen minutes later, when she pulled into the driveway of the house she'd grown up in.

The recently mown yard was surprisingly well maintained, she thought, but the house itself, sitting in the shade of several large oaks, looked in worse disrepair than ever. The asbestos siding had slipped in places, exposing bare boards beneath. The trim all needed painting, but then, it always had, she remembered. It was just another task Cal Corbett kept putting off.

She tried the front door and found it locked. The back was locked, too, and she was contemplating going to Zach's house to get the key when she remembered that the lock on the window of her old room was broken. How could she have forgotten for even a moment, considering how often she'd slipped out for one reason or another?

Unhooking the screen, she raised the window and pushed aside the small table in front of it. She caught the windowsill and, with a slight jump upward, crawled through, uncertain what to expect. The wooden paint stirrer, a promotional device from the local hardware store that she'd always used to prop the window open, was still in its usual place on the sill. Amy wedged it into place to let in the cooling breeze.

Taking a deep breath, she turned slowly, facing the room where she'd spent seventeen years of her life. Expecting neglect, perhaps even vandalism, she was surprised to find things exactly as she'd left them. Her twin Jenny Lind bed was still sitting beside the window, the ecru bedspread long before faded to white and her varnished dresser and chest of drawers—given to her mother by someone who had coated it with two coats of paint—still graced the pale-blue walls.

She remembered her mother sitting on an overturned bucket in the shade, stripping off those layers of sticky paint even though Amy maintained that the best place for the furniture was the dump.

"Sometimes you have to believe that there's something worth keeping underneath the ugliness in the world."

Sally Corbett had worked for days, getting to the natural wood. *"Look, Amy, it's quarter-cut oak. It'll be beautiful when I get it stripped and varnished."* Then she had sanded the pieces with sandpaper and steel wool. Finally, she had hand rubbed the varnish into the wood with a soft rag and the same patience and stoicism with which she tackled everything in life.

Amy hesitantly moved to the dresser that still sat next to the door. Her palm drifted across the satin-smooth finish, and she blinked back the sudden rush of tears. How had she ever been embarrassed over this? Any antique dealer worth his salt would give an exorbitant amount of money for the pieces.

"You were right, Mom," Amy said aloud. "It is beautiful."

Her blurred gaze moved upward to the mirror, where
dozens of snapshots were still stuck between the glass and
the frame. Even braced as she was for the onslaught of
memories, nothing prepared her for the rush of conflict-
ing emotions she felt as her eyes, awash with tears, moved
from one photo to the next. Happy memories were
nudged aside by bittersweet nostalgia, which was pushed
away by sorrow and a sense of having lost something she
could never find again.

There were pictures of herself at six, with her front
teeth missing; at ten, in her new Easter dress from Sears,
standing outside the high school her freshman year
wearing Russ's blue corduroy Future Farmers of America jacket; and a picture of her posing with Gail Sum-
mers in the bikinis they'd bought at the end of their
junior year.

Memories of her mother's voice accompanied each
picture. *"You're so cute without your teeth."* *"You're so
pretty in that dress, Amy."* *"Russ is such a nice boy."*
"You can't wear that thing in public."

There were pictures of all her brothers—Zach, Ben,
Mike, Lee and Jason with their prom dates. There was
one of her parents holding hands on the porch swing and
one showing the surprise on her mother's face as she'd
opened a sexy nightgown the boys had bought her the
Christmas before she died. There were elementary,
junior-high and high-school pictures, and pictures
of friends, relatives and family—an abridged version of
her life and the people she cared about.

There were pictures of Russ.

Russ holding up the big bass he'd caught in Mr.
Stonecipher's pond. Russ standing beside his first truck.
Russ dressed in white shirt, a new cowboy hat and
starched jeans, ready to go to his first rodeo. Russ smil-

ing, serious. She reached out and took down a picture of the two of them dancing at Christy Mosley's party. She remembered the party well. It was the night he'd told her for the first time that he loved her—not that she didn't already know.

Amy sniffed and licked her dry lips, tasting the saltiness of the tears that had run into her mouth. She thrust the picture back into its place and wrenched open the door, closing it behind her and leaning against it while she tried to regain control over her tears and her emotions.

She'd expected the memories. Dreaded them. But something had gone wrong, because she wasn't filled with revulsion as she'd thought she'd be. She was filled, instead, with—what? What did she feel? Sorrow that she was getting older? That those times were gone and could only be revisited in photographs?

Her haunted eyes skimmed the living room, taking in the faded floral sofa, the cracked vinyl recliner where her father had whiled away the hours after he'd had his leg amputated, and the piecrust table with the broken leg that one of the ladies from the church had given her mother. Surprisingly good with wood, Cal had meticulously glued and clamped the table leg back together, and it had held.

But she didn't want to think about her father; she didn't want to think about the past. Turning her back on the living room, she stepped into the kitchen.

"Don't track in, Cal. I just mopped."

The sound of her mother's voice came so clearly to mind that Amy gasped, her eyes scanning the room for a figure she knew wasn't there. Here, in the domain that was indisputably Sally Corbett's, the memories of her mother were intensely real. Amy imagined she could see her standing at the stove, her ash-blond hair coiled into

a loose knot atop her head, her trim figure wrapped in a
long apron, a blush staining her cheeks, while her dad,
young and handsome, stood behind her, his arms encir-
cling her from behind, nuzzling her neck.

"*Stop it, Cal. Amy's in here.*"

"*He swept me off my feet, Amy. I never knew what he
saw in mousy old me.*"

"*Stir the gravy, sister, while I take Daddy his coffee.*"

"*Here's fifty dollars from Daddy, Amy. He said
you've been looking sorta sad lately, and for you to spend
it on whatever you want.*"

Amy opened her clenched hand slowly, half expecting
to see the crumpled bills there. That was the time she was
getting ready to go to the senior prom with Russ. A time
long after the accident, after she'd begun to resent her
father. Guilt, so potent it almost stole her breath, rushed
through her. Guilt and remorse. While she was busy hating him, he'd been concerned because she looked sad.

Sinking onto a kitchen chair, Amy buried her face in
her hands and faced the truth. The resentment she'd felt
for what her father had done to her mother hadn't made
Sally resent him at all.

"*I know he drinks too much, honey, but you just don't
understand. They cut out his pride when they cut off his
leg. And you tamper with a man's pride, you got trouble.*"

A clear picture of the actual situation began to form in
Amarillo's mind.

While she'd been worrying about the hardship his re-
doeing and the resulting accident had caused her mother,
Sally had been worrying about the loss of pride and self-
respect Cal was dealing with. She'd been so busy making
things easier for him that it never occurred to her that too
much care and pampering had resulted in self-pity, when

Cal should have been working to overcome his handicap.

Sally had loved him...but maybe that love had been too protective.

The knowledge sliced through Amy with the force of the tornado that had sliced through the countryside more than ten years before. Her mother hadn't felt put upon by her dad. In spite of Cal's short temper and sullen moods, Sally had been content to shoulder the responsibility of bringing in most of the money and accepting of the headaches that went with the rearing of six kids. Because she loved him.

Had her father realized how much? Had he loved Sally half as much as she did him?

"We found them in what used to be the bedroom. It looked like your dad tried to shield Sally's body with his."

"Stop!" Amarillo cried aloud, the sound of her voice forcing the memories to the corners of the room. She clutched at her head and rested her elbows on the table, letting the tears fall freely. "Stop." The word was a ragged sob, breathed on a sigh of regret.

She wasn't certain how long she sat there or how long she cried, but she rose feeling empty, drained. Perspiration trickled between her shoulder blades and her breasts and ran in rivulets down her face to mingle with the tears. She could forgive her father's actions after the accident, but it still didn't change her mind about his selfishness, his determination to keep working the rodeo when he knew all along how much heartache it had caused her mother every time he left.

Rising and going to the drawer, she pulled out a musty dish towel and blotted the moisture from her heated face. With her emotions under control once more, she reached into the cabinet and pulled out a red-covered cookbook with a spiral binding. The ladies of the Methodist church had put it together when Amy was a baby—it held the ice-cream recipe her mother used. She tucked it under her arm and went back through the house the way she'd come, closing her bedroom window and replacing the screen, shutting the memories away so they couldn't torment her anymore.

When Russ and Tandy came home, neither commented on her swollen eyes. Even after numerous cold-water splashings and the skillful application of makeup, the signs of her weeping were still evident. Already dressed, she waited while they showered and changed, and then they drove to town for the promised dinner.

She was picking at her chicken-fried steak and talking desultorily to Tandy and Russ about nothing in particular, when a short, dumpy woman with hair tortured into a knot atop her head stopped by the table.

"Hello, Rusty...Tandy," she said with a nod.

"Hello, Mrs. Pearson," Russ said politely, though the look in his eyes was a trifle pained.

Tandy nodded shortly. "How do, Isobel?"

Isobel Pearson's dark, birdlike eyes took in Amy's appearance with one searching look. "Aren't you Sally Corbett's daughter?"

Amy forced a smile and nodded. "Yes. Amarillo Corbett."

The woman held out a plump, ring-laden hand. "Isobel Pearson."

Amy shook hands with the woman, wishing she would leave. She wasn't up to dutiful conversation.

"We here in Claude are really proud of you, Amarillo. May I call you that?"

"Thank you. Please do," Amy said.

"I suppose you're visiting your brothers."

"No," Amy corrected. "Actually, I'm staying with Russ and Tandy." As soon as the words were out of her mouth, she felt a kick to her shins from Tandy's direction. She looked at him openmouthed and received a glower in response. Confused, she glanced at Russ, who leaned his elbow on his table and propped his chin in his hand with a let's-see-you-get-out-of-this-one expression.

"I'm here for my brother's anniversary party," she tacked on for good measure, though she didn't really know why.

"Is that right?" Isobel purred. "And will your fiancé be joining you?"

Fiancé? How did she know about Wayne? Amy shook her head. "No."

"How very interesting," Isobel said, her eyes glittering. She flashed them all a reasonable facsimile of a smile. "Well, it was wonderful seeing you all again," she gushed. "And I'm looking forward to the get-together on Thursday. See you then." She pranced to the door, high heels clicking, turning and waving gaily before stepping out into the gathering darkness.

With the woman out of earshot, Amy turned a questioning look to Russ and Tandy.

"Whoo-ee!" Tandy said. "If you ain't gone and done it now!"

"What do you mean?" she asked, shifting her worried gaze to Russ. "What's he talking about?"

Russ sat there, a funny sort of smile on his face. "It's nothing, darlin'. Nothing at all. You just told the biggest gossip in the county—who also happens to do that social stuff for the newspaper—that you left your new fiancé in Dallas and were staying with me, whom she considers the most eligible bachelor in town."

"But Tandy's staying there, too. We're chaperoned."

Tandy snorted. "Hells bells! Knowin' Isobel, she'll make it sound like a menange-ah-troyz."

"What?"

Russ's smile broadened at Tandy's mispronunciation. "I believe he means a ménage à trois, Amarillo."

Chapter Eight

By Tuesday morning, Amy decided that Russ and Tandy's worries over the repercussions of their meeting with Isobel Pearson were exaggerated. If Isobel did talk, wasn't that just one of the drawbacks to small-town living? Besides, she reasoned, rising and donning her second set of Tandy clothes, the people who mattered knew the truth of the situation, and she'd be going back to Dallas Sunday, so the others didn't matter.

With the whole episode put in proper perspective, she went to the kitchen in search of her morning coffee, which was again dripped and ready. And, as there had been the day before, there was a note from Russ.

And a set of hard pastels and paper.

Amy felt the sting of tears beneath her eyelids and a tightness in her throat at his thoughtfulness. She blinked the moisture away and picked up the note.

Good morning. I guess by now you know why I
drove my truck in to the café and let Tandy bring
you home. I went in to Amarillo to the art store and
picked these up for you. Can't have you getting
bored on me, can I? I have to come in and get
cleaned up to pick Mike up at the airport, so I'll see
you about ten.

Russ

Amy drew a shaky sigh, folded the note and slipped it
into the pocket of her shirt. She peeled herself a peach
and ate it sitting in the glider, watching the horses grazing in the far pasture and thinking of the picture she
wanted to begin after she planned lunch.

She cleaned up the kitchen and took stock of the pan-
try, wondering what she could fix that would impress
Mike and Stan what's-their-names from Hollywood.
There was a box of stuffing mix and a can of artichoke
hearts that might have possibilities. The crisper drawer
revealed the makings of a super salad, complete with a
container of fresh mushrooms. With the artichokes
added and some of her mother's special dressing, anyone should be impressed, she thought with a cocky grin.
There were some extra-thick pork chops in the freezer,
and she decided to slit the chops, fill them with the
stuffing, close them with toothpicks and braise them in
gravy. She'd bake some potatoes and make a fruit salad,
and that should do it.

She was finishing up everything she could possibly do
ahead of time when Russ came home to get cleaned up.

"What are you doing?" he asked, looking over her
shoulder as she folded peaches, strawberries, bananas
and blueberries together.

"Making fruit salad," she said over her shoulder, trying to ignore the fact that his body was so close she could feel the heat radiating from him. The warmth in his eyes rivaled that of his body. Amy's hand began to tremble. "Here," she said in a reedy voice. "See if this needs any sugar."

He smiled, and the crinkles at the corners of his eyes made an appearance. "Is this a ploy to stop me from kissing you?" he asked, gripping the edge of the cabinet on either side of her and imprisoning her between the sink and his body.

Amy looked up into his teasing blue eyes and felt her willpower dissolve. Heaven help her, she wanted him to kiss her, she thought, unable to tear her eyes from his mouth. She had wanted it ever since Tandy interrupted them the day before. But as much as she wanted his kiss, something—perhaps the memory of other times they hadn't been able to stop with a kiss—warned her that this time wouldn't be any different. Still, for the life of her, she couldn't deny him the truth. "I think maybe it is a ploy," she conceded.

"Honesty, Amarillo? That's a step in the right direction." Slowly, deliberately, he took the spoon from her hand and dropped it into the sink. He moved closer to her, so close that the lower part of his body forced hers against the oak front of the cabinet. She could feel his hardness blossoming against the softness of her abdomen, and the weight of his body caused the snaps of Tandy's shirt to dig into her soft flesh. A collection of mental images of Russ's body covering hers as they made love paraded through her mind, each more vivid than the last. She closed her eyes, as if by shutting them she could block out the memories.

He put his arms around her and pulled her close, nuzzling her ear with his lips. Amy drew a shuddering breath, and her mind catalogued the scents of soap and fabric softener, even though his shirt was damp with perspiration. Tilting her head back, she raised heavy eyelids and looked up at him. If she kissed the pulse that beat a fast rhythm in his neck, if she touched it with the tip of her tongue, would he taste like soap or salt?

He lifted his hands to the front of her shirt and very slowly pulled a snap free, exposing the gentle swell of her breasts. "What are you thinking about, Amy?" he asked in a husky voice. "I can see the wheels turning in that pretty head of yours."

Another snap popped open. She knew she shouldn't let him do this, knew she was courting disaster, knew... And then his hands were on her breasts, which were covered by the merest wisp of a bra. His thumbs brushed across her hardened nipples, stealing her breath and driving away the last vestige of sanity. Unable to meet his eyes, knowing that her capitulation must show in hers, Amy shook her head in mute denial.

"Yes," she heard him whisper. Tilting his head, he deliberately set his mouth to hers in a soft, passionless kiss while his hands gently molded her aching flesh. Then, with a sigh and just as much deliberation, he released her and, grasping her shoulders, stepped away from her. She did look at him then, her forehead furrowed and her eyebrows drawn together in a question.

"As much as I'd like to pursue this course of action," he said, refastening her shirt, "I have to get to the airport and pick up Mike and Stan. And if I don't stop right now, they're likely to have a helluva long wait."

Amy wanted to deny his confident statement, but somewhere along the course of the last two days, she'd lost her desire to fight or argue with him.

"You know if you stay here, it's going to happen, don't you?" he asked, his blue eyes cloudy with concern.

She nodded. It was as if Russ wanted to make certain that she knew the consequences now that they were playing on his grounds.

"If you don't want it to happen, you'd better hot-wire that truck at the first opportunity and hightail it out of here."

"I know." He was right, and yet, as much as she knew she should leave, something told her she wouldn't.

"Don't look at me with those sad eyes, Amarillo. I can't stand it. I almost died inside when I came home last night and saw that you'd been crying."

"You could tell?"

Russ looked into her surprised, upturned face, a very real tenderness in his eyes. How could he explain that because he loved her, every emotion that touched her touched him as well? He'd instinctively known that the trip to her parents' house would upset her, but he'd also known that she needed to face the past and deal with it before she could have a future. He smiled, a little sadly, and dropped a light kiss on her slender nose. "Yeah, darlin', I could tell. Do you want to talk about it?"

She shook her head, fighting the lump in her throat that the memories brought back.

He squeezed her shoulders. "Okay." He glanced once more at the clock on the wall. "I'm gonna take a fast shower and get out of your hair so you can finish up in here."

He reached behind her into the sink and picked up the spoon, scooping up a bite of the fruit salad and popping it into his mouth. He chewed, swallowed, winked and said, "Add some sugar. Natural is nice only if it isn't sour."

He turned and walked from the room, leaving Amy with a wistful expression on her face and a feeling of expectant inevitability filling her heart.

While he showered, she finished the salad and put it into the refrigerator. She was checking to make sure she'd done everything she could for the moment when a car horn honked outside. Looking out the window, she saw the mailman and went to see what he wanted. He handed her a registered letter and asked for her signature, then he gave her the rest of the mail, which was bundled inside a folded magazine.

Amy smiled, thanked him and started back toward the house, letting the magazine unfurl in her hands. The words *Southwest Art* leaped out at her. *Southwest Art* was a magazine devoted to artists pursuing the subject of the Southwest and life-styles of earlier times, whether through paintings or sculpture. Her work had been the subject of an article a few months before, and the Hardeman gallery advertisement featured a different artist each month. Everyone in the art world—at least in this section of the country—knew the caliber of the magazine and that taking it on a monthly basis was a must, but why, she wondered as she let herself in the house, was Russ taking it?

The screen door slammed behind her, and, thinking that she would put the mail on Russ's desk, she started for his office.

"Who was it?" he called from inside the bathroom.

Amy stopped outside the door. "The mailman. I had to sign for a registered letter."

"Probably the papers on the quarter-horse stud I bought a couple of weeks ago."

"Oh." She looked at the magazine she was holding. "Russ?"

"Yeah?"

"Why do you take *Southwest Art*?"

"So I can keep up with what's going on."

"Why would you want to?" she queried through the door.

"Because painting is what you do, and anything you do interests me, and I need to know how to talk about art with some degree of intelligence."

Was that the reason he'd been able to hold his own so well at the showing? Because of her? Because he cared? The thought that he'd made the effort on her behalf pleased her. It pleased her very much. Somehow Russ didn't seem the "artsy" type. Smiling slightly, she said, "I'll just put these on your desk."

"Thanks," he called.

She moved down the hall and opened the door to a bedroom Tandy had told her Russ had converted to an office. Though she couldn't imagine why Russ needed an office—the rough stock company belonged to Tandy—it was a room she hadn't had the courage to enter uninvited.

Stepping over the threshold, she looked around with interest. It was Russ's room, all right. Plush brown carpeting and a hat rack with a Stetson hanging on it branded it that. There were bookshelves on the left, and to the right, in a prominent spot, hung *Rescue the Morning Star*. Amy stifled her initial surprise at seeing the painting he'd bought from the Hardeman Gallery a couple of weeks ago hanging in Russ's office, because here was a bigger surprise directly in front of her. A big oak desk was centered between two windows, a leather chair sat behind it, and above the chair hung one of her earliest works, *Wedding Business*, which had sold at her first showing five years before.

How had Russ gotten it? When? Why? She moved across the room and behind the desk, her trained artist's eye taking in the scope of the painting as well as the smallest details.

The young Indian maiden was dressed in fringed, ankle-length doeskin decorated with natural quillwork and traders' beads, an addition whose use blossomed along with increased trading with the whites. The girl's hands were clasped demurely before her, and she stood in front of a young trapper who was carrying a muzzle loader and was clad in buckskin breeches, a leather shirt and moccasins. Custom had it that marriages between white trappers and Indian girls were primarily business deals, with as much as six hundred dollars worth of goods often traded for the chief's daughter.

"She's beautiful, isn't she?"

The sound of Russ's voice sent her spinning around to face him. He stood in the doorway wearing nothing but a brown towel, his cheeks smoothly shaven and his hair— too long, she noticed suddenly—still damp and curling above his ears.

"Where did you get this?"

"From the Bigger's Gallery, right after the showing."

Amy looked at him, trying to fathom his reasoning. "Why?" she asked as she had once before about another painting.

"Because," he told her as if his explanation said it all, "it's us."

"Us?" she echoed.

"Yes. Look at them, Amy. Look at the man."

She looked but shook her head. "You thought the woman in *Rescue the Morning Star* was me, and now you think this couple is us. Why on earth would I paint us in both these works?"

Russ planted his hands on his hips. "Think about it, Amy."

"They're just paintings, Russ," she said, waving her hand toward the canvas at her left. "The way I've interpreted history."

"They're interpretations, all right," he agreed. A sorrowful smile curved his mouth as he said cryptically, "Granddaddy used to tell me you could lead a horse to water, but you couldn't make him drink."

"What are you talking about?"

"You're a smart girl. You'll figure it out," he said. Then he turned and left her standing behind his desk, no closer to the truth of her feelings than she'd been before.

By Thursday morning, Amy was beginning to adjust to her new routine and found herself wondering if this was how she would have spent her days if she'd married Russ. She slept as long as she liked and got up to freshly brewed coffee every morning. After she ate she threw in a load of wash, dusted, and then worked on her pictures until lunchtime. Truthfully, though the setting was different, she was spending her days very much the way she did back in Dallas. The realization was just a tiny bit upsetting.

What had she expected? she wondered, sipping her coffee while she worked on the picture of the old home place she'd sketched out the day before. Had she expected that she would be a slave to a house as her mother had? Had she been afraid that she'd be bored? Exactly why had she fought so long and so hard against the idea of coming back? And why was she now so content with her lot here, while a portion of her mind taunted her with the reminder that she should be back in Dallas with Wayne? Taunted her that she should *want* to be with Wayne.

Russ's statement about the painting she'd discovered in his office flitted without warning through her mind. She shifted uncomfortably in her chair.

It was true, she thought. He was right. The couple in the painting was her and Russ, though most people wouldn't have made the connection. How had she done such a thing and not realized it? And more importantly, what did it mean? Was it an accident, or had she subconsciously painted out her inner longing—to be married to Russ, to have the "bargaining," the trading of dreams and conditions, done with?

Amy smiled wryly. An analyst could have a field day with her hidden motives—especially the one that held her here when she could so easily pack up and go back to Dallas.

What did it mean, and why did she stay here? She kept telling herself she would stay only until after the barbecue for Zach and Mona, which meant she could leave tomorrow morning. But would she? Or would she, out of a feeling of rightness and a promise made to Russ, give him the full week he insisted she owed him?

Jason and Candace's house was only a ten-minute drive from the ranch, and when Amy, Russ and Tandy arrived at about six o'clock, the barbecue was already in full swing. That might be a good thing, she decided, since it looked as if another of those hit-and-run storms might be gathering in the north.

Amy'd never been to her younger brother's home, a medium-size brick house with a porch across the front

The cars crowding the driveway and lining the road should have been an indication of the size of this party, but when Amy led the way around to the back, she was amazed at the throng. Several men were playing a game of horseshoes, a half-dozen kids splashed in a three-foot high plastic pool, and other guests stood around long tables laden with food, while Jason presided over three barbecue grills made from fifty-five-gallon drums that leaked aromatic smoke into the air.

"Hey!" Jason cried, spying them as they came around the corner of the house. "There's my baby sister!" He put down the tongs he'd been brandishing, and, followed by her four other brothers who'd been standing nearby, came to give Amy a hearty hug and kiss. Smiling down into her eyes, Jason, who was a masculine version of Amy, asked, "Did you bring the ice cream?"

Amy returned his smile and jerked her head toward Russ and Tandy who each carried an ice cream freezer. "The ice and salt are in the back of the truck. All we need is a little electricity."

"We don't have to crank?"

"Not this time," she assured him with a condescending pat on the cheek.

Jason pressed a kiss to her forehead. "Thanks, sis." Then he stepped aside so that Zach, Ben, Mike and Lee could say their hellos. Amy hugged each of them in turn and, with a catch in her heart, thought how handsome they all were, how wonderfully, completely masculine... like Russ.

Smiling in genuine happiness at being reunited with them again, she spoke to each of their wives—Zach's Mona, a slightly plump brunette with a heart of gold; Ben's Rosemary, a rather plain woman with a marvelous sense of humor; Mike's Stephanie, a third-grade teacher who'd given him three incredible kids; and Jason's Candace, a blond bombshell who loved nothing better than to cook and clean. Between them they'd given her a total of eleven nieces and nephews, and whenever she talked to any of them, they invariably wanted to know when she was going to do her part in passing on the incredible Corbett genes.

Amy reacquainted herself with them and laughed and joked with her brothers while Tandy and Russ set up the ice-cream freezers. While Amy tended the freezing of the ice cream and more people arrived, she found herself coming face-to-face with friends and neighbors from the past.

She was regaled with praises for her success and a never-ending series of "Do you remember whens" that opened up the floodgates of her memories. She saw Judi Mason and remembered when they had gone skinny-dipping in Tandy's pond even though they'd known the guys were due to come at any time. She laughed with Sandy Calvin about the time they had taken Russ's truck and followed Sandy's boyfriend to Amarillo when Sandy got wind that he was seeing some other girl on the side—and Amy didn't even have a driver's license. She listened as two different people mentioned her parents—one who said that her mother was the nicest lady in town and one who said that her dad was the best rodeo clown in the south. Both comments brought a sense of warmth.

The only thing that briefly spoiled her evening was seeing Talia Davidson, who at one time had tried to take Russ away from her. Even though she knew it was silly, Amy felt her old jealousy creeping through her when she saw Russ carry the newly divorced redhead a coke.

"Don't worry about her," Rosemary said. "She's got the hots for anything in a pair of Levi's, but most of the guys around here have her number."

"Including Russ?" Amy asked.

"Especially Russ." Rosemary eyed Amy steadily. "Don't you know that Russ has been carrying the torch for you for so long that everyone in town thinks he's certifiable?"

Amy read truth on her sister-in-law's face. Her eyes scanned the crowd, searching for Russ and finding him near the barbecue grills talking to Zach. Russ was turned toward her, one foot on the bench of the picnic table, his forearms crossed on his knee as he leaned forward, talking earnestly to her brother. The rising wind riffled his auburn hair, and his eyes narrowed as a puff of dust blew his way. Amy imagined she could see the crow's feet appear as he squinted his gray-blue eyes.

Then, as if he could feel her scrutiny, his eyes moved from her brother's face to where she was sitting, meeting hers openly, candidly, holding a message of want and need and love. Amy's breath caught in her throat. Her tongue peeked out, slicking over lips already moist with peach-tinted gloss.

Russ said something to Zach and, straightening, started toward her. Her heart began a slow, measured beating as he moved nearer.

"Hello, Rosemary," he said with a smile. "Do you mind if I take Amy away from you for a while?"

"Not at all," Rosemary said. "I think I can handle the ice cream."

Russ reached for Amy's hand. He pulled her to her feet and laced their fingers together, turning and heading across the yard.

"Where are we going?" she asked, half-trotting after him.

"For a walk," he said over his shoulder. "Jason says everything should be ready in about ten minutes, and I thought it would be a good time to ask you to go with me to the rodeo tomorrow night."

"Go with you?"

"Yeah. I thought that since I met the people you associate with, it's only fair that you meet the people I work with."

Her heart sank. She didn't want to go, didn't want to meet other rodeo riders. And she certainly didn't want to watch him ride. He was right, though, she thought with a sinking heart. This was part and parcel of the week she owed him, so she couldn't leave tomorrow as she'd planned. She refused to listen to her mind, which whispered that even though she didn't want to go and watch him ride, she didn't want to leave, either.

"Will you go?" he asked. "Mike and Stan are supposed to have cameras there to start filming."

"You decided to do it, after all?" she asked, following him into the shadows of the hay barn.

"Yeah," he said consideringly. "You might say they bought me."

"In other words, it pays well."

"Right. Will you go?"

She nodded.

Russ sat down on a bale of hay and pulled her down beside him. "You haven't seen me ride since high school."

"I know." She cut her gaze to his. "It . . . it scares me too much," she said hesitantly, stating something that she'd suspected for a long time. She also admitted to herself that there was a world of difference between the hate she maintained she felt for what he did and the actual fear she felt for him because he did it. The truth was, that up until now she hadn't wanted to acknowledge the difference.

He put his arm around her shoulders and pulled her against his side. She didn't fight the closeness; she welcomed it.

Russ tenderly kissed the top of her shining head, inhaling the floral fragrance of her shampoo. He understood what her confession cost her and what that confession meant to their relationship. For the moment, it was enough.

"You know," he told her, his hand rubbing up and down her bare arm from shoulder to elbow, "I realized when I looked up and saw you watching me, that I haven't had you to myself since you've been here." He gave a soft laugh. "It's sort of hard to change a woman's mind if you can't get her alone."

Thunder rumbled in the distance, but Amy hardly noticed. She was too caught up in remembering the scene in the kitchen the day before and the way his hands had felt on her breasts. "You're doing all right," she acknowledged in a breathless voice.

Russ reached out and put a knuckle under her chin, lifting it until their eyes met. "Am I?"

The words held a world of uncertainty, and uncertainty didn't sit well on Russell Wheeler's broad shoulders. She smiled, a soft, encouraging smile that matched the one in her eyes. "Yes."

He moved his hands to her waist in a light grip. His head began a slow descent, and his mouth was a heartbeat from hers when the big dinner bell outside the back door began to ring, accompanied by Jason yelling, "Come and get it before I throw it out!"

With their mouths barely touching, the tip of Russ's tongue trailed along the slight separation of her lips. He didn't move when he spoke. "Jason could use a little work on his timing."

Smiling against his mouth, Amy whispered, "What's the matter? Aren't you hungry?"

"Starving," he whispered before his mouth rolled onto hers in a sweet kiss of promise. He kissed her once, twice, a third time, each kiss a little deeper, a little more heady. Amy drew a shuddering sigh between kisses, and Russ released her with obvious reluctance. "Did anyone ever tell you that you taste like sun-ripened peaches?" he queried softly.

Her eyes smiled into his. "You *must* be hungry. That's my lips gloss."

There was a look in his eyes she'd seen there before. He rose and pulled her to her feet. "I'm hungry, all right, but it isn't for barbecue."

Amy couldn't think of an answer, and the suggestive statement stayed with her throughout the meal, which everyone ate with one eye on the dark, swelling clouds. Through some miracle, the storm contented itself with ominous grumblings and held off, even though the tables had been moved beneath the carport.

Tandy had downed a plate of food then said his good-byes and mentioned to Russ that he was heading in to Amarillo with a buddy to see a movie.

The food was perfect and plentiful, and everyone complained of overeating. There was a collective groan when Candace began to dish up the desserts, including Amy's ice cream.

Exclamations of rapture were still falling from Jason's lips as he finished his second bowl and the first raindrops began to fall. In a matter of seconds the rain

had escalated into a full-fledged downpour, accompanied by an occasional flash of lightning and sullen
rumblings of thunder, reminding them that things could
get worse.

They did.

Amy, Russ and several others stayed to help carry
things inside, while most guests made a beeline toward
their respective vehicles. The wind, which had died down
some, now blew with a vengeance, sweeping the rain under the carport and drenching everyone to the skin.
Shoving the last ice-cream freezer through the back door
and telling Candace a quick goodbye, Russ grabbed
Amy's hand and yelled, "Let's get out of here!"

Hand in hand, they raced through the driving rain toward the truck. Russ dragged Amy to the driver's side,
wrenched open the door and practically shoved her inside. She scooted to the middle of the seat, and he got in
beside her, slamming the door and swearing.

"What is it?"

"The keys are in my pocket," he grumbled.

He shifted to the side, stiffened his right leg and
worked his hand into the pocket of his wet jeans. His very
tight, wet jeans. Amy's eyes climbed from the masculine
bulge to his face, a tremulous sigh escaping her lips. A
drop of water fell off the end of his nose, breaking the
sensual intimacy of the moment. She laughed softly.
Look at him! He was drenched, and so was she!

"What's so funny?" Russ asked, pulling the keys from
his pocket and inserting them into the steering column.

"You are," she said, reaching up and smoothing his
water-darkened auburn hair from his forehead.

"Well you look sorta like a drowned rat yourself," he
quipped back, unable to resist the humor in her eyes.
Actually, he doubted if Amy would look bad under any

conditions. The rain made her slacks cling to her slender thighs, and her sweater molded her breasts, the nipple taut from the chill moisture. Her short hair was plastered to her head, but it only made her brown eyes look bigger and more mysterious.

"A drowned rat?" she said indignantly, grabbing fistfuls of his shirt, intent on shaking him. The instant she touched him, she felt the warm firmness of his chest muscles beneath her palms. The teasing mood fled, replaced by stronger, more basic feelings, feelings as elemental as the storm raging around them. Her eyes struggled from the spot where her hands touched him to his eyes. She spoke, intending that the words come out light, playful. Instead, they sounded breathless and filled with wanting.

"You just wait. I'm going to get my pound of flesh for that."

With his eyes clinging to hers, Russ reached out and cupped the back of her wet head with his hand. Very slowly, as if he were afraid sudden movement might break the bond between them, he leaned down and kissed her. Electricity arced from his mouth to hers, and a bolt of lightning seared the dark sky, illuminating the interior of the truck and the surrounding countryside. Thunder boomed so loudly it seemed to echo as Russ raised his head and looked at her.

"Sweet heaven, Amy, I hope so," he breathed.

Chapter Nine

The short drive through the blinding rain was accomplished as fast as was safely possible. At some point during the journey home, Russ took her hand tightly in his, and his fingers brushed the diamond ring Wayne had given her. He didn't speak, didn't ask her to take it off; he didn't have to. Silently, Amy pulled the ring from her finger and slipped it into the pocket of her sweater. Russ, concentrating on his driving, spared her a brief glance and saw what she was doing. He didn't comment on her action but turned his attention back to the road, leaning forward and peering through the windshield into the night while the wipers waged a futile battle against the rain.

The need to hurry gripped them, but the truck's progress was hampered by the inclement weather. Russ kept telling himself that it had been more than seven months, that a few more minutes wouldn't matter, but that didn't stop the urgency clamoring through his veins, and he said a prayer of thankfulness when he turned the truck down the lane leading to the house, lured by the glimmer of the porch light visible through the sheets of water coming down.

In only a matter of minutes, now, Amy would be his. And this time he wasn't letting her go—not without a fight.

Across the seat, she shivered.

"Cold?" he asked, glancing at her.

She shook her head. "Not really. Just a chill."

He pulled the truck around to the back of the house and beneath the carport, then turned off the ignition and opened the door. The pounding of the rain on the carport's metal roof sounded deafening after the quiet confines of the truck cab. A smile of encouragement in his eyes, he helped Amy out, and they ran toward the screened-in porch. She gasped as the wind blew the cold rain toward them.

Russ flung open the back door and propelled Amy inside, slamming it closed behind them. They stood in the dim glow from the porch, the harshness of their breathing and the water dripping onto the floor the only sounds in the quiet kitchen.

She turned to him, about to say something about ruining the wax on the floor, but she never had the chance. Russ reached for her and pulled her into his hard embrace, his mouth unerringly targeting hers. Amy's lips parted, and her mouth opened, waiting for the first piercing thrust of his tongue, and, when it came, closing tightly around it.

Russ groaned; the action was reminiscent of the way her body tightened and closed around him during his actual possession of her. His hand sought the bottom of her dripping sweater, and he ended the kiss long enough to peel it up over her head. There was a soft clinking sound that both ignored before the sweater fell with a sodden plop to the floor and was soon joined by her slacks. Her wet underthings were like second skins, so tightly were they molded to her body. He was fumbling with the catch of her bra when Amy stopped him with a husky "Wait."

"Don't play games, Amy. Not now," he pleaded urgently.

"I'm not." She tugged at the buttons of his shirt with ill-concealed impatience, her hands trembling with chill and excitement. "Just let me catch up."

In spite of her clumsy fingers, Russ's shirt joined her clothes on the floor in a matter of seconds. Then her fingers slipped beneath the waistband of his drenched, form-fitting blue jeans. Russ's stomach muscles tightened at her touch, and his breath hissed on a sharp intake of air. Even though she was trembling with nervousness, the metal button was no hard task for her eager fingers.

The zipper began a slow, downward grind, and Amy felt the stirring impatience of his body beneath her touch. Hooking her thumbs in his belt loops, she struggled to rid him of the confining jeans, succeeding centimeter by slow centimeter until she got them past his hips. Peeling them down his long legs was a simple matter, and in seconds he was stepping out of them and his boots and kicking them aside.

Russ pulled her up against him, his hands winnowing through her short, wet hair, while his eyes, clouded with a blue haze of desire, caressed her face, lingering on her lips for agonizingly long seconds before his own lips found hers in a slow, sweet kiss that sent her senses reeling.

To steady her emotions, Amy moved her hands to the breadth of his shoulders, and her palms molded themselves to the muscular curves before sliding down his triceps and back again. She wanted to say that she loved him, but instead she pressed herself against his hard, throbbing body, her hands moving up and down his back and over his firm masculine buttocks in a gentle caress. Russ accepted her touch gladly, and his mouth continued to play hers with a tender tune of seduction.

It wasn't enough, she realized with a sort of frenzy. Kisses weren't enough. She wanted to touch him everywhere . . . everywhere. His body, as familiar to her as her own, was still a joy to explore, a challenge to conquer.

Her eyes closed, her hands moved between their bodies, wandering at will up his chest, skimming it lightly, blindly, memorizing the shape and feel of him through touch. She reveled in the myriad textures of his body—the soft hair tickling her palms, the corded muscles of his stomach, the firmness of his pectorals, the hardness of his biceps. She filed away the sensation of his warm skin and the contrast between the hair on his chest and that on his legs. Her fingers explored his collarbone and the hollow at the base of his throat, where his breathing rasped harshly.

Amy stood on tiptoe, leaning against him and pressing her mouth to the tantalizing hollow. He tasted of warm skin and summer rain, she thought, registering the fact that the unplanned act added new vistas to her tactile exploration. Her searching mouth found a bronze hued nipple hiding in the cloud of copper hair covering his chest. She favored it with soft, openmouthed kisses and the barest tickling of her tongue, efforts that were rewarded with a softly groaned "Amy."

Emboldened by the raw need in his voice, her fingers traced the trail of silky hair down the flat expanse of his stomach, skimming the elastic waistband and expanding both her agony and his by keeping the barrier of cotton between the heat of his body and the fire of her touch.

Her bold caresses had reduced Russ's breathing to a ragged indrawing and harsh expulsion of air that somehow failed to meet his oxygen need. He couldn't breathe, couldn't think. All he could do was feel. The nerve endings in his skin seemed to have become doubly sensitive. Every brush of her fingers, every touch of her mouth, sent quivering need speeding recklessly throughout him.

He realized suddenly that he had taken about all the passivity he could stand. Swinging her up into his arms, Russ carried her through the house to his room and eased her down onto the center of his bed. Being careful to keep his weight off her legs, he sat astride her.

Through the driving rain the outside light streamed into the room, illuminating it to a soft, dark gray. Amy was completely still, and her eyes, heavy-lidded and filled with slumberous hunger, devoured him while he feasted visually on her slim body.

He didn't know what kind of bra she was wearing, except that it was white lace and there wasn't much to it. The cups were skimpy, scalloped edged, barely covering the pert nipples that were completely visible through the lace. The panties, nothing but two pieces of triangular lace held together by a delicate sliver of elastic, did nothing but accentuate the cloud of dark blond curls hiding the very heart of her womanhood. He'd seen her before, countless times, but the sight of her slender, excrutiatingly feminine curves was his undoing. Hardly aware of his actions, Russ reached out, his big, callused hands covering her breasts.

Amy's eyes drifted shut, and her small white teeth closed over her bottom lip in an unsuccessful attempt to stifle the moan that escaped into the silence of the room.

His thumbs, moving in small, concentric circles, rubbed her nipples to pebble hardness. Then, turning her to her side and stretching out beside her, he gently pushed the aching fullness upward and lowered his head, pressing a moist kiss through the lace. There was an inexplicable excitement in the contrasting feel of lace to warm flesh against his laving tongue and, for long moments, Russ divided his attention equally between both breasts, driving them both to the very edge of an undeniable need.

When he reached beneath her to unhook her bra, Amy arched her back, giving him access. With a skill born of practice, Russ unfastened it, easing the straps down her arms and pulling it from her. His eyes drank in the sight of her smooth, creamy shoulders, the proud thrust of her small breasts, and her narrow waist with deliberate slowness.

"I love you, Amarillo," he said quietly. The words were statement, confession, testimonial, and they defeated the last bit of resistance holding Amy's emotions in check. She looked up at him with tear-filled eyes. "Oh, Russ," she whispered.

Raising her arms and looping them around his neck, she pulled him down, opening her mouth, her legs and her heart for his entrance. She felt his hand, warm and heavy against the delta of her thighs, cupping, kneading, his fingers easing aside the elastic and seeking entrance to the hidden passage of her womanhood.

Amy lifted her hips, inviting his intrusion, pressing against his hand in an effort to assuage the pulsating throb of desire while his tongue swirled with hers—both exciting but unsatisfactory duplications of the act both longed to share. She tore her mouth free from his and struggled to rid him of his briefs, while Russ did the same for her. Then, completely naked, she went back into his arms, pressing her slim body to him from breast to toe, wrapping her arms around his neck and tilting her head to accommodate the drugging touch of his mouth on hers.

Her breasts were crushed against his chest, and to Amy's heightened senses, she imagined she could feel the imprint of each and every bronzed hair. The bold hardness of his sex rode snugly in the cradle of her femininity, and their legs twined together in an effort to get even closer.

Russ's hands cupped the back of her head, his fingers digging into her scalp as his lips slanted across hers in a grinding, bruising kiss, almost, it seemed, as if he wanted to brand her as his.

And he did. This night was his chance, perhaps his only chance, to change her mind. Sex, for want of a better word, was the one thing binding them that even Amy couldn't deny. And if it was the only weapon he had to use to batter her defenses, he would.

Rolling her to her back, Russ rested his weight on his forearms, his teeth nibbling at her lower lip, while his body moved slowly against hers in a rhythmic prelude. Beneath him, Amy moved boldly, impatiently, her hand guiding the satin heat of him to the melting core of her desire.

Russ eased into her waiting warmth, controlling his body's urging to hurry. Amy's whimper of pleasure was uttered simultaneously with his soft profanity. After the briefest hesitation, his body began a slow, measured stroking, and he opened his eyes to gauge Amy's reactions. As if she could feel the intensity of his gaze, her lashes lifted, and she stared up into eyes a passionate, hazy blue.

"I love you," he said again, his voice low and throbbing with sincerity and conviction, as if the power and intensity of his love could bridge the ten-year gap of differences between them.

"I love you, too, Russ," she confessed for the first time since her senior year in high school. The words came from the heart, from the soul. Amy didn't try to monitor them or deny their truth. The time for that had passed.

His movements stopped, and Amy shifted restlessly beneath him. A ghost of a smile hovered on his lips. "I know you do, darlin'," he said. "I just wasn't sure you were ever going to admit it."

Reaching up and grasping his ears with both hands, Amy pulled him down until his smiling mouth was bare millimeters from hers. "You talk too much, cowboy. What I want is to see one of those championship rides."

Russ touched the tip of her nose with his lips. "That won't be any fun."

"Why?"

"They only last eight seconds."

Amy's eyes gleamed with naughty mischievousness. Her nails raked lightly up the backs of his thighs. "Then," she said, urging his hips to motion once more, "let's just see if you can stay the distance."

Russ's smile was lazy, confident. "Hell, darlin', that won't be any trouble at all."

After that, there was no sound in the room except that of labored breathing, whispered words of encouragement and soft moans of pleasure as Russ countered each thrust of her hips with one of his, taking them nearer and nearer the shores of fulfillment.

"Russ," she pleaded when she thought she would explode with need, "please."

"Not yet," he ground out between clenched teeth. He reached to wipe the spikes of wet hair from her forehead, uncertain whether the dampness was rain or perspiration.

"You're...driving me...crazy...." she panted, her hands gripping the sweat-slickened contours of his buttocks.

Russ didn't answer. He couldn't. She was wanton fire and icy confidence. She was country born and bred but city wise. She was his past, and by damn, come hell or high water, she was going to be his future. She was perfect, wonderful, he thought as she matched him thrust for heady thrust and the feelings held captive by his body surged stronger and harder, struggling to break the iron control of his will.

"Russ! I can't...help...I'm..." There was anguish in her voice as her hips arched upward.

The incoherent words tripped the hair trigger of his control, and Russ parried her move with a powerful surge of his body that sent them both plunging into a tidal wave of passion. Together they rode the crest, holding each other tightly, and sinking into a lethargic numbness as gentle eddies carried them back to reality.

With him buried deep inside her, they were still, eyes closed, Russ's forehead resting on hers while their breath mingled in soft, harsh panting. He recaptured one breast in his hand, as if the thought of letting her go was more than he could bear. And it was. He feathered kisses to her brows and her closed eyelids, brushing them with the tip of his tongue then moved to the bridge of her nose and the corners of her mouth.

"Do you want to talk?"

Talk? Amy thought. She didn't even want to think. Even now, with the sweat of his body mingled and drying with hers, a tiny voice buried deep inside her whispered. *Fool...fool.* She pressed closer to Russ and shook her head. "Just hold me," she said.

Russ smiled. "Sleepy?"

She nodded.

He sighed. "Me, too." He settled on one side, wedged his leg between hers, and tucked her head into the crook of his arm. "Go to sleep. We'll figure out everything else tomorrow."

Amy nodded and swallowed back the lump of emotion in her throat. Tomorrow. Like Scarlett O'Hara, she was more than willing to wait to confront the changes in her life that her inability to say no to Russ necessitated. Her cheek rested against his chest. The hair tickled her nose, but she was too tired to move. His heartbeat slowed and steadied. The rain, which had decreased to a steady downfall, flung itself against the windows in a mesmerizing cadence. A deep sigh came from her lips. Tomorrow...

At some time during the night, Amy, cradled to Russ in a spoonlike fashion, awoke to the feel of his hands on her breasts, of his mouth placing hot, moist kisses on her neck and shoulders. Sleepily, her hands covered his, holding them to her. She sighed as his mouth moved down her spine, lower and lower, before she felt the lingering touch of his tongue where her back curved into her bottom.

Then, gently, he grasped her hipbone and turned her to her back, taking her breasts in his hands again, while his mouth traveled the valley between them and moved inexorably toward her navel. His tongue dipped into the indentation, and her back arched involuntarily as he bathed the hollow with utmost care. His touch, like the rain outside, was hypnotizing. Drowsy, Amy was suspended somewhere between wakefulness and sleep, between heaven and paradise. Then, through a haze of sleepy pleasure, she felt his mouth moving even lower. She came awake instantly.

"Russ?"

His breath was a warm vapor against her as he murmured, "Shh, Amy. Let me love you . . . all of you."

Sunshine tickled Amy's eyelids, urging her to wakefulness. Sunshine. Morning. She rolled to her back, covered a wide yawn and lifted her arms over her head in a bone-creaking stretch that pulled the sheet halfway to her waist and exposed her bare breasts to the coolness blowing from the air conditioner. Her nipples puckered in protest. She was naked. Why hadn't she put on a gown? she thought drowsily. The errant thought tumbled through her mind and crowded out the lingering traces of sleepiness.

Her eyes flew open and stared up at an unfamiliar ceiling fan, giving her mind a clue to what her heart already remembered. She was naked. In Russ's room, Russ's bed. She turned her head quickly and found the place beside her empty. There was only the indentation where his head had lain on the pillow next to hers and the lingering scent of Aramis.

The smell of the sexy masculine cologne released other memories from the dark recesses where she'd buried them the night before, bringing with them a heady blush of pleasure. A soft smile tilted the corners of her mouth upward, and her eyes drifted shut. She could picture him above her and feel the heat of his body pressed to hers.

She brought her hands to her breasts and felt the hardened tips against her palms. Is this the way they felt to Russ? She fought to no avail against the memory of his masculinity sliding into her. An involuntary moan of frustration echoed through the quietness of the room.

Shocked by the wanton feelings regenerated by mere thoughts of the night spent in Russ's arms, Amy jerked the sheet back over her and sat up. She was lifting her hands to her rumpled hair when the telephone at her side pealed shrilly.

Her hands dropped to the bed, and she stared at the plastic instrument, guilt slowly filling her. She didn't want to answer it from Russ's bed. The phone rang with nagging insistence, and Amy shrugged off the feeling. After all, whoever was on the other end of the line couldn't see her.

"Hello," she said into the receiver.

"Amy?" came a deep masculine voice, a voice whose sound, along with its owner, she'd almost forgotten these last few days.

Amy tucked the sheet more tightly around her breasts and drew her legs together primly. "Wayne?"

"You remember me?" he asked. "That seems funny since you haven't called since Tennessee."

Amy wondered if there was really sarcasm in his voice or if it was supplied by her guilt. "I...I haven't?" She gave a shrug he couldn't see, and her fingers began to make tiny pleats in the top sheet. "Uh, I've been busy. Really busy. I'm helping Tandy and...his...hired-hand out."

"So I hear. I thought you were staying at your brother's, but when I called, he told me where you were. Who the hell is this Tandy, anyway?" Wayne demanded to know. This time there was no question about his tone of voice. He was angry. And, she thought with a sinking heart, rightly so.

"Tandy? Oh, he's just an old friend."

"The same kind of old friend as Russ Wheeler?"

Amy didn't want to think of Russ or what he was to her right now. She was too confused to sort out her feelings. And how dare Wayne insinuate that there was something going on with Tandy? She felt the first stirrings of anger edging aside her guilt. "Old, as in sixty, Wayne," she told him in an icy voice.

Wayne didn't speak immediately, but after a few seconds his anger emerged once more. "Well, dammit, don't blame me for being suspicious. You're the one who lied about Russ being your cousin. I don't know what to expect from you anymore."

"What does that mean?" she asked.

"That means, Amy, that your behavior since Russ Wheeler came to Dallas has been erratic at best."

"Erratic?"

"Yes. You've lied to me, you've been caught in a situation that looked to be getting out of hand, and instead of staying to explain, you rushed off to Tennessee. Then, instead of coming home, you take off to a hometown you claim to hate to attend an anniversary celebration for a brother you never talk about. This morning I find out that you're staying with an 'old friend' instead of your family—odd, since you have *five* brothers. If that isn't erratic behavior, I don't know what is."

Silence echoed through the phone lines.

He was right. She had been acting strangely. But things hadn't been this mixed up before. She didn't know what to do to straighten out her life, so she was letting it lead her by the nose.

"Don't try to smother me, Wayne. It drives me crazy with you stopping by every day and wanting to know what I'm doing every minute. I don't have to give you an accounting of my actions," she railed.

"I'm your fiancé," he reminded.

"Well, that can certainly be remedied," she snapped.

As soon as the words were out, she wanted to call them back. The anger drained from her in a second. Poor Wayne. She was taking her own guilt out on him. It wasn't fair. "I'm sorry," she said.

"Yeah. Sure."

Total quiet.

"Have you seen him?" he said at last.

The sound of Wayne's voice in her ear brought her thoughts back into line. She didn't have to ask who "he" was. Somehow, she had been expecting the question, but expecting it didn't make answering it any easier. Wayne was her fiancé, the man she was supposed to marry. The guilt she'd felt on waking returned with unbearable intensity. She couldn't tell Wayne she was staying with Russ as well as Tandy, and she couldn't tell him an out-and-out lie, either.

Her head, swimming with doubts and problems, suddenly felt too heavy for her neck to support. She raised her knees beneath the sheet and, raking her free hand through her hair, supported her head by resting her elbow on one upraised knee. "I've seen him, yes."

"When?"

Last night, Wayne. I spent the night with him. I'm still in his bed.

Her lashes lowered, as if by shutting her eyes she could shut out the question and deny the answer. "Last night."

"Where?"

There was no doubt about it, she thought, drawing a ragged breath. Wayne was going straight for the jugular. She wondered wearily if he would demand to know all the details. Last night those details had been wonderfully shrouded under an intimate cloak of rain and darkness, but when examined by Wayne's critical, angry eyes in the clear light of day, what she and Russ shared would appear sordid and wrong.

When she answered, her voice was a bare thread of sound. "He was at the barbecue." She wondered what had happened to her nice, secure world and was suddenly filled with a little-girl longing to be held in the barely remembered comfort of her mother's arms.

Again, Wayne was silent. She heard him sigh, and it sounded harsh, even over the phone. "This is Friday. You're going to miss the Historical Society luncheon."

It took a moment for it to register in Amy's troubled mind that he hadn't asked anything else about Russ. Apparently, her answers had satisfied him, or he was afraid to dig any deeper, afraid he might not like the answers.

"They'll survive without me."

"The interview with the paper is Monday afternoon. Will you be here?"

She nodded. "Yes. I'm leaving Sunday night or Monday morning."

"Positive?"

Amy stifled a twinge of irritation. "Yes."

"Well, then," he said, "I guess I'll let you go."

"Okay. Thanks for calling."

"Right."

The sarcasm was back, she thought with another mighty surge of guilt. "Goodbye, Wayne."

"Goodbye."

She started to hang up and then brought the receiver back to her ear, calling urgently, "Wayne!"

"Yes?" A pathetic eagerness filtered into his voice.

Amy swallowed. Hard. "When I get back, we need to talk."

"Sure."

He sounded defeated, a word she'd never before thought could relate to Wayne Hardeman. "Tell Bette hi for me."

"I will. Goodbye, Amy."

She heard the phone click and the hum of the dial tone. Turning slightly, she hung up her phone and turned onto her stomach, burying her face in Russ's pillow. A terrible mistake. How could she think about anything but Russ, surrounded by the scent of him? Remembering the way she fit so perfectly in his arms?

Furious—at herself, Wayne and Russ—she threw back the sheet and bounded out of bed, heading for a shower that would hopefully wash away the memories and return at least a semblance of sanity.

After a hot shower that washed away every trace of the night *but* the memories, Amy at least felt as if she could face the day and Russ with some equanimity. Nothing had changed. She doubted it ever would. She had faced and accepted the fact that Russ Wheeler's persuasiveness could override, break down or just plain old outlast her strongest defenses.

He turned her on. She'd always known it, and just because she had planned to marry Wayne, that hadn't changed. It probably never would. But it didn't change the fact that they wanted different things from life. And it didn't change the fact that she hated what he did for living. A life with him was still impossible, because th years had already proven that he wouldn't give up rodeoing.

You told him you loved him.

The thought halted her progress at the kitchen door. She had. Why hadn't she remembered before? Had she been so drunk on the taste and feel of him that she'd forgotten even that?

What was it he had said in response?

"I know you do, darlin'. I just wasn't sure you were ever going to admit it."

The words, accompanied by every nuance of emotion in his voice and face, came back with haunting clarity. Amy shook her head and started determinedly toward the kitchen, willing her mind to let go of the problem, at least until she could have a cup of coffee.

The kitchen was in order; Russ and Tandy had put their dirty dishes in the sink as usual. And, as it had been every day she'd been there, the coffee was waiting for her. And her note.

Amy picked it up, folding it open with a combined feeling of anticipation and apprehension. What would the note say today...after last night?

Amy, I put the wet clothes in the laundry. Shall I get out the ring and dust it off?

Russ

Tears filled Amy's eyes as she folded the note and stuck it into the pocket of Tandy's shirt. She was surprised at the brevity of the message, yet his few words said everything there was to say, didn't they?

The ring. A tiny smile tugged at the corners of her mouth. She could barely remember the ring he'd bought for her so long ago. It had been small and dainty—she remembered that much. Not like Wayne's, she thought, holding up her left hand.

Her bare left hand.

Panic flooded Amy at the sight of her naked ring finger. Her ring! Where was it? Her mind frantically retraced the events of the night before. She'd had it at the barbecue—several people had commented on it. Suddenly she remembered Russ taking her hand in the truck. She'd taken the ring off and put it in the pocket of her sweater... and Russ had put her sweater in the wash.

She sighed in relief and crossed the kitchen toward the door of the laundry room. The wet clothes were draped across the top of the washer. She reached for her sweater and was just about to check the pockets when she heard Russ's voice call, "Amy!"

There was no disguising the eagerness she heard in his voice and no controlling the wide smile that curved her lips. "In here!"

The sweater in her hands was forgotten as she listened to his long strides crossing the kitchen floor. Then he was standing in the doorway, his hat in his hands, a smile on his face, but a wary look in his blue eyes.

"Hi."

"Hi."

"Did you sleep well?"

She was surprised to feel the heat of a blush creep into her cheeks. "Most of the night."

Russ grinned. "Yeah, I know what you mean. There was this woman in my bed who couldn't keep her hands off—"

His voice was smothered as Amy's wet sweater hit him in the face. He caught it and tossed it on top of the other wet things.

"You shouldn't have done that, darlin'," he said, advancing across the narrow room.

Amy planted her hands on her hips. "Oh, yeah? What are you going to do about it?" she asked saucily.

Russ closed the door, isolating them in the small room that smelled of laundry detergent and fabric softener. His hands closed over her shoulders and drew her nearer. "Come here, and I'll show you."

"Russ," she said, trying to capture the hands that were deftly untying the knot beneath her breasts. "You can't do this. Tandy—"

"...is in town getting feed." The knot untied, he grasped the bottom of the shirtfront and gave a hard jerk, popping open every one of the snaps and suddenly leaving Amy bare, exposed.

His eyes met hers. "You aren't wearing a bra."

She shook her head. Had she done it deliberately? she wondered as Russ's hands grasped her waist and lifted her to sit atop the dryer. She reached out and steadied herself against his shoulders. Russ ducked his head, and she felt his mouth on her breast, felt his tongue begin a slow stroking of her nipple.

In a matter of seconds, she forgot about the loss of Wayne's ring. Forgot that she hated the rodeo. Forgot everything except that she loved him. And this time, she was afraid there was no turning back.

Chapter Ten

Thankfully, Tandy didn't come back until Russ ha⟨
once more thoroughly branded Amy as his. Afterward
they shared a shower. As she leaned weakly against th⟨
tile wall, she tiredly, bravely, faced her love, a love a⟨
undeniable as her need for air.

Russ smoothed the hair away from her face, and sh⟨
looked up at him with tortured eyes. Steam, like low⟨
hanging clouds, filled the small shower stall, but it didn'⟨
hide the concern on his face.

"Do you love me?" he asked tenderly.

Amy's amber-colored eyes filled with instant tear⟨
"God help me, yes," she choked out. "Yes."

"Is it that bad?" he asked, brushing his lips against h⟨
brow.

"Yes. No." She shook her head helplessly. "I don⟨
know. It isn't what I wanted...what I want. But I can⟨
deny it anymore. I don't know how I did this long."

Russ's face was somber as he turned off the taps. "Granddaddy always said that if something's meant to be, it'll be—whether it's tomorrow or ten years down the road. I never stopped believing that."

He smiled then. A sweet half smile that told her without words that he loved her and that hearing her confess the same for him was worth a ten-year wait.

"Oh, Russ." Her voice quivered, and her lower lip trembled with emotion.

Sliding back the door, he reached for a huge charcoal-gray towel, using it to blot her face and shoulders and to brush the streaming hair from her face. He seemed to be concentrating solely on what he was doing until he said, "Now, if I can only make you see that I'm not like your daddy."

Amy, who was reciprocating his actions, recalled the things he'd done for her while she'd been there—all the little kindnesses, small proofs of his love that would never have crossed Cal Corbett's mind. "You're nothing like my dad," she said, realizing at last that it was the truth.

Russ grinned and set her out of the tub and onto the floor. "Two down, two to go, then."

Amy took the towel from him and began to rub her short hair vigorously. "What do you mean?"

"How do you feel about small-town living?"

Her eyes narrowed in mock anger. "Don't push it, Wheeler," she said.

"C'mon, darlin'," he teased with a grin, "admit that it isn't so bad."

"Actually, it isn't." She sighed and gave him a side-long glance. "Why do you think that is?"

"I suspect it has a lot to do with growing up and realizing that happiness equates to people, not places."

She thought about that for a moment and decided he
was right. As she'd discovered, her life at the ranch was
very similar to her days in Dallas—with the exception of
the social life, which wasn't a real problem, since dinner
parties had never been her favorite thing.

"What else did you set out to change my mind about
when you kidnapped me?" she asked, thinking of his
two-down-two-to-go comment.

"Set out to change your mind? Is that what I did?" he
asked with feigned innocence.

"You know it is."

Russ grew suddenly serious. "Can't you guess what the
other is, what the problem has really been the last ten
years, Amy?"

Of course she knew. She'd always known. "The rodeo."

"Yeah," he said, taking the towel from her and wrapping it around her still-damp body. "Have I changed
your mind about that?" he asked, securing the ends over
her breasts.

She loved him and recognized now that she probably
always would. She'd more or less come to terms with her
parents' problems since she'd been back, but she could
still remember the horror on her mother's face when
she'd heard that Cal had been injured. She looked up at
him, fear and sorrow mingling in the depths of her brown
eyes. "Sorry, cowboy. Not yet."

Surprisingly, her answer didn't seem to anger him.
Maybe, she thought, they were through with anger.
Maybe they'd said all the hurtful things they had to say.
She looked up at him, wistfulness in her eyes as he bent
and tenderly kissed her swollen lips.

"I'm not asking you for anything you can't give willingly, Amy. I just want you to try to be openminded about this weekend."

An endearing earnestness molded her features. "I'll try."

"Good enough." There was a twinkle in his blue eyes as he said, "After the rodeo, I've got a little surprise for you."

"What kind of a surprise?"

"If I tell, it won't be a surprise, now, will it?" he taunted.

"Beast!"

Happier than he'd been in years, Russ laughed and swatted her on the fanny. "Let's get dressed. We've got a drive ahead of us."

The rodeo was in Oklahoma, and Amy and Russ made the whole trip holding hands and talking about the past and what had really been going on in their lives during the last ten years.

"Do you remember the first time I made love to you?" he asked as they neared the Oklahoma border.

Amy raised her eyebrows. "As Tandy always says, 'Does a bear sleep in the woods?' It was graduation night. After the party."

"Right. You seduced me."

"I what!" she cried indignantly.

"Seduced me."

"I did not."

"You were drunk."

"I wasn't drunk, Russell Wheeler."

"What do you call it?"

She didn't answer.

Russ shot her a teasing glance. "As I was saying, you were drunk. Drunk and sexy as all get out."

"When did you know you loved me?" he asked ten miles farther down the highway.

Amy thought for a moment. "I guess I've always loved you, in one way or another." Her eyes were serious, and her voice held incredulity, as if she'd just that moment realized the fact.

"Yeah. Me, too."

She thought some more. "I think I realized it was for real when I saw you out with Talia that time."

"Really? I only went out with her because you were being a brat and giving Glen Sawyer the rush."

Amy smiled, a smile that was guaranteed to cause trouble. "Oh, yeah," she said dreamily, "Glen."

"I'll get you for that, Amarillo Corbett."

"Promises, promises."

They were driving through a small town when she asked, "What about you?"

"What?"

"When did you know you loved me?"

"Well," he told her thoughtfully, "I don't remember a moment of revelation or anything, but I knew it was for real by the time I was out of high school. Then I thought all I had to do was bide my time until you finished."

She gave his hand a squeeze, understanding how her plans to go to New York must have upset him.

"I do remember the first time I lusted after you."

"Russ!"

"Hell, darlin', I've had the hots for you ever since that time we went fishing at Mr. Stonecipher's pond and got to horsing around and you fell in. You should have seen yourself. Your hair was slicked back from your face, and the sun seemed to...I don't know. You just looked so grown-up all of a sudden." He laughed wryly. "And then there was the fact that you didn't have on a bra, and that sopping wet, white T-shirt was pretty...revealing."

"Russ! I was barely fourteen."

"Yeah, but my eighteen-year-old hormones failed to make the distinction. I still remember the way that shirt clung to you and the way your nipples looked...." He took his eyes from the road long enough to sneak a peek at her. "The same way they get when I touch you."

Amy gave him a coy, sidelong look. "I have a confession."

"What?"

"That's when I began to have these erotic dreams about you, too."

"Erotic?"

"Well, I didn't know at the time what they were called. There must have been something in your eyes, because after that day I began to daydream about you kissing me. And when I went to sleep, I dreamed you took off my shirt and touched me. And when the time came that you really did, I thought I'd die, it felt so good." She gave him a worldly, confident look. "And, Wheeler, the only thing I was drunk on the night I graduated was you."

They talked about what had happened to people she'd known in Claude since she'd gone—Mrs. Vernon who'd sold eggs, Mr. Peterson who'd sold Amy her first lipstick at the drugstore, and Mrs. Farmer who'd made her prom dress. She asked about his mother, of whom she'd always been fond, and was pleased to find that she was doing some traveling since Russ's father had died and the family farm had been turned over to his older brother.

Amy told him about her time in New York and how she'd worked at getting her career established. Russ, in turn, told her about the year he won All-Around Cowboy, the publicity he'd gained from it, and how tough an act it was to follow.

By the time they got to the arena, Amy felt the kind of happy glow that follows a prolonged visit with an old and dear friend. Besides being her lover, Russ was exactly that, she realized, a good friend.

The parking area roiled with dust as trucks pulling horse trailers arrived and the horses and cows used in the rough-stock events milled around in the holding pens.

Russ's plan to introduce her to some of his friends was thwarted when, almost as soon as they got out of the truck, Mike and Stan approached, anxious to begin shooting on the documentary. They dragged Russ off to the side to explain the script and to prep him with what they planned to do during the shoot.

Amy spent the afternoon tagging along, marveling while they shot what seemed like miles of film—most of which, if she understood correctly, would be cut and trashed. She watched and listened to Russ as he conveyed his considerable knowledge about life on the road and in the spotlight.

She learned that, like Russ, many rodeo riders supplemented their income with jobs on a ranch. If they were lucky, they got on with an outfit where the boss didn't mind if they were gone two, three and sometimes four days a week. But if they weren't lucky enough to find someone that easygoing to work for, their chances of ever making it big were pretty slim.

He explained the feeling a contestant experiences when they've taken off work, driven for hours to get to a rodeo and paid the entry fee, only to get thrown coming out of the chutes. It wasn't, he told them with an easy laugh, an occupation for anyone fainthearted or easily discouraged.

On the other hand, if a cowboy did well, all he had to worry about was how to spend his money and which buckle bunny to choose from. A buckle bunny, he said with a grin, was a female rodeo groupie, a woman who wanted to date a cowboy just so she could claim the prestige of having his newest, biggest and shiniest belt buckle.

The interview changed pace then. Russ sat on the top rail of one of the holding pens, elbows resting on his knees, his hat pushed to the back of his head, and Stan asked point-blank why he rode.

Amy found herself listening with as much interest as Stan.

Russ smiled, a crooked kind of smile that looked at once embarrassed and yet strangely proud. Reaching up, he grasped the crown of his hat and pulled it down to shade his eyes. He cleared his throat and, looking directly into the camera, broadened his smile. "It may sound corny, but...cowboys have always epitomized the true American spirit."

Amy bit back a smile of her own. He was good, she thought. Very good. He *should* go into acting. He exuded enough masculinity to come across as a man's man, while that devastating smile and slow Texas drawl were guaranteed to increase feminine pulses.

"Did you ever take part in sports at school?" he was asked. "Ever look up to football or baseball stars?"

Russ laughed and shook his head. "I never was much on team sports when I was growing up. As I said, my role models were guys like Monty Henson and Larry Mahan.

I guess I like that one-on-one competition—just me and the stock against the clock.''

"Is there a single incident that stands out in your mind that made you know for certain that rodeo was the place for you?''

"Oh, yeah," he said, a thoughtful expression on his rugged face. "When I was a kid, my dad worked for a stock contractor. I used to hang around the ranch and watch them working with the broncs and bulls. Then, when I was seven, he took me with him to the Mac-Alester Prison Rodeo. I don't know. There was something about it—the noise, the excitement, maybe even the roughness—that appealed to me.''

Amy sat with her chin cupped in her palm, mesmerized by the intensity of feeling in Russ's statements. As she listened, she began to understand why he was the man he was. It was the first time she'd ever set aside her prejudices long enough to really listen to how he felt. And the longer she listened, the sorrier she was that she hadn't done it years before.

Finally, Russ called a halt, telling Stan that he had to have a little time to himself before the actual start of the rodeo. He introduced Mike and Stan to some other riders, including a retired bull rider by the name of Vernon Greerson, who traveled the circuit for no other reason than to watch his twenty-one-year-old grandson ride.

Then, leaving them to their own devices, he looped an arm around Amy's shoulders and gave her a brief kiss. "I'm sorry about all that," he said, waving his arm in an encompassing gesture.

"It's okay. I enjoyed watching and listening to you.''

"What do you think?''

"Of the documentary or the man?'' she teased.

He shrugged. "Both.''

"I think the man will make the documentary memorable."

"You're prejudiced."

"Possibly."

Russ escorted her to the truck and got her a cola out of the ice chest.

Amy took the cold drink and gave him a dirty look. "I was dying of thirst. Why didn't you tell me these were in here?"

"You didn't ask."

"Cute, Wheeler," she quipped sarcastically.

Russ mimed a kiss in her direction, popped the top of his own drink and took a healthy swallow. Then he clasped her hand and led her to the parking area.

"Where are we going?" she asked.

"To meet some friends. Listen up, Amy. I'm about to teach you something about rodeos."

Amy schooled her features into a studious demeanor. "Teach away."

"The people we're going to meet right now compete in the timed events. They tend to hang out around the horse trailers and trucks when nothing's going on. Later, I'll take you over behind the bucking chutes, where the rough-stock riders congregate. Got it?"

"Rough-stock riders are bronc-and-bull riders." She remembered that much from her dad's rodeo days.

"Right."

"Elementary," she told him with a lofty air that earned a laugh and a quick hug.

Hand in hand, she and Russ approached a tall man who looked vaguely familiar. When the man heard Russ's voice, he turned, and Amy found herself staring into the memorable, sky-blue eyes of Cody Jarrell, the gum-popping pilot who'd shanghaied her at the Nashville airport.

"'Lo, Rusty," he drawled, giving Amy a jaunty salute. "Ma'am."

"Mr. Jarrell, artist-abductor extraordinaire, I presume?" Amy said, a hint of laughter in her voice.

Cody looked at Russ and cocked his head toward Amy. "Glad to see you calmed her down, Rusty."

"It took some doing, I don't mind telling you," Russ got out before Amy's elbow gouged him in the ribs. "What're you doing here, Cody?"

"I flew Mel Townsend up from Houston. Gene drove his horses up."

"Some of the timed-event riders have someone haul their horses from place to place and they fly wherever they're going later," Russ explained to Amy.

"That must be expensive."

Russ shrugged. "It's a pretty expensive sport."

"You got that right," Cody agreed, cracking the piece of gum he was chewing.

Feinting a blow to the pilot's shoulder, Russ said, "We'll see you later. I'm going to take Amy around and introduce her to some folks."

"Right," Cody said, offering Russ his hand. He nodded to Amy. "Nice to see you again, ma'am."

"Same here," Amy told him sincerely. "Before I go I'd just like to ask you one thing."

"Sure."

"How did you do it?"

"Do what?"

"Convince me you were taking me to Dallas?"

The crow's feet at the corners of Cody's unbelievabl blue eyes appeared along with his smile. "I believe it' called sophistry. Not lying, just not telling the whole truth and letting the imagination fill in the rest.''

Amy shook her head, a disbelieving smile curving her lips.

For the next hour, she met dozens of Russ's friends and acquaintances. Then they got hamburgers at the concession stand and ate sitting on the tailgate of the truck, sharing an order of fries and talking quietly. She was relaxed and happy, and she wasn't certain when anything had tasted so good. They were just finishing when Russ noticed that Mike and Stan had the minicam rolling again.

''They're interviewing Vern Greerson. Do you want to listen?''

Amy wiped her fingers and washed down her last bite with a sip of iced tea. She gave a sigh of repletion. ''Sure. Why not?''

A safe distance from the interview area, Russ lifted Amy to the top of the board fence and settled beside her. Vern Greerson's voice carried clearly, even over the occasional restless shuffle of the cattle in a nearby pen.

''I was the old-timer of the circuit, I guess. I bull-dogged until I was forty,'' Vern was saying, scratching his cheek in a gesture that betrayed his nervousness. ''I quit ridin' bulls a long time before that, though.''

Amy listened, finding herself fascinated, as she had been all day, by the determination in these men to outlast the beating of a clock.

''Why did you stop bull riding?'' he was asked.

''One of my friends got hurt real bad,'' Vern explained, crossing his arms over his chest. ''He was a clown. Cal was probably the best damn clown that ever hit the rodeo.''

Amy's mind exploded in a whirlwind of questions. Cal?

"Maybe you've heard of him?" Vern continued. "Cal Corbett. Got killed in a tornado several years back."

Amy's head began to spin, and, as if he knew what she was going through, Russ's arm circled her shoulders to steady her.

"Anyways, I got hung up, and before I even got loose, Cal was on his way. I hit the ground wrong and broke my pelvis. Cal was out there waving his red bandanna in the bull's face before the critter got a chance to work me over."

Vern lifted a work-worn hand and scrubbed it down his face as if the memories were too much to talk about. "There I was in the middle of the arena, the medics trying to get me onto a stretcher and Cal and Snipe trying to keep the bull off us. You know, bein' a clown is about as dangerous as riding those durn bulls. Course, they gotta have a knack for gettin' laughs, too, so Cal was cuttin' up some.

"I don't mind tellin' you I was hurtin' like hell, but I recollect him gettin' down in a four-point stance, wigglin' his butt for laughs and pretending to be the bull by pawin' the ground."

The tears gathering in Amy's eyes overflowed and trickled down her pale cheeks. Russ held her tighter and took her hand in a crushing grip.

"The bull charged, and Cal waited until the last possible minute to make his move. Then, when he did—" Vern swallowed "—his foot got tangled in the lariat looped around his neck that he'd been usin' for rope tricks earlier. He lost his footing, and the bull picked him up and slung him over his back. It was one of those freak things, but the strap of Cal's overalls got hung on the bull's horns, and he kept tossin' Cal around like a sack of feed. I remember there was a lot of blood—he got a kidney punctured—before he got untangled and the bull started really working him over.''

Vern took a white kerchief from his pocket and mopped his perspiring face. There was a suspicious huskiness in the big man's voice as he said, ''He was in the hospital for a long time. Had to have the kidney removed and his leg took off and everything.''

Through the blur of her own tears, Amy watched Vern Greerson take a fast swipe at his own eyes. Then he looked at the producer with riveting directness. ''Cal Corbett saved my life, and I'll never forget it.''

There was a curious quiet among the documentary personnel, and, by tacit agreement, Stan turned to the cameraman, who was already lowering the minicam from his shoulder.

Without a word, Russ leaped from the fence and reached to lift Amy down. Then, he pulled her into his arms and pressed her face to his chest, heedless of the curious looks they were attracting from the bystanders as he offered her what measure of comfort he could.

His own heart ached as the moisture of her tears wet the front of his shirt. She had needed to hear the story from a perspective other than the bits and pieces her mother had probably doled out to her as she'd tried to deal with her own pain. She had needed to cry the tears that were long past due. She'd come a long way this past week, but her hurts had festered for so long that only the catharsis of tears could wash away those last, lingering traces of bitterness.

Finally, when he'd begun to wonder if they ever would, her tears slackened and she raised her head to look at him, her brown eyes swimming and her eyelashes clumped into wet spikes. She took the handkerchief he offered and tried to speak around the small sobs that still racked her body. "H-he saved th-that man's l-life, Russ... My d-dad was a... h-hero."

Russ's big hands cradled her face, smoothing back the short hair clinging to her damp temples. "It looks that way."

"D-did you know?"

"Yeah, I knew, but I guess I thought you knew, too. Obviously, you didn't."

"I knew he was trying to keep someone else from getting hurt. That was his job. But I guess until just now I never really thought of it as saving someone's life and putting your own on the line."

Russ smiled in understanding and leaned over to kiss her hot forehead. "Feel better? Want me to get you a cool cloth?"

Amy stepped back, shaking her head. "I'm fine." She wiped the traces of her tears with her fingertips and attempted a smile. "Really."

The look in his eyes told her he had his doubts.

"Russ," she said. "Why didn't my mother ever tell me any of this?"

"Who knows? Maybe she was too torn up at first, and maybe later she just wanted to forget it. Maybe she even felt some resentment toward him and the rodeo."

Amy shook her head. "Not Mom. She was a saint. I never heard her say anything but good about my dad."

"She was a good woman," Russ agreed. He took the damp hankie from her and stuffed it into his back pocket. "Look, darlin', I hate to leave you like this, but I promised Shorty I'd help him with the stock, and it'll be time to start soon. Do you feel like finding a seat?"

She sniffed, nodded and pointed to a place midway up the bleachers. "I'll sit right up there."

"Okay." He lifted her chin with the knuckles of a loose fist, lowering his head and giving her a kiss of exquisite sweetness. "See you later."

Amy watched him go, her heart filled with so many emotions she could hardly sort them out. There was a sense of sadness because she'd let her misunderstanding and her bias keep her from really getting to know her father as she'd grown older. While Cal's act of heroism didn't change the mistake he'd made after the accident, now she had a better understanding why these men did what they did.

The urge—the need, even—to outlast the eight-second clock was the same urge and need that compelled her to chronicle the past with her paintings. By bringing her on this overnight trip, Russ had managed to make her understand what he'd tried to explain so many times before. Like Cal, like Vern, like herself, he had no choice but to follow his dream, to accept the gauntlet thrown down by life.

She made her way slowly to the grandstand and climbed to the spot she'd pointed out to him. When had she begun to resent her father? When had his weaknesses overcome the good she'd known in the past?

"He's killing you, Sally."

Her Aunt Vicki's voice, whispering a statement from the past, spun through Amy's mind, transporting her back to when she was in the eighth grade, a year after her father's accident....

Sally Corbett was in the kitchen, ironing and talking with her youngest sister. Vicki, dressed in Houston haute couture and sipping coffee from the china cup Sally kept especially for her visits—Vicki hated drinking from mugs—looked to Amy, who was sitting worshipfully across the table from her.

"He's a good man, Vicki," Sally said, never looking up from the shirt she was ironing. "He's been through a lot."

"He should have stopped rodeoing years ago. Good grief! He's traveled all over the country and came home just long enough to get you pregnant six times. Look at you! You look twice your age."

"It's what's inside that counts, Victoria." Sally glanced pointedly at Amy. "And I'd appreciate it if you'd keep your feelings about Cal to yourself when the children are around."

Vicki's cup clattered to its saucer. "Fine. It's your life. If you like living this way, that's your problem."

"The vows said 'for richer, for poorer, in sickness and in health, till death do you part'."

Vicki shook her head, knowing there was no way to get around Sally's principles. She rose and refilled her cup, and, as she sat back down, she pinned her niece with a questioning look.

"What about you, Amy? Do you want to be a housewife?" she asked with a dazzling, crimson-lipped smile.

"I want to be just like you," Amy said.

Vicki reached across the table and patted her hand. "You have a lot of artistic talent, you know. You could go straight to the top."

"Don't go putting fancy ideas in her head, Vicki...."

But it was too late; the seed was already planted. From that time on, every time she came, Vicki cultivated the tender shoots of Amy's discontent. And when Sally and Cal were killed in the tornado, it was only natural for

Vicki to step into the breach and offer to take full responsibility for Amy's future....

Looking back, Amy was able to see her aunt through the eyes of an adult instead of a worshipful child, and she realized that even though Vicki's plans were often calculated, her intentions were good. It had been love and genuine concern for what she felt was her sister's unhappy plight—plus the fear that it would happen to Amy if she stayed in the close-knit community—that prompted Vicki to be so careful in shaping Amy's life.

Amy didn't blame her; her aunt had done what she thought was right. And up until recently Amy had been satisfied, except for her relationship with Russ, a relationship she hadn't been able to bring herself to either accept fully or deny.

The crackling of the public-address system alerted Amy that the rodeo was about to begin and brought her wandering thoughts back to the present. She was about to be baptized by fire, Amy realized with a sickening lurch of her stomach, about to watch Russ do what he did the best, the very thing she was scared to death to have him do. She drew a deep breath and reminded herself that she was here willingly. She'd definitely come a long way.

The rodeo participants paraded in single file for the Grand Entry. She watched the riders take their horses through the complex, winding paces, the American flag leading the way. Then, with all eyes on the flag, the spectators were asked to rise for the national anthem. Standing there with her hand over her heart as the familiar song played, Amy once again felt tears stinging her eyes. What could be more American, she asked herself, than a sport that originated in this country, a sport that had evolved from an American way of life?

As the music ended, everyone settled themselves while the announcer stated much of what she'd just been thinking, adding that the cattle drives after the Civil War had brought about the need for a tough breed of man and horse to battle the dangers of the open range. It was this unique breed of man, he said, who became the living legend known as the American cowboy.

"These leather-faced men were masters at what they did, and the riding-and-roping contests at the end of the day became the forerunners of today's rodeo."

The crowd around Amy roared its approval.

Amy listened as he named the clockers, and a pang shot through her heart when he introduced the clowns, dressed as usual in huge overalls, their faces decorated with greasepaint. She laughed with the rest of the spectators at the tired but still effective bandanna trick—one clown grabbed a bandanna from another's pocket and several yards of red handkerchiefs emerged after the first. Slowly, without even being aware that she was really enjoying herself, she let the ambience of the evening draw her in.

The events were fast-paced and exciting, but she held her breath when it was Russ's turn to participate in the saddle-bronc riding. She was amazed when he tuned in to the horse's bucking pattern only seconds out of the chutes. The choreography between his working of the reins and his spurring required incredible balance and skill. When he made it to the eight-second whistle with a clean, high-scoring ride, she began to relax. When he won the event, she was ecstatic and actually looking forward to the bareback-bronc riding when it came up. When he took first place in that event, too, she wondered why she'd ever been worried. He was very good at what he did, as she should have known.

The sky grew darker as night fell and the rest of the events were run. Amy was pleasantly tired when time came for the last event, the bull riding. Only two riders before Russ stayed on for the required time, and when his turn came up, she was optimistic. Like the other rides, the high-point rider would be the winner.

She watched Russ in the chutes for what seemed an amazingly long time. She knew from what he'd explained to her on the drive that he was taking extra care with getting his rigging just right.

She went over the steps in her mind, imagining Russ doing them. First, he would put his gloved hand into a handhold, and a chute helper would tighten the flat, plaited bull rope around the bull. Then he would put the rope across Russ's palm, loop it around the back of his hand and return it to Russ's fist. It was Russ's job to hang on with a death grip throughout the ride.

At last, she saw him nod. The chutes opened, and the bull charged out, head down, hind feet kicking skyward. Russ's hat flew off with the first jump, and his bronze hair gleamed beneath the lights. He rode with his left arm high; if it touched him or the bull he could be disqualified. Amy watched, her heart in her throat. She was beginning to think Russ had everything under control, when the bull lurched suddenly into a spin to the left, catching him unprepared. Russ went sailing to the right.

"No!" she cried, leaping to her feet, her complaisance fleeing on the heels of a sudden panic and a renewed realization that this was the most dangerous event of the rodeo. Amy thought she saw his feet touch the ground but could hardly tell . . . all she knew was that the dreaded had happened. Russ was hung up.

Chapter Eleven

The pungent aroma of smelling salts assaulted Russ' nostrils, bringing him to instant, if groggy, consciousness. He tried to open his eyes and found that his vision was blurred in one eye and sight in the other was gone. Even half-conscious, he felt a keen sense of panic.

"Keep your eyes shut," he heard a gritty, masculine voice say from above him. "I need to get this blood cleaned up."

"What's your name?" another, more pleasant voice asked.

"Russ Wheeler."

"Open your right eye. That's good. How many fingers do you see?"

"Four. What is this? Twenty questions?" Russ asked irritably.

"Something like that," the agreeable voice said and then added, "I think he's okay."

Okay. Russ, whose mind was still toying with full consciousness, had a lucid thought. Amy. He had to let Amy know he was okay. He opened his eyes and saw a big, rough-looking man looking down at him. Two thoughts more or less crowded into his mind at once: he could see. His head was swimming, but he could see. And this guy looked like a professional wrestler, not a paramedic.

"This is going to need some stitches," the gravelly voice said.

"Yeah."

"Put a butterfly bandage on it," Russ told them testily. "I've got to get out of here." Taking them by surprise, he swung his feet over the edge of the gurney and sat up. The world listed to the left, and he swayed erratically with the imagined movement before the gritty-voiced man caught him and lowered him back down.

"You're not going anywhere but the clinic, because a butterfly bandage won't cut it with this one."

Russ couldn't have cared less about stitches. His head was clearing more and more, and all he cared about was getting to Amy. "I've got to see Amy," he said, looking up into the face above him.

The man's gaze shifted. "Are you Amy?" Russ heard him ask.

"Yes."

Russ tried to turn his head toward the sound of her voice—her trembling, barely audible voice—but someone had a firm grip on his head.

"Amy?"

She moved into his field of vision. "I'm here, Russ." She took his hand, her eyes bright with moisture and wild with fear. One look into those eyes did more to clear his head than a bucket of smelling salts could have. "I'm okay," he told her.

"I can't stand it," she said, her voice quavering.

"Shh...I'm okay," he said again. He squeezed her hand tightly. Dear God, he wondered, why did this have to happen now, when everything was going so well? "Do you hear me, Amy? I'm all right."

She nodded, but her eyes held a faraway look.

Russ's heart sank. He was losing her, and heaven knew he couldn't take it again. Not this time.

Less than two hours later, after one in the morning, they were on the road, headed toward Claude. Russ wanted to go home, but filled with painkillers, he hadn't been in any shape to spend the next few hours at the wheel. When Amy volunteered, he had been worried about her falling asleep, but she assured him that sleep was the furthest thing from her mind.

She had tanked up on coffee while they stitched him and checked him for broken bones, and once she was reassured that he was fine except for the cut above his left eye and a plethora of bruises over his body, she had felt the knot of worry inside her loosening. Still, she didn't know how he could be worried about her falling asleep when her mind kept replaying those few heart-stopping moments when he'd been thrown.

In the end she won. She drove while Russ slept.

Distance was measured off by the green mile-marker signs along the highway. The radio played softly, but she couldn't have said what she heard. From time to time Russ shifted and moaned. The yellow center line dividing the asphalt highway mesmerized her as hour followed hour. As if suffering tunnel vision, she was keyed into some numbing mode, her attention set, locked in, bordered by the white lines that edged the road that unrolled before the probing headlights of the truck.

She didn't stop, even though she could have used more coffee and the use of a rest room. She didn't want to wake Russ. In spite of her good intentions, the evening began to take its toll, and she started to get sleepy, managing to stay awake only by telling herself again and again that she could make it to the next small town and the next.

It was almost six when she pulled into the driveway of the ranch, and by then, the blessed numbness had given over to an aching weariness. She pulled the truck beneath the carport, put the gearshift into park and turned off the ignition. Russ shifted restlessly, the cessation of movement rousing him from his sleep.

His eyes opened slowly.

"We're here." Her voice sounded weak, as spent as her body and mind felt.

He tried to sit up and groaned, a sound she had to bite her lip to keep from echoing.

"Stay put," she commanded, opening her door and rounding the hood of the truck. She opened Russ's door, offering him the support of her slender body.

He tried to smile, but it was a poor imitation. "I'm really fine, Amy. Just sore and hung over from the pain pill."

She didn't answer, and it became a matter of male pride that he allowed her to help him only by opening the door of the screened-in porch.

Tandy met them at the kitchen door, took one look at Russ's crippled gait and bellowed, "My Gawd! What happened?"

"Nothing much. I just got hung up and banged my head against the bull's somehow or other."

Tandy cackled with misplaced glee. "No broke bones. You'll be all right."

"Yeah. Got any coffee?" Russ asked, limping across the kitchen.

Amy, standing in the doorway, couldn't believe the casual exchange. Didn't either one of them understand how serious this was? Didn't they realize he could have been killed or maimed? Didn't Russ care that part of her had curled up and died when she saw that bull tossing him around like a doll?

She must have made a sound, because Russ turned from the coffeepot toward her, the look in his eyes eloquent and pleading. *Dear God, Amarillo, I love you so much...so much. Don't leave me...not again.*

I can't deal with this. I can't.

Tandy, reading the separate, silent pleas, slipped quietly out the door.

"Coffee?" Russ asked at last, breaking a silence that seemed to border infinity.

She shook her head, fighting the recurring need to cry.

He turned, and in blatant disregard to her answer, poured two cups of the fragrant, steaming brew, holding out a cup, which she took without thinking. "I'm going to spend the next fifteen minutes in a hot shower," he told her, urging a smile he was light years away from feeling. "Do you mind helping me out of these jeans?"

If I keep her with me, she can't run away.

I can't bear to leave him. Not now. Without a word, Amy followed him into the master bedroom, the room where she and Russ had taken each other with such sweet abandon.

Russ downed a scalding mouthful of the coffee, swore and set it on top of the dresser. Then he sat down on the bed and, leaning over, grasped the boots to pull them off, which he did with barely concealed grimaces and grunts of pain. His unwavering gaze snared hers. Wordlessly, he unsnapped his shirt and pulled it off, revealing a torso mottled with bluish bruises, places where the bull had stepped on him.

Amy couldn't help her gasp of horror.

Russ looked across the room into the mirror at his reflection, his eyes finding hers in the silvered glass. "Not too pretty, huh?"

"No."

He rose and crossed the room, taking the coffee cup from her nerveless hands. Kissing her forehead, he commanded softly, "Get undressed, Amy. We could both use a hot shower."

It did sound good, she had to admit. She slipped out of her slacks and blouse while Russ peeled off his socks.

"Can you give me a hand with these?" he asked, unbuttoning his jeans. "The boots about got me."

Recalling the pain on his face as he'd taken the boots off, Amy went to him, hardening her heart to her own pain while she unzipped his jeans. She helped him ease them down, kneeling to pull them off over his bare feet. Then, with her hand cupping his hair-crisped calves, she allowed her gaze to travel up over his bruised legs.

Her fingers trailed up his thigh, brushing the bruise there with feather lightness, while her mind, contrary to her will, reran for the hundredth time a picture of the bull's wild romp. Two tears spilled down her cheeks, and, leaning forward, she kissed the mottled flesh.

She felt the comforting warmth of Russ's hand on her head. Dragging her tear-glazed gaze upward, she looked into blue eyes alight with tenderness. "Amy, don't. Please," he begged, pulling her to her feet.

"You could have been killed!"

"I wasn't."

"Russ..."

"Amy..."

They spoke at once, both wanting, needing, to make the other understand, both feeling the progress they've made slipping from them with each breath they drew, both hurting so badly inside that they could hardly bear the pain.

Russ placed his forefinger over her lips and took her by the shoulders, propelling her toward the bathroom. Confined inside the small shower cubicle, they didn't speak. Russ leaned against the back wall, his head tipped back, while the hot water sluiced over his battered body. Amy leaned against the side wall, her arms crossed over her breasts, her tortured eyes roaming his body at will, storing away the images—how his biceps bulged even in repose, the narrowness of his waist and the lean strength of his legs.

Beneath his closed eyes, Russ's mind whirled. He was tired. Mentally, physically, emotionally, and he had a gut feeling that the worst was yet to come. There was nothing he could say to change how she felt. He'd already used all his arguments several times over. He could tell her about the "surprise," of course—that he was going to stop rodeoing after this season so he could take Tady's place as a stock contractor. But somehow the words choked him.

Call it masculine ego, stubbornness or just plain stupidity, but he couldn't cave in now, not after all they'd been through. Even though telling her would ease her mind, he felt that she had to come to grips with what she felt for him and the degree of that feeling. It was simple. He wanted her to accept him for what he was. She either loved him or she didn't. And if that love wasn't big enough to see them through this, then it would never work, anyway. Maybe that's why he'd never stopped rodeoing, even though it might have made a difference in their relationship.

He opened his eyes to look at her and found that she was watching him, her folded arms hiding her breasts from his gaze. "I love you," he said, the words vibrating from his very soul.

Amy's eyes filled, and two tears spilled down her wet cheeks.

"Do you love me?"

The steadiness of her gaze faltered and fell from his.

Silence. "Amy..."

Angrily, she brought her eyes into direct contact with his. "Yes."

"Yes, what?"

"Yes! Yes! Yes, dammit!" she screamed, lunging from the tiled wall and raking back the sliding door.

Before she could step out, Russ grabbed her shoulders and hauled her back against his chest. He turned her to face him. Hot water poured over them, slicking their hair to their foreheads, streaming in small rivulets over their faces and splattering the tile floor.

Russ turned off the water in an automatic gesture, never taking his eyes from hers. "Marry me."

Amy's eyelashes swooped to conceal her thoughts from him. She'd known he would ask her again, sooner or later, and she'd prayed it would be later, when she'd had a chance to absorb the changes in her feelings. Behind her closed eyes, in slow motion, she saw the bull lunge to the left, saw Russ sail to the right, saw his arm almost jerked from its socket while the bull bucked and kicked . . . and then trampled him in the dirt.

She opened her eyes to look at him, and instead of answering, she made a declaration of her own. "Stop riding."

A funny, sad sort of smile quirked Russ's mouth. Her response clarified the situation immediately. Now all he had to do was figure out how he was going to spend the next ten years . . . the rest of his life. "I plan to," he told her, willing to part with that much of the truth. He released her and stepped from the shower, reaching for a towel.

"When?" she asked from behind him.

He looked at her over his shoulder. "Soon."

Tell me you'll stop now. Tonight. "Stop now, Russ, and I'll marry you," she said, hating herself for even voicing her thoughts.

Russ sighed. "Ultimatums, Amarillo?" he asked quietly as he toweled himself dry.

She sniffed and swallowed the lump of emotion clogging her throat. Then she lifted one shapely bare shoulder. "If you want to call it that."

He stared at her, pretending to give the matter serious consideration, but what he was really doing was fortifying himself for the final break. What was it about a good defense being a good offense? He nodded his wet head. "Yeah," he told her. "I think I do want to call it that. Granddaddy always said that what was good for the goose was good for the gander."

Her eyebrows drew together in a frown. "Meaning?"

"Meaning, I don't like the time you'll have to give to promoting your work, so why don't you give up your painting?"

Fire flashed in her eyes. "It isn't the same thing."

"Isn't it?" he asked coolly.

"No!" she yelled, dropping all semblance of control. "It isn't!"

Unlike Amy, Russ kept his tenuous control under tight rein, allowing his anger to manifest itself only in sarcasm. "How is it different, Amy? Tell me that."

"My work doesn't put my life in danger."

Russ's cool vanished. "Yeah? Well, you could get hit walking across the streets of Dallas—and, my God, the crime rate there is terrible," he told her, tossing his towel to the floor and stalking to the bedroom.

"I don't want to hear all those pat answers!" she cried to his retreating form.

"And I'm sick of trying to justify my life to you!" he yelled over his shoulder.

Still more wet than dry, Amy whipped the towel round her body and tucked it over her breasts. "Face it, Russ!" she said, storming into his bedroom to find him calmly pulling on pale blue briefs, an action whose very normalcy infuriated her because it seemed to underscore his unconcern.

Planting his hands on his hips, he asked, "Face what?"

"That you go out there in front of hundreds of people and pit your skill against a dumb animal because being big-shot, All-Around Cowboy pumps up that damnable male ego of yours and makes every woman in the arena wonder how well you ride in private."

In a gesture that sent her anger soaring, Russ shifted his weight to one leg and crossed his arms over his brawny chest. "Well you know what they say: 'If you ain't a cowboy, you ain't shit.'"

Amy offered him a false sweet smile. "Granddaddy again?"

"Sam Shepard," he offered tersely.

"Sam Shepard?"

"Yeah. The ultimate statement from his movie, *Foo For Love*, the title of which," he told her as he pulled a pair of worn jeans from a drawer, "I'm beginning to think about sums up my life."

As much as she could see his point, his proud attitude still hurt. She balled hands into tight fists that gouged her nails into her palms. "Damn you," she said quietly watching while he pulled on the denim pants and zipped them.

He flexed his shoulders and, reaching to massage the muscles at the back of his neck, met her fiery gaze with a stoic one of his own.

Amy thought he'd never looked more handsome, more masculine. She couldn't remember loving him more than she did at that moment when he seemed hell-bent on destroying her.

"We have to face the fact that you're you and I'm me and we can't change each other." His chest bare, he spread his arms wide, offering her all the warmth and strength there. "This is the real me, Amarillo. Take it or leave it."

Fury fled. And in its place came the realization she'd tried so hard not to face. She was about to lose him again . . . for good. She stared into the stormy blue of his eyes, the only thing betraying his feelings, and felt her world crumbling around her.

"I want to Russ . . . I really do, but . . ."

"But you can't. I understand . . . I guess this is it, then," he said.

Yes, Amy thought, *I guess it is.* He stood there, immobile, not offering to make it any easier for her. To save her soul, she couldn't think of a single thing to say. Instead, she turned and started toward the door.

"Amy!" he said as she turned the knob.

"Yes?" Her voice held a sad hopefulness.

"I'm going to get some sleep. Have Tandy drive you to the airport."

He was not only going to make it hard for her, he was actually sending her away. It was truly over then, she thought dully. She watched as he reached for an object lying among the pile of change on his dresser.

"You might need this," he said, tossing the twinkling object toward her. "Catch."

She reached for it automatically, her fingers closing round something small and hard and sharp. Opening her clenched fist, she found herself staring down at the ring she'd been so worried over yesterday morning—until Russ had come home and made her forget everything. Wayne's ring. She lifted her head to tell him that she wouldn't be needing Wayne's ring at all, but the room was empty. Russ had fired his last salvo, made a direct hit to her heart and retreated to neutral territory.

* * *

It didn't take long for Amy to get her things together
Despite the flood of tears that got in the way, it took her
only ten minutes to get dressed and throw her things into
her suitcase. Somehow, as if he'd known he'd be needed,
Tandy was nearby, waiting.

He didn't say a word as he hoisted her bag into the bed
of the truck; he made no pithy commentary about her
tears. All he did was mutter something that sounded like
"Dang fools!" and spit a stream of tobacco juice toward the tire.

Without a word, Amy climbed inside, sitting stiffly in
the seat and twisting the leather shoulder strap of her
purse as Tandy ground the gears and headed the truck
toward the highway. She didn't look back at the house
She couldn't.

If she had, she would have seen Russ standing in the
window, a fistful of curtains crushed in each hand, his
own tears sliding down his tanned cheeks.

The trip to Amarillo airport was made in record time
Amy's tears dried, and her heart had ceased to ache. Now
it lay like stone in her chest, heavy, dead. Tandy stood
nearby while she bought her ticket, and he saw to it that
her luggage was checked. Then he stood with his hand
in his pockets, shifting from one foot to the other.

Amy, wrapped up in her misery, was hardly aware of
his presence.

"Did he tell you he wasn't going to ride anymore?"

"What?" she asked, the sound of Tandy's voice
bringing her momentarily back to the present.

"Did Russ tell you he was going to stop riding?"

"*Stop riding.*" The memory of her ultimatum rang
clearly through her mind.

"I am. Soon."

How soon is soon, Russ? she wondered. Next week? Next year? "Yes," she replied.

Tandy scratched his bearded face in contemplation. "I can't believe it didn't make any difference. What is it you're wanting, girl?"

One part of her told her it was none of Tandy's business, but another part, the part that remembered him from childhood, reached out to the comforting familiarity he offered. "For him to love me enough to..."

"To what? Give in to yer whims? You'd hate his guts in less than a year."

Would she? Amy shook her head. "Leave it alone, Tandy."

"All right. I will. But you can't have everything your way."

First the fight with Russ, and now this. "I don't want everything my way," she said in dismay.

"Don't you? I'm beginning to believe that you think Rusty's good enough to bed but not to wed."

It was as if he'd slapped her. "That's ridiculous!"

"Is it? Seems to me you want a relationship with him as long as it doesn't interfere with your job, your friends or your tidy little life. What's wrong with you lovin' him enough to take him as he is?"

Amy groped for the arm of the chair behind her and sat down—hard. She couldn't take much more of this...she really couldn't. "Go home, Tandy," she told him, her eyes filling with tears once more. "Just please go home."

"Fine. I will." He turned to go and had taken no more than five steps when he turned back to face her. "Yer a young woman, Amarillo. You've got a lot of nights ahead of you. It'd be a shame if you had to spend them alone."

"Russ isn't the only man in the world," she flung at him in a desperate move toward salvaging a morsel of her self-respect.

"I let someone get away from me thirty years ago, and there's never been anyone who could take her place. If you don't marry Rusty, you'll never marry anyone," Tandy said sagely, "and you know it."

Amy watched him as he turned and left her alone. Her teeth sank into her bottom lip as she fought to hold herself together. If she could just keep from making a fool of herself until she got home, she'd crawl into a hole and never come out.

The plane trip seemed interminable, the taxi drive to her apartment even longer. Amy let herself into the apartment and set the suitcase near the door. Looking around the familiar domain made her feel empty. Where was the sense of coming home she should be feeling?

Changing into shorts and a big shirt, she went into the kitchen to find something to eat. It was well past noon and it was hard to believe that she hadn't eaten since the hamburger and french fries she'd shared with Russ at the rodeo the night before. She smiled wryly. Surprisingly she hadn't collapsed into tears as soon as the door shut behind her, and if food was uppermost on her list of priorities, she couldn't be in too bad a shape—could she?

She found some Swiss cheese that was drying out around the edges and a semistale loaf of rye bread that made an adequate grilled cheese sandwich. The milk was stale, there were no cold drinks and she didn't want to make any tea. Eyeing the bottle of Sangria near the bar of the refrigerator, she threw caution to the wind and poured herself a generous portion.

Then, sitting cross-legged in front of the coffee table, she ate, hoping the replenishing of her fuel supply and a long nap would give her the strength to face what she had to do next. She wouldn't think about how she would get through tomorrow and the day after that. All she could do was take one day, one moment, at a time. Theoretically, she thought with a sense of hopelessness, it should work.

By the time she finished eating, the sleepless night had caught up with her, and she gave silent thanks that she hadn't slept the night before. At least she was guaranteed a few hours respite from the reckoning with herself she knew was coming. She pulled back the pink satin sheets and kicked off her sneakers, falling onto the bed with a sigh. In a matter of minutes she was deep in a blessedly dreamless sleep.

Amy was awakened four hours later by a loud ringing. She groaned in protest and reached blindly for the alarm-clock button. The ringing didn't stop. She groped for the phone and muttered a sleepy "Hello," but that didn't stop it, either.

"Someone's at the door," she murmured aloud, pushing herself to an elbow and raking a weary hand through her tousled hair. Who on earth knew she was home? She lowered her feet to the floor and made her way down the steps to the door, clicking the lock and swinging it open with one hand while she stifled a yawn with the other.

"Amy?"

At the sound of the masculine voice, her eyes flew open and her mouth snapped shut. Wayne! She fought back the groan of dismay that threatened. "How did you know I was home?" she asked instead.

Wayne stepped inside, shut the door behind them and drew her into a tight embrace. He looked down at her, an indulgent smile on his face, their fight of a little over a week ago obviously forgotten. "I called that Tandy fellow you were staying with, and he told me you'd flown home earlier. By the way, whatever happened to, 'Hello, Wayne. I missed you?'" he asked before he lowered his mouth to hers.

Amy didn't fight the kiss, but she couldn't reciprocate, not with the memory of Russ making love to her so fresh in her mind. She knew now why Wayne's kisses failed to move her. She belonged to Russ, body and soul. As Wayne ended the kiss and lifted his mouth from hers, Amy wondered a bit desperately if she would ever be able to respond to another man's touch.

"What's the matter, darling?" he asked.

Without answering, she left him and went into the bathroom. When she came out, she took his hand in hers and opened it, palm up. Then, with her eyes begging for forgiveness, she pressed her engagement ring into his hand and closed his fingers around it.

Wayne unclenched his fingers, saw the sparkling canary diamond, and looked at Amy with disbelief. "Amy..." he began, his voice unsteady, his hand trembling the slightest bit. "What does this mean?"

"I can't marry you, Wayne," she blurted. "I'm sorry but I can't."

"Can't? B-But the wedding is just three weeks away. What..." His voice trailed away as comprehensio dawned, a comprehension that spawned a quick and violent anger. He grabbed her shoulders and shook her slightly. "It's that damned cowboy, isn't it? You're going back to him."

"No," Amy assured him, "I'm not going back to Russ."

Wayne's voice was filled with disgust. "If you think I believe that—"

"It's true." Amy twisted her hands together. "I'm not going to lie to you, Wayne," she said earnestly. "I do love Russ."

Wayne dropped his hands to his sides and turned away, going toward the living area and sitting on the sofa.

Hating herself for the dejected slump of his shoulders, Amy followed him, sitting down on the coffee table facing him. Wayne was staring at the ring. She took his hands in hers.

He looked up; their eyes met, and there was a suspicious glitter in Wayne's. "I love you."

Amy squeezed his hands. "I know. That's what makes this so hard. I love you, too, but as a good friend, not a potential husband. You're a wonderful man, and you need a woman who'll give you all the happiness you deserve. I can't."

He smiled wryly. "Then why did you take my ring?"

"I told myself I loved you," she said, as much for her benefit as his. "I had myself convinced that I did, but it wasn't the right kind of love. I know you're angry at Russ over this, but in all fairness, I was beginning to figure out that something was wrong even before he came back into my life."

"I pushed too hard, didn't I? I came around too much and invaded your space."

"Sometimes, yes," she agreed. "But that isn't the real problem. If I'd really loved you, I wouldn't have minded—don't you see? I don't expect you to understand, but Russ and I go way back, Wayne, and we've always loved each other, I guess. It's just that there are things we can't seem to get worked out. We've tried everything—not seeing each other, a part-time affair, being together. I don't know," she said with a sigh. "It seems hopeless."

"If you aren't going to marry him, marry me. You don't have to love me—"

Amy's hand came up and covered his mouth. "Don't say that. Everyone deserves love. Don't settle for anything less, Wayne. I won't let you settle for anything less."

He swallowed. Nodded. Then he stood up, pulling her to her feet. He brought her hands to his lips and pressed a kiss to each palm. She could tell the tremendous effort he was making to rally when he gave her a forced smile. "You're still going to let the gallery handle your work aren't you?"

"For as long as you like," she promised.

He cleared his throat. "Good." He patted her hand and let them drop, turning and going to the door, his back straight, his step brisk. Before it closed behind him he turned and said, "Don't forget the interview tomorrow."

"I won't. I promise," she told him with a weak smile.

The door closed behind him, and the small click echoed deafeningly in the emptiness of her heart. So was over now, she thought. Everything. All of it. Drawing a shuddering breath, she rose and went back up to her bed, stretching out and covering her eyes with her forearm.

There was nothing left to do but fall quietly to pieces.

Somehow, she made it through the evening and the night, lying awake and wondering how anyone could love as much as she did and still have it go wrong. Was Russ right? Should she love him all-or-nothing? Should she be willing to push her fears aside and let him pursue his dream?

"Cal Corbett saved my life."

"Your mother was a good woman."

"I remember the first time I lusted after you."

"Marry me, Amy. I love you..."

... love you ... love ...

... you..."

She fell into a restless sleep, memories fighting for their place in her heart, tears in her eyes and Russ's name on her lips.

Chapter Twelve

Amy stood in line for the ticket at the Dallas/Ft. Worth airport, contemplating how she'd survived the week since she left Claude. If it hadn't been for the interview, she might not have made it through Monday. And, if it hadn't been for a flurry of work that lasted from daylight each day until past midnight each night, she never would have made it at all. As it was, when she realized that her subject matter was Russ—working, riding, in repose—she almost died anyway, from remorse.

On Wednesday morning she'd placed a call to Darcy Lightfoot to see if she could go to Tennessee early to start on Darcy's portrait. Thankfully the country singer had told her to come on Friday afternoon. Now, as she stood in the ticket line, nothing between her and the hills of Tennessee except a ticket and a couple of hours, she found herself wondering if Russ's eye was better and i he bruises were fading. She chewed her inner lip. It was Friday again. Would he be riding this weekend?

Her mind recanted its position for the hundredth time since she'd left Claude, but her heart told her that she'd made a mistake. The ache in that tender, hurting center of her emotions showed no sign of abating, and she realized with a start that she was as worried about him right now, in Dallas, as she had been being there with him.

Was she a fool for not going back and at least having his love to temper the worry? And if she did go, was her love strong enough to withstand the agony she'd be subjected to each week, knowing there was a chance he could be badly hurt?

"May I help you, please?" the petite girl with the golden tan and curly, sun-streaked hair asked.

Amy put her credit card on the counter and opened her mouth to say she wanted a round-trip ticket to Nashville, Tennessee, but instead, heard herself saying, "Amarillo, please."

"Thank you. Will that be round-trip, ma'am?"

"No. One way."

The girl, whose name tag said Nicole, began to punch the computer keys with lightning speed while Amy vacillated between wondering where a phone was to call Darcy and tell her of the change in her plans and turning to go back home to the comfort of her apartment. What if Russ was really finished with her this time? She was just about to take back her hasty decision and change her destination to Nashville, when the girl slid the ticket into the airline's envelope and handed it and her credit card back. Too late. Amy could almost smell the smoke of her burning bridges.

"Thank you," she said, taking the ticket automatically.

"The flight leaves in forty minutes," Nicole said with another smile. "Thank you; have a nice trip."

Amy nodded and turned away, looking for a telephone.

Faster than she would have liked, she was disembarking at the Amarillo airport. With her stomach churning in apprehension, she rented a car and drove the thirty-odd miles to the ranch. It was almost six by the time she pulled the rental car beneath the carport, which was empty of the Dodge and Tandy's old Silverado.

She got her suitcase from the seat, praying Russ wouldn't pitch it and her out on her ear, and carried it onto the screened porch. Shading her eyes against the evening sun, she scanned the area behind the house. No one was around, or if they were, they were inside the barn.

She tried the door and found it unlocked. Thank goodness Claude wasn't like Dallas! The cool breath of the air conditioning wafted over her, and Amy stepped inside, eager to escape the afternoon heat.

"Tandy!" she called, crossing the kitchen with her burden. "Russ! Is anybody here?"

Silence answered her, and with a sigh of relief, she carried her suitcase to the room she'd vacated less than a week ago. Strange, that this room, which didn't have a thing of hers in it, should feel more like home than her own apartment. She shook her head to rid it of the fanciful comparison and hefted her suitcase to the bed. Five minutes later, she was dressed in jeans and filling the coffeepot.

While the coffee dripped, she rummaged around in the refrigerator for something to eat, reasoning that she might as well make herself at home. If Tandy and Russ had gone to the rodeo, they wouldn't be back until the wee hours, if at all. It was possible that he had gone to a two-day event, and if he had, she had a long wait ahead of her, over twenty-four hours to change her mind and fly back to Dallas.

But she didn't think she would.

One sandwich and two cups of coffee later, Amy cleaned up her dishes and wandered around the house, worried about Russ's reaction to finding her there. On a sudden impulse, she opened the door to his room, hoping, she supposed, that she would feel closer to him there. Memories assaulted her from every direction, and Amy beat a fast retreat. Seductive memories were the last thing she needed right now.

Thinking suddenly about the paintings she'd done and determined to see if Russ was right, she entered the paneled room.

She sat down behind the desk and swiveled around until she had a clear view of *Rescue the Morning Star*. Pride washed over her. It was good, she thought. Darn good. She remembered how intensely she'd painted when she started, working long, hard hours—too many hours—doing research and detailing with special attention to the maiden. She'd wanted it to be perfect for...for whom?

For the brave. Amy laughed aloud at her mind's answer, and the sound seemed to blaspheme the quiet of the office.

"You're definitely losing it, Amy my girl," she murmured aloud.

It sounded crazy, but there had been a tension between the two subjects from the beginning. It was there in the woman's eyes, which seemed to beg for help, and the brave's, which answered, "I will."

Thinking of Russ's comment that the main subjects in both paintings were the two of them, Amy studied the pictures carefully. The women could both be she, even though they had flowing black hair. And the men—she cocked her head to the side—well, that was Russ's nose... and his chin... and...

Russ was right. She had painted the two of them. Why? If the woman in the painting was pleading for help, it was because she was being sacrificed for the tribe's well-being. Anyone would want to cop out on that one if they could, but it had nothing to do with *her*. Why on earth did *she* need to be rescued?

Amy groaned and left the room, despairing of her sanity. The painting depicted her interpretation of an actual historical event. Nothing more, nothing less. It had nothing to do with her and Russ. Nothing.

Suddenly tired, she headed for her bedroom. Although it was only a little after eight, she felt she could sleep around the clock. Donning a cotton night shift, she turned on the ceiling fan and slipped beneath the cool percale sheets. She would see Russ in the morning, and everything would be fine. She was asleep in minutes.

Amy came awake instantly. From habit, she'd pulled the sheet over her head at some time, probably when the early-morning sun threatened to wake her. She opened her eyes slowly. Even though her head was covered, she could tell that it was full daylight. She started to lower the sheet, but before she could, it was grasped and yanked down to her waist. Gasping in surprise at the sudden action, she cowered against the pillows, her eyes widening in shock. Staring back at her, was a single, round eye—the barrel of an ancient Colt.

"Damnation!"

Tandy. The sound of the harshly muttered epithet spoken by a familiar voice sent a message to Amy's brain. *Relax.* She did—marginally.

"What in the Sam Hill are you doin' here, Amarillo?"

Amy's eyes moved slowly from the barrel of the gun to his face. "I'll tell you if you'll put that thing away."

Chagrined, Tandy blushed to the roots of his carrot-colored hair and dropped the gun to the bedside table with a clatter. "It ain't loaded noways."

Amy sat up in bed, a frown drawing her eyebrows together. "If it wasn't loaded, why did you have it?"

"You didn't know it warn't loaded, did you?"

She shook her head. "No. But why on earth did you pull a gun on me?"

"How'd I know it was you? I come home at daybreak to find a strange car under the carport. You coulda been a robber."

Amy smiled gently. "Tandy, robbers don't usually park their cars under the carport or go to bed in a house they're robbing."

"Oh," he said, blushing again. "Guess you're right." He stood there a moment, then exploded again. "What in the hell are you doin' here, anyways, Amarillo? Where have you been? I been trying to call you for hours."

"Whoa!" Amy said, holding up her hands, palms outward. "One thing at a time. I've been here since late yesterday evening, waiting for Russ to come home." Her eyes moved automatically beyond Tandy to the open doorway, then moved back to his. "Where is he, anyway?"

Tandy's eyes shifted uncomfortably from hers, and he reached up and scrubbed a gnarled hand down his face.

The simple gesture spoke volumes to Amy, who was filled with a sudden, inexplicable fear. "Tandy...where's Russ?"

Tandy swallowed. "He got hurt at Pampa. They moved him to the hospital in Amarillo."

"What!" Amy began to scramble to the edge of the bed. "What happened? Is he hurt badly? He must be if he's still in the hospital. Tandy! Tell me!"

"Settle down," Tandy said, going to the window and looking out.

Amy forced herself to sit still, but her hands, clenched tightly in her lap, twisted into a tight knot. "Is he all right?"

"He's gonna be, I guess." He shoved his hands into his back pockets. "He got stomped on—a lot worse than before."

Amy blanched.

"Broke his leg in a couple of places."

"Dear God," she breathed.

"And got kicked in the face."

Amy dropped her head into her hands, visions of Russ's handsome, laughing face bleeding and ruined. "How bad is it?" she asked when there was enough air in her lungs again to force the words out.

"Coulda been a lot worse. Doc said if he'd been a quarter of an inch closer, it woulda shattered his cheekbone. Didn't break nothing, though. I waited around a while, till they took him outta intensive care and the ophthalmologist got through seein' him.''

Ophthalmologist! Amy recoiled, as if from a blow herself, and a moan of pain fluttered from her lips. ''Is . . . his eye all right?''

''They were worried about it for a while, but they felt pretty good about it when I left. He's got a mess of stitches, and they said he might want to see a plastic surgeon later on. Looks like he's gonna have a U-shaped scar on his cheek.''

Amy sat staring at her twisted fingers, trying to assimilate the extent of Russ's injuries while Tandy continued to stare out the window. Finally, she turned and looked at him over her shoulder. ''How did it happen?''

Tandy turned slowly, and when he did, there was undisguised censure in his eyes. ''After you left the other day, one of those drunk fronts moved in. Lasted all week. He wasn't in no condition to ride.''

''Drunk fronts? Russ doesn't drink.''

''Wrong. Russ doesn't usually drink, because he knows how much you hate it,'' Tandy clarified. ''The only times I've ever seen him drink is after he came home from spending time with you.''

Fresh pain rushed through her. How could Russ have continued to love her if that love hurt him so much? she wondered.

For better or worse . . .

You're right, Mom, she thought. Amy wondered why it had taken her so long to find that out.

''How come you came back?''

There was no denying the hint of belligerence in Tandy's voice. He never had been good at hiding his feelings. It was Amy's turn to blush. "I came back because I love him."

Tandy snorted in disbelief. "How come I have a hard time buyin' that?"

"It's true."

He moved from the window and came to stand in front of her. "What changed yer mind, Amarillo? If Rusty told you he was givin' up ridin' and goin' into the rough-stock business after this year didn't change your mind, what did?"

"What do you mean?" Amy asked, looking up at him.

"Just what I said. You told me yourself that Rusty said he was quittin', but you left anyway."

Amy shook her head. "No. What did you mean about Russ going into the stock-contracting business? He didn't tell me that."

"Can't imagine why not. The truth is, Amy, that if Russ manages to win the National Finals, or winds up one of the top money winners, he'll be able to pay me off completely."

"Pay you off? For what?"

"He's buyin' this place from me."

Amy couldn't believe her ears. "Since when?"

"Ever since you left, ten years ago, he's put every penny he could scrape up into it. He's driven enough miles to so many rodeos it shoulda been against the law. Hells bells, I'da give the place to him, but fer my baby sister, Suzy in Omaha—her husband died a few years back, if you'll remember."

Amy didn't remember, but it didn't matter. "Russ is buying MacGregor Ranch from you?" she repeated, as if to solidify the possibility in her mind.

"Yep. It and all the buckin' stock. We come up on an agreement and a price that was fair to us both."

"But why?" she asked.

"Are you completely crazy, Amy? Russ knew you hated the rodeo, but it and ranchin' is all he knew, and he sure didn't have no ranch to offer you. I was gettin' older and was tired of doin' everything by myself, so we struck a deal. Then, the more successful you got, the harder he pushed himself."

"But why?"

"You really ain't too smart, girl, or you're blind. He did it so he'd have something to offer you if you ever come to your senses, that's why. Why do you think we redid the house? Wasn't my idea. Russ wanted it to have everything you were used to havin', so you might think about stayin' on."

Tears filled her eyes. Tandy was right. She was stupid *and* blind not to realize how much Russ loved her and not to see that the value of that love far outweighed all the success she'd garnered.

Tandy was staring at a spot across the room. "Don't really matter none if he makes the finals or not. Rusty don't know it, but except for what I'm leavin' to my sister, Suzy, I'm leavin' it all to him, anyhow."

"You're leaving everything to Russ? Why?"

"Ain't got no kids of my own, so why not? He's like a son to me."

Amy nodded. She could see that. Anyone could. A sudden thought occurred to her. "Tandy?"

"Yeah?"

"Why haven't you ever married?" she asked, remembering his comment about letting the woman he loved get away.

"Never could get the gal I loved to say yes," he told her. "Sorta the same problem Rusty has with you, 'cept my woman couldn't break away from her daddy."

"Is she still around?"

"Yep," he said with a nod.

"Do you still . . . care?"

"Nosy little critter, ain'tcha?" Tandy said testily. "No. Can't say I do. Took me a lifetime, but I got over her. And you'd best watch out, missy, that what happened to her don't happen to you."

"What's that?"

"Got meaner'n a snake the older she got. Bitterness just pooled up inside her like water in a well." He looked into Amy's eyes, anticipating her next question before she could voice it. "Yes, you know her—some. Her name is Isobel Pearson."

"Isobel!" Amy cried, unable to imagine Tandy ever caring about someone like Isobel Pearson.

"Yes. Used to be one of the sweetest girls around," Tandy said, going to the door. "Just hate to see the same thing happen to you."

Chastened by Tandy's tale, Amy was more determined than ever to set things right with Russ. After a quick cup of coffee and a quicker shower, she left Tandy to catch up on his sleep and drove back to Amarillo to see Russ.

When she told the nurse on duty that she was his fiancée, she had no trouble being admitted, even though it wasn't visiting hours.

"You must be Amy," the thin, gray-haired nurse said, leading the way to Russ's private room.

"Yes."

"That's good. He's pretty heavily sedated, but when he starts coming around, he calls for you."

The news lightened the burden on Amy's heart a little. "Is he going to be all right?"

"He's doing very well, considering what a beating he took," the R.N. told her. "Dr. Samuels was concerned about the blow being so close to the eye, but there's no apparent injury to the optic nerve, and they're relatively sure there's been no permanent damage done." She opened the door and indicated that Amy precede her into the room. "As far as the leg—" she smiled "—let's just say that he won't be riding any bulls for a while."

Together, she and Amy approached the bed, where Russ lay on his back. His leg—covered in a cast from his toes to his thigh—was outside the covers, his bare chest was wrapped in gauze, and the left side of his face, the same side he'd injured the night she'd gone, was swathed in white bandages.

"What's the matter with his chest?" Amy asked, going to the opposite side of the bed and taking one of his hands in hers.

"A variety of minor cuts and abrasions," the nurse replied.

The nurse took Russ's wrist between her capable fingers to check his pulse. Satisfied, she lowered his hand back to his stomach and tried to rouse him. "Mr. Wheeler. Mr. Wheeler, can you wake up a minute?"

Russ's lashes fluttered as he tried to open his eyes.

"Wake up, Mr. Wheeler. You have company. Amy's come to see you."

When he heard her name, his mouth twitched as if he was trying to smile, but the effort was aborted at the grimace stage. He forced his unbandaged eye open upward. The usual brightness was gone, dimmed by the effects of the painkillers, but when he saw Amy standing there, a glimmer of happiness appeared. Then sleep claimed him again. Amy felt a prickling of tears.

Blinking to hold the emotion at bay, she glanced at the R.N., who smiled.

"He'll probably sleep most of the next few days, but you're welcome to stay with him if you like."

"Thank you," Amy replied.

The nurse left, and Amy pulled a chair nearer the bed. Is this how her mother felt when her father was hurt? she wondered. Had prayers for his well-being tumbled from her lips? Had she begged, as well as prayed? Had she tried to make a deal with God, making promises she knew she couldn't keep? Had she asked Him why it had been Cal instead of herself—the way Amy was doing now?

Swallowing the lump clogging her throat, Amy took his hand in hers and, leaning over, pressed her lips to his uninjured cheek. She felt his hand tighten on hers for a fraction of a second, heard him breathe her name on a soft expulsion of air. Then she sat down beside him, prepared to wait however long it took for him to wake up and know that she was there for him.

Prepared to wait forever.

Chapter Thirteen

The sound of a rhythmic pounding roused Russ from his medication-induced sleep. Gradually, he became aware that the thumping was the sound of his heart. The lucid part of his mind told him that if his heart was beating, he must be alive, which was something of a miracle if the events flitting through his mind had actually happened. The memories—from the drinking to the moment the bull threw him—became sharper as his mind fought its way clear of the painkiller, unfurling with a random, crazy pattern, like paper streamers at a New Year's Eve party.

He shifted uncomfortably and moaned as a burning pain seared his left leg from his hip down. His stomach spasmed in sudden nausea, and he sent a prayer winging heavenward that the pain would hurry up and knock him out or kill him, whichever would rid him of the agony faster. Grimacing, he clenched his teeth together until the sickness abated.

Warm flesh touched his hand, closed around it. A hand. Small. Soft. Feminine. He struggled to open his eyes and learned that his right eye was bandaged shut, and his face, like his leg, hurt like hell. Before he could focus his uninjured eye, he caught the faint whiff of a familiar perfume. Amy's perfume. Blinking, he struggled to sit up and felt her hands on his shoulders in an effort to restrain him.

"Lie still, Russ."

Her voice, calm and soothing, swept over him like a benediction. His eyes closed, and he did what she asked because he was too weak to do anything else. Amy was like a drug the doctor had prescribed for the pain, and her presence effectively ended the hurt he'd felt in his heart for so long.

"Does your leg hurt, Mr. Wheeler?" he heard the nurse ask.

He nodded and drifted off again. He hardly felt the prick of the needle.

The next time he woke up, it was dark in the room, except for the sliver of light that escaped beyond the door of the bathroom. He was still, trying to get his bearings and take stock of his injuries. His leg was broken, of course. Even though the pain was bearable at the moment, he knew it could rapidly get out of hand. He yawned and felt the pull of adhesive tape on his cheek. Lifting a hand to his face, he fingered the patch of gauze covering his eye and his cheekbone. It didn't take a high IQ to figure out that *toro* had branded him with a hoof-print.

He was body sore, but that usually went along with getting thrown and being banged around. Russ lowered his hand back to his stomach, damning his weakness. He was still groggy, but his mind was clear enough to recall that he'd been hurting like hell for... how long, now? It was clear enough to remember bits and snatches of conversations with doctors, nurses, Tandy and Amy.

Amy! Had she really been here or was the memory of her touch, her scent and the love in her voice just wishful thinking—hallucination?

An almost imperceptible sound sent his good eye flying open again, and he turned his head toward the source. Fully dressed, her head dropping at an unnatural angle, Amy slept in the vinyl chair beside the bed. His first reaction was sympathy. She looked so uncomfortable. He ought to wake her and tell her to change positions, to thank her for coming, to tell her he'd missed her.

Missed her. Amy had been gone. Why?

It's your damned male ego.

The words came from the darkest recesses of his mind and triggered a chain reaction of memories that outlined the week following her leaving with perfect clarity. Dormant anger surged to fresh new heights. His nostrils flared in fury, and his leg began to throb in tandem with each aching beat of his heart.

What was she doing here? The answer came directly on the heels of his question. Tandy. The old coot just couldn't keep his nose out of anyone's business. No doubt Tandy had called as soon as he could and told her he'd been hurt, and Amy, out of some perverted sense of duty, must have decided that it was her place to come and see just how badly. Well, dammit, he didn't want her here. He wanted her gone from his life forever.

Glaring at her, Russ started to ring for the nurse, but Amy shifted and sighed and crossed her arms over her breasts. He was afraid she would wake up, afraid she wouldn't. She didn't. Even as he watched, she settled down and began to breathe in an even, measured tempo.

He stared at her, the anger driving away the last vestiges of the painkiller. The room's fuzzy edges became sharper, more focused, but unfortunately, so did the clean, feminine lines of Amy's face. He could see her tousled ash-blond hair, the classic line of her nose, the tender bow of her mouth, the roundness of her chin, the gentle swell of her breasts.

Even with the pain in his leg increasing with every second, Russ couldn't help the surge of desire that instigated another wave of anger at himself and her. A muscle in his jaw tensed. Dear God, what was the matter with him? Was he some sort of masochist who kept going back for more, the very kind of weak person he despised? Where was his pride and that damnable male ego he was supposed to have?

His leg was throbbing as the seconds passed and turned into minutes, the minutes feeling like hours. He didn't wake her. He watched her sleep, both hating and loving her, while his pain—physical and mental—became a live thing that tore at his heart and bathed him in perspiration. He didn't call for the nurse and the sweet surcease he knew she could bring him. He needed the pain to purge Amy from his life, from his heart.

By the time he heard the whisper of the nurse's crepe soles and the swish of the door opening, some sort of mentally induced numbness had taken over him, body and soul. He stared up into the cool, professional eyes of the night nurse, his own eyes calm but burning with a deep-rooted pain.

"Get her out of here," he said quietly.

The nurse was trained to spot changes, however small, and though Russ spoke lucidly, there was no hiding the sweat beading his forehead and dampening the hair falling over his forehead. Ignoring his command, the L.P.N. reached for his wrist to check his pulse. "You're hurting pretty badly, aren't you, Mr. Wheeler? Let me check your blood pressure, and I'll go get you a shot."

Sounds of the quiet conversation roused Amy from her exhausted sleep. Had Tandy come back? She opened her eyes and pushed herself into a sitting position. Russ was awake and obviously talking to the nurse, who was wrapping a blood pressure cuff around his arm. A sleepy smile curved Amy's lips. If he was awake enough to carry on a conversation, he must be better.

Russ turned toward the sounds of her waking in time to see the smile. His heart lurched, and then out of a need for self-preservation, he hardened it to the consistency of granite.

"What are you doing here?" he snarled.

Her smile vanished. "I've been here with you for three days."

"Who called you to come?" he asked, his voice wounding and rusty from disuse. "Tandy?"

Amy shook her head. "No. No one."

In his fury, the implications of her denial escaped him. "Well, you can go on back to Dallas, city girl," he said. "No one wants you here."

"Mr. Wheeler," the forgotten nurse interrupted. "Settle down. Your blood pressure is sky-high."

Russ turned on the innocent bystander with light-ning quickness. "If you want my blood pressure to go down, get her—" he jerked his thumb in Amy's direction "—the hell out of my sight."

Amy's heart dropped to the bottom of her soul and shattered into a million, irreparable pieces. She had expected his anger, but she hadn't expected this...this hate.

"Russ, I came back because I love you," she said ear-nestly, her eyes filling with tears.

A malicious smile curved Russ's hard lips. "Well, that's too bad, Amarillo, because you're too late. I was too stupid to know that the eight-second buzzer rang a long time ago. Hell, I just kept hanging on, taking the beating when I could have gotten off."

"Russ..." She reached for his hand, but he jerked it away. Her eyes, wide and disbelieving, locked with his.

"Go home, Amy. No one changes how they feel over-night, and I don't want you here." His voice was filled with cold finality.

The tears welling in her eyes began to slide down her pale cheeks. "You're upset and in pain," she said, grab-bing at excuses as she gathered her purse and swiped at her eyes with her fingertips. "I'll go for now, but I'll be back."

"Don't bother."

"I said I'll be back!" she cried. Then, embarrassed by her outburst, she covered her mouth with her trembling hands. Her gaze flicked to the nurse, who stood impo-tently by. "I'm sorry," she choked out.

The nurse nodded, and Amy rounded the bed and fled the room. She had gone no more than a few steps down

he corridor when the nurse's voice stopped her. Still
crying, Amy turned.

"He's in a lot of pain," the white-uniformed woman
explained. "It makes them crazy. He doesn't know what
he's saying."

Amy's smile was tremulous, bitter. Her eyes awash
with tears, she said, "Oh, he knows what he's saying. He
knows exactly what he's saying." She turned and started
for the elevator, her steps as heavy as her heart.

"No one changes how they feel overnight."

Russ's words, flung to her in anger, became her talis-
man over the next two weeks. If they were true for her,
weren't they true for him as well? If she couldn't start
loving him enough to make it work, could he stop loving
her just because he wanted to? She didn't think so.

Besides, she hadn't changed overnight. Her metamor-
phosis had been a gradual changing over the last few
years. Russ's part in her life might have been sporadic,
but his place in her heart had been as constant and eter-
nal as the morning star, no matter how hard she tried to
deny it.

The last few weeks had been the key to her understanding her love fully, something she hadn't been able
to do until Russ brought her home and forced her to face
her past.

Her mother, Tandy and Russ had all been right. Love
originated in the heart, not the mind, and, by its very
nature should be unconditional, a realization Russ had
reached long ago. He had never tried to dictate conditions for his love, never asked anything of her but that
she should love him in return—unlike the conditions
she'd set for him.

She even understood the painting now. Most people would think she was crazy, but Amy believed she had used herself and Russ as the subjects of *Rescue the Morning Star* because, on a subconscious level, that's what she wanted—rescue from a life that was becoming increasingly unsatisfactory.

It would have been untruthful to say that she had sacrificed her happiness for her aunt's goals and ideals, but it was true that in many ways her life had been shaped for Vicki's satisfaction, not her own. The newfound understanding freed her and opened her mind and her heart to her love and to hope, even though Russ was being extremely difficult.

The first week after he'd told her to go was the worst. Whenever she went to see him, he demanded that they make her go. The second week, somehow shamed into submission by Tandy's sharp tongue, he consented to her presence but refused to talk to her. Amy hoped that when he got home, things would be different.

"No one changes how they feel overnight."

Things weren't different. The day he came home from the hospital he thanked her politely for the time she'd spent away from her work and wished her a cool farewell. When Amy had replied that she was going to the ranch to take care of him, he had exploded with anger again. Tandy, calmly chewing his cud of tobacco, told him not to be a damn fool—*somebody* had to take care of him for a while. Surprisingly, Russ settled down after that, accepting her presence with more grace than Amy had expected. Still, even though he needed her because Tandy had the ranch to run, he confined his communications to asking her to get something for him or telling her he could do it himself.

The only thing that kept Amy from going back to Dallas was the look in his eyes when she turned suddenly to catch him staring at her. There was no malice or disgust in them then. Instead, there was a considering quality, as if he were trying to figure out what she was up to, as if he were trying to decide whether he should trust her actions.

Then there was the day she'd gone back to Dallas to get more of her things. Russ had seemed glad to see the back of her, but when she'd returned that evening, there was no mistaking the glimmer of gladness in the ice-blue coolness of his eyes before he'd turned away with a show of indifference.

It wasn't his nature to act the way he was acting, and Amy was smart enough to realize that he was doing it as a means to protect himself from any more hurt. In a way she couldn't blame him. Ten years was a long time to carry the torch for anyone. She was thankful he had.

The only time she was certain she still affected him was when she helped him dress every morning. Amy made certain she touched his chest when she buttoned his shirts, made sure she touched him everywhere she could as often as she could without being too obvious. His clenched jaw and the reckless don't-push-me-too-far look in his blue eyes were her only clues that he wasn't as unaffected as he wanted her to believe.

All in all, she was relatively happy. She painted. She cooked and cleaned and took care of the house as if it were her own. She made Russ oatmeal cookies and began taking care of his paperwork. She insinuated herself into his life in so many little ways, it would be hard for anyone to oust her. And all the while she planned and plotted and watched and waited for the perfect time to make her move. The perfect time to catch him off guard so that she could force the issue of picking up the dangling reins of their relationship.

"Tandy, are you going to drive Russ in for his doctor's appointment this afternoon?" Amy asked one morning when Russ had been home from the hospital about a week, some three weeks after his accident.

"I got to go look at those two yearlings at the Carpenter place over near Oklahoma," Tandy said, sipping his sugar-and-cream-laced coffee. "Looks like you'll have to take him." He glanced at Russ with a complacent grin. "That sure oughtta make her day, Sunshine."

Russ glared at him over the rim of his own cup.

He was looking better, Amy thought, refilling all the mugs and sitting down across from him. The swelling on his face was minimal now, and the bruises were fading to an unattractive greenish yellow that was scored with a livid red scar where the bull's hoof had found its mark. The white of his eye was still red in the corner, but he could see as well as he ever had—thank God.

After breakfast, Tandy left for his appointment with the Carpenters. She and Russ left for the doctor's appointment at two o'clock, Russ still griping because they had to slit the seam on the leg of a new pair of Wranglers. Amy only smiled and drove.

"What about the documentary?" she asked as they left the city limits of Claude.

Confined to the interior of the car, unable to pretend the question was meant for Tandy, Russ had no option but to answer. He folded his arms across his chest and glanced at her profile. "Stan said that even in a cast, they

ould use me as the main commentator. Mike even kind
f likes the idea of me being hurt.''

Surprised, Amy looked over at him. Russ had dropped
is guard for a moment, and there was an honest-to-
oodness smile toying with the corners of his mouth.

"He said it lent a certain authenticity to the piece. Gave
t a sense of reality.''

Amy smiled back, and when Russ realized what he'd
done, he instantly donned his cloak of indifference. Amy
didn't let it faze her. She went right on talking, and there
was no way Russ could keep from answering. By the time
hey got to Amarillo, he had loosened up in spite of him-
elf, even volunteering to take her to a favorite Chinese
lace for dinner before they went back home. When they
ot to the street of the doctor's office, Amy passed it by.

"Whoa,'' Russ said. "You missed the turn.''

Amy looked at him innocently. "I have a couple of
hings to do before we go. It's early yet.''

Russ glanced at his watch. "Early? Amy, it's ten till
hree.''

Amy's smile was serene as she rummaged around in her
urse with one hand. To Russ's astonishment, she pulled
ut Tandy's battered Colt and laid it in her lap.

"My God, woman! What are you doing?'' he de-
nanded.

She laughed then, a low, sexy sound that sent Russ's
bido tripping. "Why, darlin','' she said, mimicking his
one to a tee, "I think they call it kidnapping.''

"What!'' Russ exploded. "Amarillo, are you crazy?''

"As a matter of fact, I am,'' she told him. "I'm crazy
ver you.''

"Sure. Until the going gets tough,'' he accused sar-
astically.

"Tough?" she echoed. "Well, I got news for you. I doesn't get much tougher than it's been the last few weeks. You've yelled at me, cussed me, ignored me, in sulted me and generally made my life hell."

"If you can't stand the heat, get outta the kitchen," he quipped.

"I'm still here, aren't I?" she shot back, whipping th car into a Holiday Inn.

"What are we doing?"

Amy turned off the ignition and got out of the truck "I'm going to go in there and register us for the night.' She glanced at his crutches and shoved the gun back int her purse. "You stay put. Of course, if you decide to take off, I won't have any trouble catching up with you."

"What's the purpose of all this?"

"I haven't been able to get your attention any othe way, so I had to do something to make you listen to me And now we're going to thrash this out once and for all." She slammed the door shut and headed for the hotel of fice. Russ watched her go, his emotions wavering from anger to disbelief to downright admiration.

In less than five minutes Amy had him inside th room—on the lower level so he could manage with hi crutches—and was pulling the drapes closed.

"What about the doctor?" he asked, making his way to the bed and easing down onto the bedspread.

"You need to pay more attention to detail, Rusty. You appointment is for the day after tomorrow."

"Did Tandy know about this little scheme?"

"Yep," she said, smiling. She sat down in the chair and, dragging her purse onto her lap, reached in and took the gun out again. The look on his face when she pointed it at him was comical.

"Don't point that damn thing at me!" he roared.

"Take off your shirt," she said calmly.

"What?"

"You heard me, cowboy."

"Put down the gun and I will," he bargained.

Amy laid it on the table beside the chair, and Russ obediently took off his shirt. When he was finished Amy reached for the top button of her blouse and began to unfasten it.

"What are you doing?" he asked hoarsely.

"What does it look like I'm doing?" she retaliated, sliding the blouse off one shoulder.

"Driving me crazy."

Amy smiled sweetly. "Now you get the picture." She stood up, took off her blouse and jeans and walked toward him with a look in her eyes that Russ knew from past experience meant trouble. When she reached him, she put her hands on his shoulders and pushed him back against the bed.

Russ looked up at her, a twinkle he couldn't disguise in his eyes. For the first time in weeks Amy felt a glimmer of hope.

"I figured out the painting," she told him.

"You did?" Russ's voice was husky with the desire coursing through him.

"I decided that the painting was my plea to you to save me from myself, which you did when you kidnapped me." She reached to unfasten her bra, drawing the straps down over her arms and tossing it to the floor.

Faced by her partial nudity, Russ felt the last of his defenses crumbling. He loved her. There was no ignoring it, no denying it. Maybe what she felt for him wouldn't last forever, but what he'd put her through the last few weeks proved that she could take a lot.

Hooking her fingers under the elastic of her panties, she wriggled her hips, and the brief triangle of lace slid down the length of her legs to the floor.

Russ sighed. He was scared to death to trust her with his heart again, but it was beginning to look as if he didn't have a choice.

"You rescued me from a life that was good but not really what I wanted or needed." She placed a knee on either side of his prone form, and, being very careful not to hurt his injured leg, she rested her bottom on the rapidly hardening bulge of his manhood. She forced herself to remember that lust wasn't love. Leaning over him, she pressed a series of kisses to his flat brown nipples. Then she rested her cheek on his chest and relaxed against him, praying that she wasn't too late, that he would give her another chance.

"I love you, Russ Wheeler, and, contrary to your behavior of the last few weeks, you love me."

"That's never made any difference before," he reminded her.

"I know. I don't have any excuses, but I think I have the answers now—inside me."

He didn't speak. For long moments there was no sound in the room except the strong beating of his heart beneath her ear. Just when she was beginning to think she hadn't reached him, she felt his hands on her back. Then his arms closed around her, holding her tightly to him.

"I'm not sure you can stay the distance," he said.

Amy heard the fear in his voice. She lifted her head, probing his anxious eyes with the directness of hers. "After seeing what my mother went through, I wasn't sure, either, Russ, and that's why I would never try before. But I've finally learned one thing."

"What's that?"

"I'd rather have a life with you and the fear than to have a life without you. I'm only half-alive without you, and we've wasted so many years already. I want to be with you for all our tomorrows."

Russ reached up and cradled the back of her head with his hand, pulling her face down until his lips touched hers. "We aren't guaranteed tomorrow, Amy. I've earned that the hard way. If you can give me each day, one day at a time, that's enough."

"I can handle that," she said with a smile.

"Can you give me the next hour?" he asked. "The next thirty minutes?"

She smiled. This was the Russ she knew. The arrogant, macho cowboy who'd proven he could stay the distance. "What about your leg?"

Russ gripped her hips and pressed her harder against the denim covering him. His answering smile was sexy, naughty and completely irresistible. "I guess it's time to see if you have the makings of a cowgirl."

The next morning, Amy pulled into a combination gas station and convenience store on the edge of town to get some gas and some aspirin. She'd been so intent on spiriting Russ away, they'd gone off and left his pain pills. And, after the night they'd just spent, his leg was killing him. Leaving the gas pump running, she started inside to pay for their purchases, but turned suddenly, an embarrassed look on her face.

"Get in my purse and hand me my billfold," she said, leaning through the open window.

Russ stuck his hand in her purse and came into contact with the cold steel of Tandy's gun. Very gingerly, he put it on the seat.

Amy laughed. "You don't have to be so careful. It's not loaded."

Russ's disbelieving eyes met hers. "Not loaded? Do you mean you made me strip... practically raped me at gunpoint, with an unloaded gun?"

"So it would seem," she told him with a smile.

"Where did you learn to be so sneaky?"

"Cody Jarrell," Amy confessed. "And it's called sophistry—you know, not telling the whole truth and letting the other person fill in all the blanks."

Russ bit back a grin and shook his head. "Remind me to tell Cody thanks."

Amy rounded the truck, told him to roll down his window and kissed him. Thoroughly. When she pulled back, he dragged a deep lungful of Texas air. Dawn was ushering in a new day, and even though the morning star still shone in the east, the rising sun sought out the golden highlights in Amy's hair. He brushed the wispy strands away from her face, his heart filled to overflowing.

"Are you sure, Amy?" he asked, afraid to trust so much happiness. "I don't think I can take any more of these on-again-off-again affairs."

She smiled, and in the smile was love and joy and promise. "There won't be any 'off' again, cowboy. This time is forever."

* * * * *

Silhouette Romance

LONG, TALL TEXANS

A Trilogy by Diana Palmer

Bestselling Diana Palmer has rustled up three rugged heroes in a trilogy sure to lasso your heart! The titles of the books are your introduction to these unforgettable men:

CALHOUN

In June, meet Calhoun Ballenger. He wants to protect Abby Clark from the world, but can he protect her from himself?

JUSTIN

Calhoun's brother, Justin—the strong, silent type—has a second chance with the woman of his dreams, Shelby Jacobs, in August.

TYLER

October's long, tall Texan is Shelby's virile brother, Tyler, who teaches shy Nell Regan to trust her instincts—especially when they lead her into his arms!

Don't miss CALHOUN, JUSTIN and TYLER—three gripping new stories coming soon from Silhouette Romance!

SRLTT

Silhouette Intimate Moments

At Dodd Memorial Hospital, Love is the Best Medicine

When temperatures are rising and pulses are racing, Dodd Memorial Hospital is the place to be. Every doctor, nurse and patient is a heart specialist, and their favorite prescription is a little romance. This month, finish Lucy Hamilton's Dodd Memorial Hospital Trilogy with HEARTBEATS, IM #245.

Nurse Vanessa Rice thought police sergeant Clay Williams was the most annoying man she knew. Then he showed up at Dodd Memorial with a gunshot wound, and the least she could do was be friends with him—if he'd let her. But Clay was interested in something more, and Vanessa didn't want that kind of commitment. She had a career that was important to her, and there was no room in her life for any man. But Clay was determined to show her that they could have a future together—and that there are times when the patient knows best.

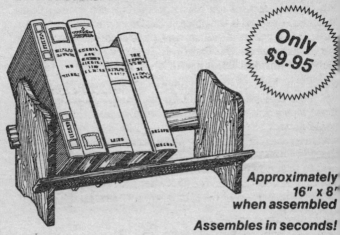

COMING NEXT MONTH

#469 ONE LAVENDER EVENING—Karen Keast
Exactly one hundred years from the night her great-grandmother opened her home—and heart—to a desperado, a stranger appeared on Elizabeth Jarrett's doorstep. And a legendary love affair was about to be relived.

#470 THE PERFECT TEN—Judi Edwards
Melody expected little from life—until dashing David Halifax, with his perfect combination of brawn and brains, bred hope in her heart . . . and taught her the dangers of sweet anticipation.

#471 THE REAL WORLD—Kandi Brooks
Jennifer had loved Racine Huntington, the boy next door; she didn't even *like* Race Hunter, superstar. So, she couldn't possibly let his fantasies blind her to reality again . . . .

#472 IMAGINARY LOVER—Natalie Bishop
For Candace McCall, the biological clock had turned into a time bomb! Once Connor Holt discovered her condition, how could she convince him that she hadn't set a baby trap?

#473 DIVINE DECADENCE—Victoria Pade
Allyn Danner made her living on desserts, but she wasn't sweet on love. Financier Ian Reed was willing to back her . . . if she'd satisfy his taste for a lifetime of loving.

#474 SPITTING IMAGE—Kayla Daniels
Claire would do anything to keep her adopted daughter . . . but did that include marrying Mandy's natural father? How could she trust Jason's sudden love when he, too, desperately wanted Mandy?

AVAILABLE THIS MONTH:

#463 DANCE TO THE PIPER
Nora Roberts

#464 AMARILLO BY MORNING
Bay Matthews

#465 SILENCE THE SHADOWS
Christine Flynn

#466 BORROWED TIME
Janice Kaiser

#467 HURRICANE FORCE
Lisa Jackson

#468 WHERE ANGELS FEAR
Ginna Gray

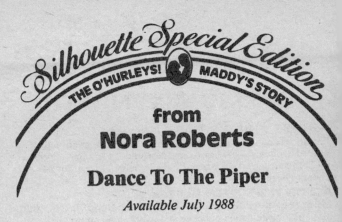

Silhouette Special Edition

THE O'HURLEYS! MADDY'S STORY

from
Nora Roberts

Dance To The Piper

Available July 1988

The second in an exciting new series about the lives and loves of triplet sisters—

If *The Last Honest Woman* (SE #451) captured your heart in May, you're sure to want to read about Maddy and Chantel, Abby's two sisters.

In *Dance to the Piper* (SE #463), it takes some very fancy footwork to get reserved recording mogul Reed Valentine dancing to effervescent Maddy's tune....

Then, in *Skin Deep* (SE #475), find out what kind of heat it takes to melt the glamorous Chantel's icy heart. Available in September.

THE O'HURLEYS!

**Join the excitement of
Silhouette Special Editions.**